TIT FOR TAT
AND OTHER TALES

TIT FOR TAT

AND OTHER TALES

BY

HAROLD ACTON

HAMISH HAMILTON
LONDON

First published in Great Britain 1972
by Hamish Hamilton Ltd
90 Great Russell Street London W.C.1

SBN 241 02064 6

All the characters in this book are fictitious and are not intended
to represent any actual persons living or dead.

Printed in Great Britain by
Western Printing Services Limited, Bristol

CONTENTS

CONTENTS

AUTHOR'S NOTE

Four of these stories first appeared in *Winter Tales* (Macmillan), *The Spectator*, *New Writing* and *The London Mercury*, and I take this opportunity of making my acknowledgments to the Editors —in the last case to the genial memory of Sir J. C. Squire.

Hoping to be allowed some credit for his imagination, the author declares that the characters in these stories are impeccably fictitious.

THE GIFT-HORSE

'EVERARD is the most munificent of men. Few confirmed bachelors are—in my experience. He's always loading me with lovely presents.'

'He must have a crush on you, darling. Though he is ready to come round for a meal, he has never given me a thing.'

'Perhaps you make him feel like an extra man. Everard has his pride. He doesn't care to be exploited.'

'An invitation to dine is hardly exploitation.'

'That all depends. A meal may have invisible strings attached to it. Everard realizes his entertainment value. Without apparent effort he makes a party go. And everybody knows his taste is exquisite.'

'You mean his appetite. Last time he helped himself to so much asparagus that there wasn't enough to go round.'

'Surely that's rather flattering.'

Everard had in fact confided to Hilda that he only went to Rosemary's on account of her cook. 'I'd put up with a lot of boredom for a perfect *blini*,' he added.

Rosemary wore an aggrieved expression. 'I can't deny that my cook has merits. But one resents being treated like a restaurant. I don't think I'll ask him again.'

Hilda tittered. 'You'll change your mind when you need another extra man.'

'Darling, how well you understand my foibles. Tell me more about the presents he showers on you. Are they practical or merely decorative? Let's have a peep.'

'The odd thing is that he's morbidly shy about them. He begs me not to show them. "I got this just for you," he always tells me. "I don't want to make other girls jealous." '

It was Rosemary's turn to titter. 'Jealous of that old bag of bones?'

'At least they are bones of contention. Two opulent widows have been running after him for years.'

'Amazing! That throws a new light on him. Do you know these widows? Who are they?'

'One is a Mrs. Hibbard of Cap Ferrat. The other is our country neighbour Grace Fotheringham whose husband was an ambassador to I forget where. Everard divides his summers between them. They're wildly jealous of each other.'

'Why doesn't he marry one of them and settle down? There's something so dreary about old bachelors.'

'Everard can live off his friends, and most of them can well afford to keep him.'

'He has never even offered me a cup of tea. It's high time he gave me something. What has he given you now?'

Hilda led her towards a cabinet filled with bric-à-brac, such as ivory netsukes, snuff-boxes and snuff-bottles. 'Nearly all these', she remarked, 'were presents from Everard.'

'My word, quite a little museum! I can see I shall have to cultivate him more often. He's certainly a connoisseur. Why that's Meissen, or is it Dresden? And I've always had a penchant for Fabergé.'

Hilda picked up a jade frog with ruby eyes. 'Everard brought me this the other day.'

Rosemary fancied she had seen it before, she couldn't think where. Loretta Perkins collected Fabergé: perhaps she had seen one like it in her menagerie of *chi-chi* animals? Its familiarity continued to nag at her but she said nothing except: 'Aren't you lucky! Obviously he's mad about you, darling.' Her eyes skimmed the shelves and rested on a snuff-box in the shape of a butterfly. For a moment she caught her breath. Surely it couldn't be a replica of hers? She turned it over in her hand and stroked its wings as if to question it. Could she be mistaken? She recalled with a pang that she had not noticed it lately. 'Was this another of Everard's gifts?' she asked.

Hilda nodded coyly. Rosemary resolved to rush home and investigate. 'You've not done too badly,' she observed. 'I must see what I can do, turn on the charm before it is too late. Did Everard inherit these bibelots?'

'I've no idea. More likely he picked them up in antique shops.'

'Picked them up' was the operative expression, Rosemary reflected. 'Somehow one doesn't connect him with a family. He seems to have sprung from nowhere.'

'I know nothing of his antecedents. He never mentions them.'

'One longs to discover more. These objects prove that he has considerable flair. I'll ring him up this evening.'

'He's in the South of France with widow Hibbard.'

'How tiresome. I need an extra man for *Norma*. Ralph has refused to sleep through another opera.'

'Rosemary, you're incorrigible.' The rivals parted gaily, each brushing the other's cheek with varnished lips. But Rosemary was inwardly apprehensive, for she could not banish a suspicion that the snuff-box belonged to her. In all her visits to sale-rooms she had never spotted its equal. She tried to recall the last occasion when Everard had come to dinner. Had it been a week or a fortnight ago? He had been a frequent guest but she had never liked him. She remembered with distaste that he was apt to stroke her furniture and turn her plates upside down. Yet it was difficult to believe that he would go so far. . . . And if he had taken it, what was the point of giving it to a mutual friend? She could hardly wait to solve the teasing riddle.

On her way home she wondered about Everard's relations with Hilda. What on earth did they see in each other? Big bouncing Hilda and wizened Everard: they formed an incongruous pair. She tried to analyse her attitude towards them. It all boiled down to their serviceability. Everard was a useful fourth at bridge, and he put Ralph in a good temper. She was suddenly reminded that he had given Ralph a repeater watch by Bréguet which he prized so highly that he wore it on a platinum chain. Evidently he preferred Ralph to herself. Could Everard be 'queer'? Her feminine instinct decided that he was sexless—except when he gazed at articles of virtu (which he pronounced with an exasperating French accent). Then a covetous gleam would moisten his slate-grey eyes and his fingers became predatory claws. She had noticed this when she had shown him her *famille verte* parrots. He had clutched them with quivering hands and broken into a sweat. 'Staggering,' he had muttered. 'I hope you'll leave them to me in your will.' As if he had the faintest chance of surviving her!

While she was running upstairs the telephone tinkled. Hilda again. 'Everard has been on my conscience,' she explained. 'I shouldn't have shown you his things. Please forget and say no more about them. He's so sensitive I'd hate to hurt his feelings.'

Rosemary was inclined to answer that the presents might equally be on Everard's conscience. 'Of course I won't breathe a word,' Rosemary assured her insincerely. She raced into her sitting-room, followed by yapping Ming and Ching, the white Pekinese she called her guardians. Usually she greeted them in pidgin English which they pretended to understand, but this evening she was too flurried to notice them.

One glance at her rosewood console table proved that they had been unable to guard her butterfly snuff-box. She stood gazing at the vacant spot where it had rested as on a flower and a pang of misery shot through her like neuralgia. It was as if she had lost a dear cousin whom she might have overlooked now and then but who had remained a kindly presence, a permanent comfort in the background of her over-organized existence. Gone! For a moment its image flickered before her. She stretched out a hand to grasp it and realized with a sob that it was no longer there. The butterfly had taken wing and flown out of the window, all the way to Hilda's flat. Tears welled into her eyes. Then she stamped her foot defiantly. 'No, this can't happen to me. I'll get it back even if it means a rumpus.'

After the first shock of anger and disappointment she thought: 'Hilda's bound to return it when I prove it's mine. Everard must have swiped it, the old brute.'

There could be no other explanation. Marshall, her maid, was completely beyond reproach. Rosemary dashed to the telephone but Hilda was out. Fortunately, perhaps, for in her actual state of nerves she might talk recklessly. Supposing Hilda refused to surrender it? She might be convinced that Everard had offered it in good faith. Rosemary would have to consult Ralph when he returned from the City. His advice was occasionally sound.

Ralph rang up to inform her that he had been detained at the office: she need not keep any dinner for him, he would sup at the club. How typical: he was never available when he was needed. At other times he was apt to blunder in her way. Then a bright idea occurred to her. Why not pursue her investigations with the owner of the Fabergé menagerie? Loretta Perkins also belonged to Everard's circle of hostesses. Lips open to her inseparable telephone, she cooed: 'Loretta darling, at last!'

Loretta barked back: 'Who's speaking?'

'Who else but Rosemary. Don't you recognize my voice?'

'Forgive me, dear, I didn't. It sounds altered, tense. What's up? It's ages since the Nureyev episode. I was wondering only this morning at the hairdresser's, whatever has happened to Rosemary? And now that you have rung up I can see that something *has* happened. Is Ralph being naughty again, or is it one of the boys? I'm so lucky to be free as air. No worries of that kind.'

'Gracious, how you jump at conclusions! You're wide of the mark this time. What I wanted to ask in strict confidence was, have you been missing things?'

'Missing exactly what? Please be less cryptic. I don't follow you, dear.'

'I mean items from your collection.'

'Now that you mention it I can't find my Fabergé frog. It's the least valuable of my pets, but that is no consolation. I simply doted on my froggy-woggy.'

'Have you reported it to the police?'

'Heavens, no. They'd terrify my Spanish maid. I couldn't get along without her.'

'I'm almost sure I've spotted your frog as well as a snuff-box of mine.'

'Darling, how thrilling. Where?'

'You'd never guess. At Hilda's.'

'Incredible! How on earth did she get hold of them?'

'In perfect innocence. They were presents from a man.'

'That doesn't sound so innocent to me. I've always suspected that Hilda had a lover. Who is he? Don't keep me on tenterhooks, please!'

'I don't like to blurt it out over the telephone. But isn't it a coincidence that your frog should sit next to my butterfly at Hilda's, and that both were presents from the same individual?'

'For goodness' sake stop stalling. Who is this slippery bedfellow of Hilda's?'

The overworked telephone revolted and the line was cut off. Having found another clue, Rosemary did not care. When the instrument rang again she failed to reply. Presuming that it must be Loretta, she chuckled to herself, for it amused her to keep her inquisitive friend in suspense. While the telephone tinkled on and on she gazed at the console table where her butterfly box had rested—how many years?—six or seven at least without any interference. She had taken its presence so much for granted that she had ceased to notice it until today when it had appeared to flutter its wings at her in Hilda's cabinet. She mixed herself a Bloody Mary and as she sipped it her longing to recover the treasure afflicted her like a toothache. She had no appetite for dinner, nor could she concentrate on the latest Simenon. The radio merely irritated her; those complacent voices jarred on her jangled mood.

Forlornly she sat waiting for Ralph with Ming and Ching snuffling beside her on the sofa. She was dozing off when Ralph lurched into the room and kissed her with brandy breath. The dogs yapped in protest against the disturbance. At once Rosemary related the details of her visit to Hilda.

'You and Loretta had better stake your claims,' he said. 'I'm sure Hilda won't make any fuss about returning the loot.'

'I wish I could feel sure. People often grow more attached to trifles than to their friends. I do myself.'

'Come, come, you never noticed its absence any more than I did. Hilda will deliver the goods but it's dashed awkward for Everard. A common or garden thief wouldn't behave like that. To pinch them and give them away to a mutual friend—it doesn't make sense.'

'He's always the first to arrive at a party, usually before the host. Quite a haul can be made in those few minutes.'

'Before challenging him you must be cautious. Yours may not be the only snuff-box of that type, or Loretta's the only frog.'

'To me the case is crystal clear. I'm convinced.'

'Let me round him up for a chin-wag before you take action. Kleptomania's a disease. Not being a psychiatrist I'll ask Dr. Cooper to collaborate.'

'If the snuff-box was yours I believe you'd do nothing about it.'

'I've always had a soft spot for old Everard. He gave me my Bréguet repeater, like the one the Iron Duke gave his A.D.C. after Waterloo.'

'You'd better look out or you'll be had up for receiving.'

'Righto, I'll keep it under my waistcoat. I don't intend to part with it.'

'And I don't intend to part with my butterfly.'

'Don't worry, dear. I'm sure you'll get it back.'

But Rosemary did worry. The distinct image of Everard snatching her treasure kept her awake at night: she resented it more than if it had been stolen by an ordinary burglar. The impudence of his presenting it to Hilda, who hadn't the slightest notion of its value. You only have to lose a thing to appreciate its rarity, she mused.

While Everard was tanning himself in the South of France there was little she could do. Rosemary decided reluctantly that she would have to bide her time.

II

'Everard dear, you shouldn't. I don't expect such presents and you can't afford them. I read in the paper that one was sold for several thousand guineas the other day. Do keep it and I'll be much happier. All I want is your company and you ration it too severely.'

'You know how deeply I'm attached to you, Nesta. Haven't I proved it again and again? Lady Catersham was furious with me for leaving her.'

Nesta Hibbard gazed at him with sad spaniel eyes. She saw him as Horace Walpole, herself as Madame du Deffand. Though she was not yet blind she was older than Everard—at an age when every additional year counts as double. She regarded him as an arbiter of taste. He had selected and arranged her furniture; he had helped to choose her dresses, hats and shoes; he advised her on food and wine. She seldom went shopping without him, and how she revelled in those expeditions! He imparted the last touch of refinement to her receptions and she was flattered when he was mistaken for her husband. With his languid air of distinction he impressed her friends.

'When will Everard be arriving?' they asked her. 'We must throw a party for him.'

And to those who celebrated his regular visits to Cap Ferrat he brought some trinket from England in token of gratitude. And they all exclaimed, 'Dear Everard, how you pamper us!'

'It's a homeless heirloom,' he replied. 'I'm delighted it has found a home with you.'

Nesta's friends called him her beau and quizzed her on the subject: 'When shall we hear the chime of wedding bells?'

These friends were scattered along the coast in marzipan villas and hotels where they tried to prolong the *dolce vita* of good King Edward's heyday. They turned a deaf ear and a blind eye to the antics of astronauts and other futuristic phenomena.

'Extra-vehicular activity, ahem!' snorted Captain Gutteridge.

'I'm jolly glad I've known a better world. I'm an old-fashioned romantic and proud of it.' With a quavering voice he burst into song: 'Give me the moonlight, give me the girl, And leave the rest to me.'

'Soon all will be over between men and women,' sighed Maggie McGrew. 'No more loving, only laboratories.'

'Lavatories? Never mind. You and I needn't bother about that, eh Maggie, so long as we're alive and kicking together.'

The veteran sailor hugged the retired heroine of many a shocking divorce. 'Nothing's over between *us* at any rate. I'm looking forward to this evening's rubber. Let's hope Princess Polly won't revoke as usual. It's time she treated herself to a new wig. I'm tired of looking at that bundle of straw on her head and wondering when it will slip off.'

'I've a good mind to raise a subscription for a new one. We could send it to her anonymously.'

'Are you going to Prince Vladimir's beano at the casino?'

'Of course. It will be a riot. He's had a remarkable run of luck lately.'

Everard introduced a spice of variety into the routine of these voluntary exiles who periodically shared Browning's nostalgia: 'Oh to be in England, now that April's there!' But it was another England they remembered.

When he was in London Everard's gossipy letters about social events, which seemed far more vivid than the newspaper columns from which they were culled, were recited by Nesta to a spellbound group of cronies. A legend had gained credence that he was the offspring of a duke. Nesta never denied it, and Everard remained reticent though he hinted that the trinkets he bestowed were relics of an ancestor's collection. Their supply, however, never seemed to dry up, and each had some subtle *rapport* with the recipient.

On this occasion he had offered Nesta an eighteenth-century Staffordshire figure of a rosy-cheeked lass whose crinoline might have been designed by Miró with suggestive dots and squiggles. It looked surprisingly modern, yet Nesta, who considered herself an authority on Staffordshire salt-glazed stoneware, knew it was authentic.

Everard had never been prone to introspection and he rejected psycho-analysts as quacks, but in so far as he could analyse his impulse to collect he was attracted to beautiful objects indiscriminately and his preference inclined towards the pretty, the decorative and the useful. The attraction was beyond his power of control. For practical reasons the object had to be of limited dimensions. Once in his possession he had no selfish desire to keep a thing entirely to himself: he would gloat on it until he had absorbed its shape and design into his system, like a poem learnt by heart. He wanted others to enjoy it even more. Who better than his frequent hosts at home and abroad? Since he was not 'demented with the mania of owning things' he could appreciate a fine bibelot either here or there. It was gratifying to feel that he could have kept it but had parted with it in a spirit of munificence. It gave him a keener pleasure to recognize in the house of a friend some cameo or miniature or Baccarat paperweight that had been his for even a short while. He relished the element of risk involved in its acquisition far more than if he had bought and paid for it.

In the past he had presented Nesta with a miniature attributed to Hilliard, a diamond spray-brooch, a fan by Conder, a Battersea enamel snuff-box with Corydon playing bagpipes to Amaryllis (Everard and Nesta), a Chinese cloisonné phoenix, a Meissen Harlequin and Columbine (Everard and Nesta again), a Chelsea ink-stand, a small bronze dancing figure from Tibet, a minute painting on copper of a Dutch carousal and, less appropriate despite its quaintness, a Lambeth delftware barber's bowl adorned with scissors, comb, razor, leeches and other instruments of his trade: the assortment was rich, original and varied.

'I wonder you get them through the Customs free of duty,' Nesta remarked.

'They are only trifles,' Everard replied. 'The Customs are after bigger game—or cigarettes. By the way, I haven't forgotten your Harem Puffs, the amber-scented ones.'

'You absolute angel. You haven't forgotten my favourite vice. I must kiss you for that.'

With a grimace that was comically demure Everard permitted himself to be moistened on the cheek by his infatuated hostess. Dante, her Florentine majordomo, glimpsed them over his cocktail tray and thought: 'Ridiculous, at their age! But it cannot go much further.'

Dante disliked and distrusted Everard. He disliked him because his tips were so niggardly that he had to refuse them out of self-respect. He distrusted him since he had caught sight of him creeping out with a parcel when the old lady's silver coffee-pot had vanished. Fearing that he as an alien servant might fall under suspicion, he had immediately reported its disappearance to the Signora and proposed to summon the police.

'I bear an honoured name, and I would not have it tarnished by reason of a coffee-pot,' he declared. 'I keep a strict eye on the staff, but I cannot spy on the Signora's guests.'

'Are you suggesting that one of my friends would walk off with a coffee-pot?' Nesta retorted indignantly.

'Why not, Signora? You are so hospitable and the Riviera abounds in sharks.'

'Be more precise, Dante. Give me an example.'

Dante smiled at her compassionately. 'I could give you many, Signora. There's the Countess who crams her bag with your cakes after your bridge-teas, pretending they are for her poodle. She also empties the chocolates from their paniers after dinner. And the Marquise fills her case with your scented cigarettes. And only yesterday I saw Mr. Gifford leave the house with a big parcel. I could not presume to inspect the contents, but it had the same dimensions as your coffee-pot.'

'Not a word against Mr. Gifford. He is one of my closest friends.'

'With your permission I must vindicate myself. In the matter of missing silver all fingers will point at your major-domo. The responsibility is mine.'

'I trust you completely, Dante. Surely that ought to suffice.'

'A day may come when you will cease to trust me. A teapot may follow the coffee-pot, spoons may follow knives and forks—and I repeat I feel responsible, Signora. I desire my character to be cleared in advance.'

'I'm sure my coffee-pot will turn up,' said Nesta. 'In any case I forbid you to call the police.'

'Then I shall demand an affidavit that you absolve me from blame.'

'Won't it do just as well if I raise your wages?'

The prospect of more emolument induced Dante to relax, and a smile effaced his frown of discontent. Nesta knew that smile which signified: 'I'm at your service so long as I'm rewarded.' She sighed with relief. Dante was a necessary luxury but she wanted no truck with the French police. She, too, had noticed the rapacity of certain guests, but she bore them no resentment. On the contrary, it wrung her heart-strings when Daisy made a clean sweep of her cakes and Natasha bagged her cigarettes, for it meant that they must be poor in spite of their veneer of affluence. Most of them lived on and at the casino. When in luck they made a splash, especially the White Russians, with *zakouski* and vodka all round and music, music, music. Their vicissitudes provided Nesta with distraction during Everard's absence. Often they brought equivocal partners to her house, but one had to be tolerant in a cosmopolitan clique. Dante was not exaggerating their peccadilloes, but Nesta was annoyed with him for daring to cast a slur on her favourite.

Madame du Deffand had complained that she only met fools and knaves or people who made her feel a fool herself. Horace Walpole was the unique exception. Nesta was well over seventy and Everard over sixty, yet Nesta fondly imagined that their relationship was similar. Everard seemed as brilliant to her as Horace to the blind Marquise. Dante must be jealous, she thought; only that could account for his outrageous hint. Everard had nicknamed him Cerberus.

'Sometimes he looks as if he is going to bite my head off,' he remarked.

'Nonsense,' said Nesta. 'Everybody adores you. You're just like a member of the family.'

Since Dante had sleuthed him into a boudoir where Nesta kept her Old Dresden (her generic term for porcelain), Everard grew wary of the prying butler. Though he had spotted several figurines that would appeal to Grace Fotheringham he was never given a chance to remove them. His padded suitcase was still empty after a fortnight's stay. On previous visits he had never failed to fill it.

Fortunately Maggie McGrew had enough Dutch and Georgian silver to fill a shop-window. And Natasha had not yet parted with all her icons. While the others were absorbed in bridge he might unhook a pocket-sized one on his way to the loo. A weakness of the bladder—'Excuse me if I powder my nose'—had often served him as a plausible pretext. Perhaps in aiming at the coffee-pot, which was larger than his usual quarry, he had been over-ambitious. If nothing else materialized he would have to try for the tea-pot, and if Dante caught him he would say that its handle needed soldering.

In the meantime he accompanied Nesta to luncheons and dinners where he met the same futile people and to dressmakers and other shops along the Riviera. As Nesta was slow to make up her mind he spent many a wearisome hour in shops exclusively feminine. But he was never idle, for a pretty pincushion, a pair of scissors or an ashtray would catch his eye, and among the mirrors, models and hawk-faced attendants it was excellent sport to transfer it into his pocket. He seldom departed without a souvenir.

Aware of his influence over their lavish customer, the proprietors would present him with a gardenia for his button-hole, a silk handkerchief, a bottle of eau-de-Cologne or after-shave lotion. As a reward for his counsel Nesta would say: 'Now I must get you something nice. Your clothes are far too conservative for the Côte d'Azur. Let me find you something gay.'

Everard objected that a well-tailored man should never be conspicuous. He wore a necktie, for instance, that might have passed muster for Old Etonian, except that the stripe was a *soupçon* bluer and broader. But Nesta was so insistent that he had to yield. It gave her additional pleasure to renew his wardrobe. Pyjamas and silk dressing-gowns were heaped on the counter. She tested the material and supervised the measurements. 'They'll imagine I'm being kept by you,' Everard murmured.

'That's what I'd love to do, dear, if you'd only let me,' she replied, squeezing his limp hand.

Not a bad haul for an afternoon, he reflected, but I've definitely earned it. What other man of his age had the patience to linger while she tried on this and that for hours on end? They always dressed for dinner and the women spent half the day wondering what they should wear at night. Of course, Nesta consulted Everard who preferred her in orchid mauve.

At Maggie McGrew's he had to compete with Captain Gutteridge. After a few dry Martinis Maggie's drooping eye began to rove towards other males, including Everard, whose friendship with Nesta teased her curiosity. Thanks to the Captain, she refused to believe that anyone was too superannuated for a frolic. At a certain hour and in a certain light—her lamps were ingeniously shaded—wrinkles became blurred, the pouches vanished. When mouth met mouth the eyes were apt to close and youth appeared eternal.

Everard's manner with her was formal yet flirtatious. He kept her guessing. Under the table at dinner her foot pressed his and he returned the pressure, but her drooping eyelid signalled that she was already half-seas-over. She invariably wore white kid gloves to conceal her knobbly hands. Yet she chain-smoked through meals, dropping ashes over the lobster mayonnaise, burning holes in the table-cloth and sometimes in her gown. Jim Gutteridge, acting as host at the end of the table, was so accustomed to the effects of her tippling that he overlooked them. She might make passes at others but she was his for keeps. Sure of his prowess, he knew exactly what she wanted, the when and the how and the where. Privately he considered Everard a tame old tabby-cat, good enough for Nesta but on the shelf where sex was concerned. No cause for rivalry there! As he and the consul sat over their port Everard excused himself, 'to spend a penny'.

'Spend tuppence for me,' Jim chortled with a wink and continued to discuss his recent golf scores.

The bathroom adjoined Maggie's bedroom. Seeing that the coast was clear Everard tiptoed in to reconnoitre. The accumulation of silver on her dressing-table made his mouth water. It was twice the length of Nesta's, spread with an array of brushes, combs, hand-mirrors, boxes of all dimensions, candelabra of classical nymphs holding cornucopias, a George II basket containing lotions in cut-glass bottles, and two graceful sauce-boats of the same period containing hair- and safety-pins. Everard made a lightning inventory. All this for the toilet of a raddled old dipsomaniac! There was an *embarras de choix*, and he had to decide which were the most manoeuvrable. There was an irresistible cigarette case of platinum and gold which fitted his breast pocket. The boxes might make his dinner-jacket bulge. However, he decided to take that risk with two of the smallest. One was shaped like a high-heeled shoe—just the thing for Grace's collection. Maggie would be too squiffy to notice their absence before tomorrow. A lingering appraisal of the sauce-boats—perhaps he could return for them later—and he rejoined Jim Gutteridge and the consul in the dining-room. On his way out to join the ladies, giving precedence to the captain and the consul, he slipped a salt-cellar into his trousers. Otherwise it was an evening of conventional pattern. They played bridge till one o'clock with copious 'night-caps' in between. Everard was the only sober member of the party.

A couple of days later Maggie confided to Nesta that she was going to sack her maid. 'We can't prove it yet but I'm positive that she's been pilfering. I've lost several bits of old silver recently and the cigarette case given me by King Fuad. I miss that most of all: it brought back blissful memories. The police are watching her movements, but it's an uncomfortable feeling to keep a maid one cannot trust.'

'How I agree,' cooed Nesta. 'Maids bother me so that I'd sooner fend for myself. I'm lucky to have Dante; it's like having a private detective in the house. Everard calls him Cerberus.'

'I envy you,' sighed Maggie. She had attempted to bribe Dante into her service with a promise to double his wages but he had declined. He disapproved of drunken dowagers on the loose.

The news that Maggie's maid was under suspicion would have encouraged Everard to capture the sauce-boats had not Maggie mentioned that she had locked up her silver, except the bulkier pieces, too heavy to manipulate. He would have to be content with his paltry percentage. Yet something in the air of Cap Ferrat made his fingers itch for booty.

Natasha possessed a glowing Madonna of the Novgorod School in a jewelled frame which would fit his 'special' pocket like a glove. But she told him candidly that she could not organize a party for him as her luck at roulette had failed her.

'Don't dream of it. A tête-à-tête over tea would be much nicer. I'll bring the tea-leaves myself, a packet from Fortnum's. Your native samovar will do the rest.'

Broke though she was, Natasha would not take him at his word. She provided enough *pâté de foie gras* sandwiches and chocolate éclairs for a school treat and arranged half a dozen tables for bridge and poker. Her bed-sitting room was packed with greedy gamblers. The icons beside her bed were hidden by a Japanese screen so that it was not difficult for Everard to glide behind it while his hostess was attending to her other guests.

Maggie was still maundering about her maid and the cigarette case which King Fuad had given her on board the royal daha-beeyah. 'So far the police haven't been able to trace the stolen goods. I'm afraid I won't see them again.'

'You console me for not having a maid,' said Natasha. 'In Petersburg I used to have dozens but I never lost anything before the Revolution. And here I have nothing to lose except my family icons, and I'm told they are *démodés* whenever I try to sell them.'

'Do show them to me,' said Nesta. Everard could have slapped her at that moment.

'Let's finish our rubber first,' he said testily.

When the game was over and the losses were subtracted from the gains it was time for everybody to dress for Prince Vladimir's banquet. To Everard's vexation Nesta offered to fetch Natasha in her limousine. When he returned an hour later he found her in a flood of tears.

'I shall not go to Vladimir's, I'm too *angoissée*,' she wailed. 'The most precious of my icons has disappeared. It has been in my family for generations. Somebody must have taken it while we were playing bridge this afternoon. I have had to give a list of my guests to the police.'

Everard urged her to attend the party, though she wept on his shoulder and cried: 'Who could be so heartless as to steal one of my last heirlooms, the one I valued most of all. It is a complete mystery. The police are not interested in helping a poor refugee. Besides, they do not understand what a Russian icon signifies. They laugh in my face and suggest that I keep *louche* lovers. I shall never see my holy relic again.'

'I promise to find you another,' said Everard soothingly. 'There's a little shop near the British Museum which specializes in Oriental antiques.'

'Thank you for the generous thought. But it is the sentiment attached to my icon, the prayers that have been said before it by my parents and grandparents, which make it so dear to me.'

Everard commiserated with her, as if unaware that the object was in his hand-bag. His conscience did not prick him in the least. He knew that Nesta would provide compensation.

Natasha was too typical a Slav to behave like a wet blanket and Prince Vladimir was an exuberant master of revels, so that she soon recovered her ebullience, whereas Everard and Nesta grew more phlegmatically Anglo-Saxon. Everard could see nothing to tempt him and Nesta was depressed at the prospect of his departure.

'I wish you could stay here for ever,' she told him.

Everard's mask froze into Horace Walpole's, impassive and aloof. 'I should like nothing better,' he replied, 'but I can't disappoint the old folks at home. I have my faults but I have never let anyone down.'

'Except me,' said Nesta bitterly. 'I love you more than all the others put together. And life is so short. Haven't you been happy here? You know there is nothing I would not do for you . . .'

Nesta's whole face quivered and her elaborate make-up seemed in danger of cracking.

'You are the dearest of women,' Everard replied, 'and you have given me a marvellous time. Unfortunately I have my social obligations.'

'I'm ready to give up the South of France for you.'

'I'm too fond of you to demand such a sacrifice. You'd never cease to regret it. In London you'd be an exile, and you'd hate me for it. I'll be back whenever you really need me.'

'I always need you. Couldn't you manage to stay another week?'

In spite of his remarkable staying power Everard had begun to long for England. Even Nesta complained of the Riviera now and then: 'I don't know what society is coming to.' Everard considered that it had come to a stagnant pond where a family of frogs, neither French nor by Fabergé, croaked continually: 'I ask you to lunch (or dinner), You ask me to lunch (or dinner), I owe you a lunch (or dinner), You owe me a lunch (or dinner), I wonder why So-and-so hasn't asked me to lunch or dinner lately.'

Everard became slightly less greedy by reaction. But since Nesta called him cruel he was forced to relent. He might yet add a souvenir or two to his collection.

III

Parting from Nesta had always been sticky and this time she made it worse by a hysterical fit of weeping. The scene left a disagreeable after-taste. Everard's social round was meticulously planned—a week here, a fortnight there—but his longest visits were reserved for Nesta Hibbard and Grace Fotheringham. These ladies were coevals, but whereas Nesta was superficially cosmopolitan Grace was proud of being 'county' to the backbone.

'I sink or swim with Britain even if the Commies take over,' Grace asserted. 'Let others cry stinking fish and emigrate. Here I am and here I stay.'

So comfortable was her house, so sylvan her park, that her immobility entailed no sacrifice. Not even Everard could have inveigled her abroad, and Everard, as she often proclaimed, was her favourite man. His visits to Fotheringham Hall were no less eagerly expected than his visits to *Mon Repos*.

Owing to a frugal diet, regular hours and abundant fresh air, Grace had preserved a big round baby face without the aid of cosmetics. She devoured several newspapers but read little else; she had no Madame du Deffand delusions and Horace Walpole was hardly a name to her. But her affection for Everard was a steady flame. All her neighbours remarked that her eyes were brighter when he came to stay; he flattered and amused her simultaneously. His accounts of society on the Azure Coast were as good as a play and she was delighted with the unpredictable souvenirs he brought her.

Everard enjoyed more freedom with Grace than with Nesta. There was no snooping Dante at Fotheringham Hall. He could prowl all over the place to his heart's content. If one of Grace's bibelots disappeared he never heard it mentioned. And the house was crammed with small, choice, portable objects. The late Sir Geoffrey had had a penchant for jade; his forbears had collected miniatures; and Grace had amassed a singular assemblage of tiny shoes in porcelain, ivory, silver and other materials. The rooms were gay with pink as the predominant colour. The furniture was sprawlingly Edwardian. The sofas could have been converted into beds; chests of drawers were scented with lavender and pot-pourri filled bowls of *famille rose*. It was the ideal setting for an old-fashioned musical comedy. The food was wholesome and suited Everard better than the flesh-pots of Cap Ferrat.

Grace met him at the little railway station and held out both her chubby hands in welcome. Under a huge picture hat her whole face beamed at him.

'Dear Everard, at last!' she exclaimed. 'It has seemed such a long, long time. I was afraid you'd been seduced by one of those sirens you described in your delicious letters from the Riviera.'

'I was there for business rather than pleasure,' he replied, not untruthfully.

'I hope it was a success. You're looking splendid.'

'So are you, Grace. Honey and flowers—the same fresh Gainsborough beauty. By Jove, it's a tonic to set eyes on you again.'

Though Grace lacked a Dante, she possessed a bull terrier called Pongo which growled at Everard with peculiar animosity—peculiar because it was so amiable with her other guests. Once it had given him a nasty bite so Grace deemed it advisable to leave her pet at home on this occasion. As if it blamed Everard for depriving it of a drive in the car, Pongo growled at him so viciously that Grace had to expel it from the room. Everard was slightly unnerved by the incident but Grace's cucumber sandwiches restored his equanimity.

'I've been looking forward to this like a schoolboy to his hols,' he said. 'The Riviera's all very well in small doses but I've had enough of it. Business apart, I can't think why I wasted so much time there.'

'Nor can I, Everard. Anyhow better late than never. I'm delighted you could tear yourself away from so many temptations. Hilda Betterton was inquiring about you yesterday. She has had a tiff with Rosemary Filson and wants your advice.'

'What about, I wonder?'

'Oh, some present you gave her which Rosemary declares was stolen from her drawing-room.'

Everard grinned uncomfortably. 'Shall we be seeing Hilda?'

'She asked us over for dinner tonight but I'm afraid I was selfish. I wanted to keep you all to my wee self.'

'Perfect, that was just what I was hoping. Hilda would be *de trop*. Do you often see Rosemary Filson?'

'Not since she stayed with Hilda last year. Frankly I couldn't bear her, and I'm not the least bit interested in all the names she drops.'

'I agree. Her social success is entirely due to her cook.'

'I'm afraid you'll find mine very plain after the French cuisine.'

'I'd sooner eat mutton with you than *foie gras* at Cap Ferrat.'

'Flatterer. Another sandwich? There's also some gentleman's relish. You must be famished after your journey.'

Everard did not need to be asked. He had had no luncheon in anticipation of this tea.

While he dressed for dinner Everard wondered whether he should present Grace with the icon as well as the shoe-shaped box or reserve the former for a later visit. The icon might look barbaric among the English miniatures. He cursed his folly for giving the snuff-box to Hilda: he had done so when he had felt unwanted and unloved. She had kissed him and told him how popular he was, and she had scolded him for his reckless generosity.

The shoe-shaped box seemed more appropriate. He always chaffed Grace about her 'shoe-fetish': it was one of their private jokes. 'You ought to be psycho-analysed,' he told her.

'For loving you?' she retorted.

His gift evoked gurgles of delight. 'I'd lost hope of finding another,' she explained. 'But how can I accept such a rarity?'

The usual friendly squabble ensued. Everard forbore from answering that she would pay for it in other ways.

His remarkable staying power was best exemplified at Fotheringham Hall. Between croquet in the afternoon and backgammon in the evening he did a little gardening with Grace to stimulate his appetite for her solid meals. He always took two helpings of the boiled silverside of beef and the maids encouraged him to eat more. 'Another dumpling, sir? Cook will be disappointed unless you finish them off.'

'Thanks, but I haven't room.'

'Come on, sir. There's only gooseberry fool and a savoury to follow.'

After dinner he sat beside Grace while she knitted bedcovers for the hospital. It was an idyllic existence. Having despatched his bread-and-butter letters, Everard could relax from this arduous labour. His company made Grace more sociable and he escorted her to local entertainments which were altogether cosier than those at Cap Ferrat.

The only fly in his ointment was the weekly letter, page after rambling page, from Nesta who continued to bewail his absence and beseech him to return. 'Life is meaningless without you,' she wrote. 'I'm unutterably bored. *C'est une maladie de l'âme.*'

Madame du Deffand again! And like Horace Walpole, Everard threatened to stop writing unless she pulled herself together. It was absurd to pretend that she didn't have loads of fun. Wasn't she the virtual Queen of Cap Ferrat? Why couldn't she send him the latest news of her court? Had Maggie's missing silver turned up, and had her maid been arrested? Had Natasha recovered her icon? He smiled at his cynicism as he scribbled his moral lecture. Nesta should count her blessings. The woes that afflicted the rest of humanity had spared Cap Ferrat.

Not at all, she replied. Forest fires had been raging in the neighbourhood and now there were thunderstorms like hurricanes; the airport at Nice had been flooded and Communism was on the rampage; the lower classes were ruder than ever, even the shopkeepers and waiters in restaurants were apt to be uncivil.

'You have Dante to protect you,' he retorted. 'And with so many congenial friends—how's Jim Gutteridge by the way?—you need never spend a dull moment.'

But Nesta's cronies were failing fast: Maggie had gone to Vichy for her spleen, Jim Gutteridge had had a stroke, Natasha was suffering from blood pressure and had fainted in the Casino just when she was winning at roulette. Nesta herself was worried about her palpitations: she was trying a saltless diet which destroyed her appetite. Everard was reminded of the salt-cellar he held in reserve: perhaps he would give it to Hilda.

Health was the one subject banned at Fotheringham Hall.

Grace never mentioned it and she discouraged others from doing so. Hilda came over to dine as soon as Grace decided she could no longer monopolize Everard. When he presented her with Maggie's salt-cellar Hilda thanked him less effusively than usual. 'How pretty,' she remarked, 'and how sweet of you to call me the salt of the earth, but I can't go on depriving you of family heirlooms.'

'I thought it would brighten your breakfast tray. I'm getting on in years you know, though I keep my age a secret. This will remind you of me when I am gone.'

'Do take it,' said Grace. 'Everard chose it specially for you. He'll be hurt if you refuse it.'

'It's much too grand for me.'

'What rot. Why look a gift-horse in the mouth?' Grace prompted her.

'Perhaps Rosemary will claim it like the snuff-box.'

'You shouldn't have shown it to her,' said Everard. 'I particularly asked you not to. She's the most grasping woman I know. Of course she'll try to winkle it out of you.'

'Rosemary and I were at school together. I'd hate to quarrel with her on account of a snuff-box. I can see that she wants it desperately.'

'Let her want it. It is yours since I gave it to you.'

'That's the trouble. She swears it is hers.'

'If I were you, Everard, I should send her a lawyer's letter,' said Grace. 'Threaten to prosecute for slander.'

'Evidently she's taken leave of her senses. But Ralph's a sensible fellow. Trust him to put things right.'

'Rosemary wears the trousers. What she says goes.'

'She struck me as odious,' said Grace. 'Don't yield an inch. One must be firm with neurotics.'

'I'd hate to quarrel with a lifelong friend,' Hilda repeated miserably.

'Her behaviour doesn't sound very friendly to me,' said Grace. 'Spreading horrid lies about the kindest of mortals. Never mind what she says, Everard. We'll stand up for you, won't we?'

'It's not agreeable to be slandered by a woman who pesters one to dine with her,' said Everard gloomily.

'You should never have gone,' said Grace.

Everard was inclined to agree but he blamed Hilda's indiscretion. He couldn't remember if he had given her anything else of Rosemary's.

Hilda lacked the courage to add that Loretta Perkins had also put in a claim for her Fabergé frog. Since Grace and Everard were both so insistent she accepted the salt-cellar, but she wondered if it would lead to further friction.

Far from spoiling his dinner this episode stimulated Everard's appetite and he helped himself twice to the treacle pudding. Hilda's reluctance to accept the salt-cellar had amused him. 'Next week you must dine with me,' she said.

Everard luxuriated in the placid routine of Fotheringham Hall. The weather was autumnal for August and frequent showers drove him indoors but even the climate was exhilarating after the pitiless glare of the Riviera. Everard was as happy indoors as in the garden for he could browse to his heart's content among Grace's bric-à-brac. Chimney pieces, cabinets and tables were so overcrowded that it was easy to camouflage the displacement of an object. A spell of wet weather revived his acquisitive instincts. He picked up an assortment of Christmas presents which more than compensated for his losses at backgammon, since it was his policy to let Grace win. A meal with the vicar was unexpectedly remunerative though the apostle spoons were more manageable than the Victorian tobacco jars, always acceptable to pipe-smoking friends like Jim Gutteridge. One must take what comes one's way, he reflected, furtively slipping a couple of spoons into his pocket while the vicar was saying grace.

As the weeks went by he began to think it strange that he heard nothing more from Hilda. If he rang her up it would look like fishing. He mentioned this to Grace who telephoned with the gymkhana as a pretext. Her maid replied that Hilda had gone to bed with a chill. Grace had no patience with illness which she suspected was imaginary in nine cases out of ten. However, she called on Hilda with a basket of nectarines from her greenhouse. Somewhat to her surprise it was Hilda who opened the front door.

'My daily's out shopping,' she explained. 'Fortunately my temperature's down. Anyhow it was nothing serious. The fact is I'm shy of meeting Everard since Rosemary Filson and Loretta Perkins are both dunning me for the return of the presents he gave me. Though I'm not possessive I hesitate to send the things back. It would seem an admission that Everard pinched them. I simply don't know what to do.'

'Keep them, of course. It sounds like a conspiracy to me. Would you trust Rosemary's word against Everard's? I wouldn't trust that woman round the corner.'

'One can't help loving Everard, but he has put me in a quandary. Both Rosemary and Loretta are positive about their claims. It's all so unpleasant that it has given me nightmares.'

'Snap out of it, Hilda. Those women are taking advantage of your gullibility. You only have to look at Everard to see that his conscience is clear. Though he hasn't said as much I suspect he's offended by your neglect. I told him you were seedy and he wanted to send you a Russian icon which he says has healing properties. Isn't that typical?'

'Once bitten twice shy. I want no more of his presents. They're getting too hot to hold.'

'Look here, Hilda, if you consider yourself a friend you mustn't come to terms with the enemy. Stick to your guns!'

'I suppose I must ask him to dinner but it will be a strain. I can't deny that I'm shaken.'

'I won't bring him unless you promise to stand firm.'

'I don't see how I can keep his presents in the circumstances. If I only had Rosemary to deal with . . .'

'That's quite enough. I thought you had more gumption.'

Grace sailed out of Hilda's cottage like a proud ambassadress after the failure of an important mission. She said nothing about it to Everard, whom she found playing patience in the library after extracting an inscribed first edition of *Alice's Adventures in Wonderland* from one of the shelves. He had searched in vain for

Through the Looking-Glass but perhaps that was asking too much: he knew 'The Walrus and the Carpenter' by heart and felt a certain affinity with the Walrus, who was 'a *little* sorry for the poor oysters'. Lewis Carroll's classic, which was lost on Grace, would cheer up Nesta in the midst of her palpitations.

Dear Grace! Her house was incomparably pleasanter than Nesta's and there were fewer hospitable houses at Everard's disposal since the war. At bottom he was profoundly insular and Fotheringham Hall was an enclave of insularity. If Grace should ask him to marry her—and she often seemed on the verge of doing so—he was prepared to accept, but alas, it was only Nesta who made the advances. Grace was content to leave things as they were with Everard in seasonal attendance. Perhaps he should exert a little pressure and withdraw his countenance when it was most desired. . . .

Lady Catersham, an acquaintance who lived in Hampshire, served him as a useful alibi. He had never stayed with her but thanks to his vivid imagination he came to believe that he had. Grace was resentful of Lady Catersham since he invariably referred to her as the perfect hostess.

With every semblance of regret he told Grace one morning that he would have to cut his visit short. 'I've had an S.O.S. from Lady Catersham,' he announced, 'who implores me to help her with a charity bazaar. The date had to be altered on account of the rector's retirement. As I promised her ages ago it wouldn't be cricket to let the old girl down.'

'Where do I come in?' Grace exclaimed peevishly. 'I was expecting you to stay at least another fortnight. In fact I've booked you for a number of engagements. Would you jilt me for a charity bazaar?'

'Please don't put it that way. Of all my friends you are the nearest and dearest. But poor Lady Catersham is eighty-five and looks it. I've known her since "Hallo Ragtime" days. As she's a martyr to sciatica she has been more helpless than usual since the death of Miss Murchison, her lady companion. I'm one of her executors, you know.'

'It's too bad,' said Grace tearfully. 'To throw me over for an old hag with one foot in the grave.'

'If you think I'm letting you down, I'll put off Lady Catersham.'

'Yes, do, for my sake. Tell her I also have my charity bazaars. I'm sure she has plenty of nurses to cope.'

'We ought to be married,' said Everard with a weary smile. 'You treat me as if we were.'

'At our age that would be silly. I'm not so young as I look.'

'You are too young, that's the snag. I'm the antique.'

Grace pressed his hand. 'Aren't things marvellous as they are? You can come here whenever you like. Wedlock is a padlock, my dear. I'll be a wife to you in all but name.'

'Thank you,' he muttered. 'I shouldn't demand more as I have so little to offer—only myself, a grizzled bachelor. And yet . . .' He gazed at her sentimentally.

'You silly boy. If you want me to pop into bed I'm ready to do so, but it wouldn't be much fun for either of us. One must be realistic.'

'That I've never been. I'm a hopeless romantic.'

Grace pressed his hand again. 'Well, it is my duty to rescue you from Lady Catersham. She's becoming a bad habit.'

But after dilly-dallying another week Everard grew restive. It was obvious that Grace had no intention of proposing. In a mood of acute frustration he sent himself a telegram saying that Lady Catersham had taken a turn for the worse and hoped to see him before her condition became critical. Showing this to Grace, 'I'm afraid I've got to go,' he said glumly. 'I'd never forgive myself if I deserted my old friend on her deathbed.'

'She'll probably be unconscious by the time you reach her,' Grace replied. But he wore so dismal an expression that she had to relent. 'I'll let you go on condition you return within a week. No lingering by the deathbed, mind you. At our age it is bad for morale.'

A few days later Everard called on Lady Catersham from the

village inn where he was staying. Having borrowed some of her crested writing paper he composed a fictitious account of his visit. He alleged that Lady Catersham had begun to recover as soon as she set eyes on him. Now that she was well enough to be taken for drives in her Rolls he was at liberty to return to Fotheringham Hall. If this were still convenient, would Grace kindly send an answer to his London address.

The reply, when it came, left him stupefied. Grace advised him to leave the country before he was charged with larceny on several counts. He could keep the miniatures and other purloined souvenirs of Fotheringham Hall but he must not suppose that he would be welcomed there again after such an abuse of her hospitality—an abuse so flagrant that it was unpardonable. Further communication with her was superfluous.

Though the shock was intense Everard decided to bluff it out. He still regarded Hilda as a rock of loyalty. To her he telephoned in his distress. Had Grace taken leave of her senses? he asked. He could not imagine why she had written him such a letter. They had parted amicably; she had even begged him to return. And so forth.

Hilda spoke to him gently but firmly. She, too, advised him to disappear until Rosemary and Loretta had forgotten and forgiven the losses they had suffered at his hands. At present they were so delighted to recover their treasures that they had withdrawn their threats to prosecute him. They had visited Grace together and insisted on her checking her inventory of heirlooms. She had done so reluctantly and the proof of Everard's perfidy had made her blow up. Hilda had had much ado to dissuade her from denouncing him to Scotland Yard. 'I've never seen her in such a rage,' she said. 'You had better return to Cap Ferrat, at any rate till the eruption dies down. But I implore you to curb your too generous instincts.'

Everard did not wait for further advice. He packed up his traps and caught the next plane for Nice. After some deliberation he kept his relics from Fotheringham Hall. Nesta would appreciate the miniatures. One of them might plausibly be described as a portrait of Madame du Deffand before she went blind. He would tell her that it had belonged to Horace Walpole.

IV

Nesta was at the airport to welcome him. 'What a wonderful answer to my prayers,' she exclaimed.

The sunlight accentuated her myriad wrinkles coated with a pale pink powder which clung like hoar-frost to the fuzz on her double chin. Everard shuddered when she kissed him with sagging lips. She mistook this for emotion.

'I had to come back to you,' he said. 'Your letters worried me, especially those palpitations you wrote of. So I've descended on you like a bolt out of the blue.'

'More like the Archangel Gabriel,' she gushed. 'I've been missing you terribly and that caused the palpitations. Now we'll have to make up for all the time you've been away. Everybody's pining to entertain you. Maggie's still at Vichy but all the rest are here. . . .' She chattered on with feverish gaiety. 'How well you're looking, but you've lost weight. You must sunbathe on the terrace. I'll get Dante to spread a lilo for you. . . .'

Everard's thin lips twitched into a mechanical grin. Already the prospect of an indefinite sojourn at *Mon Repos* depressed him.

Dante noticed that his luggage was heavier than usual and that there was more of it. A born diplomat, he greeted Everard with an exaggerated bow. But he drew his own conclusions and watched Everard more closely than before. He seemed to dog his footsteps. 'Anything I can do for you, Monsieur?' he would enquire, peeping round the door of whichever room Everard chanced to occupy.

'When I need you I shall ring the bell,' Everard answered huffily.

'*Entendu, Monsieur*. Can I offer you tea or a cognac with seltzer?'

'Perhaps a cup of tea later on. Now I think I'll lie down for a rest.'

From his room he could hear Nesta telephoning to all the Toms, Dicks and Harrys of her acquaintance. He saw himself condemned to a ruthless routine of bridge and cocktail parties. Yet the alternative, an endless tête-à-tête with Nesta, would be even more lowering. Conversation with her soon became a grinding effort: he found himself racking his brains for some fresh topic. When the stream of local gossip had run dry—and this was chiefly concerned with the bodily ailments of her cronies—there was little left to say. With Grace talk had flown spontaneously and the intervals of silence were never strained. The rhythm of each day and night at Fotheringham Hall was regular, almost melodious, and never wearisome, whereas Nesta felt obliged to keep moving, never mind where.

Everard regretted bitterly that he had overplayed his hand. Perhaps he should have returned the miniatures, but that would have been equivalent to an admission of weakness. He had refrained from answering Grace's ultimatum. Her anger was bound to subside. She was too big-hearted to nurse a grievance: after a few months she would only remember the rosier features of their twenty-year-old friendship.

As time went on it was Everard who nursed the grievance. Grace's resentment was out of all proportion to his offence, if offence it could be called. His nostalgia for Fotheringham Hall made *Mon Repos* all the more intolerable. He missed the lavender cosiness, the breakfast kedgeree, the dumplings with the silverside of beef, the claret cup flavoured with borage. He even missed the charades and guessing games which at least required mental activity.

At Nesta's the cocktails dulled the palate for good wine. But they enabled one to face the interminable evenings. Nesta's coterie vegetated in the same vacuum. Natasha had a bright new wig but in other respects she was down on her luck.

'We Slavs are superstitious,' she told Everard. 'Since losing my icon I have never won at roulette.'

Everard was reminded that her icon was upstairs in his dispatch case.

'I've brought you a little talisman from London,' he said. 'I hope it will change your luck.'

He went to fetch the Novgorod icon, carefully wrapped in tissue paper and tied with ribbon, and handed it to Natasha. She opened it in a flash.

'A miracle!' she cried. 'I had given up hope. My heart overflows with joy.' She kissed the holy image and then she kissed Everard. 'A million thanks, most chivalrous of friends! But where oh where did you discover it?'

'In a curio shop not far from the British Museum.'

'Poor Serge must have sold it for his dope, but I'll say nothing. I'm too happy to see it again.'

While she dabbed her tears Nesta slipped a few thousand francs inside the icon's frame. 'Now Natasha, run off to the Casino and try your luck. If it fails you this time . . .' She left the sentence unfinished. Natasha would gamble as long as she breathed. Nesta regarded her as one of her permanent charities.

'No, I'd rather give a party for you and Everard. It will have to be at the Casino as I only have a tiny bedroom now.'

'You'll do no such thing—until you've broken the bank.'

'I'll break it yet,' said Natasha with a chuckle.

Everard raised his dry Martini to 'the girl who'll break the bank of Monte Carlo'.

Never before had he been so certain that it was more blessed to give than to receive. But he could not help regretting Grace. Whether she could live contentedly without him remained to be seen. He was sure that he would not be easier to replace than her miniatures. He even pictured her imploring his forgiveness. She would cry a little on his shoulder and offer her cheek to be kissed; he would assure her that bygones were bygones and that he bore her no bitterness, none whatever. A grand and glorious reconciliation would follow at Fotheringham Hall with boiled silverside of beef and all the trimmings.

In the meantime he enjoyed a minor satisfaction when he presented her miniatures to Nesta as well as the inscribed first edition of *Alice in Wonderland* whose disappearance Grace had failed to notice though it was worth five thousand pounds.

'What a heavenly book! It takes me back to my age of innocence.'

'We'll read it together and fancy ourselves in the nursery, boy and girl. Don't you adore the Tenniel illustrations?'

For Nesta it was as if an eternal spring had dawned. Everard would quicken the languid pulse of her life. Very gracefully, very domestically, they would grow old together.

For Everard it was like entering a golden cage, watched by a circle of predatory cats. He felt he was being punished undeservedly for his tenderness of heart.

A MODERN VESTAL

IT WAS annoying to discover that I would have to share a car and its driver-guide with three other tourists. The guide introduced us: Mr. and Mrs. Rufus Quigly and Miss Dingeldein.

'Miss Flora Dingeldein,' the latter amended with emphasis on the Flora, as if it made all the difference. I had seen them swilling Coca-Cola in the airless lounge of the Merida Hotel. The trio sounded boisterous considering the mildness of their beverage and the intensity of the heat, otherwise they were not particularly noticeable.

Owing to Mr. Quigly's bulk it was decided that he should sit in front with the driver-guide. I was privileged to share the two ladies: Mrs. Quigly, blue-haired and bespectacled but festively garbed like many American matrons of her generation, with butterflies printed all over her frock and a tiny winged hat about to take flight from the summit of her mountainous hair-do, and Miss Dingeldein, a buxom woman in her forties with a spray of bougainvillea in her parted raven hair. Miss Dingeldein wore a black and orange outfit and when she pulled off the jacket it appeared like a bathing costume, the plump arms and shoulders astonishingly bare beside me. At any moment one felt that her breasts would pop out.

The guide was very voluble at the wheel. His name was Frederico and he invited us to call him Fred. Having spent some time in the north, he spoke a fluent Latin brand of English, and he had absorbed a variety of fact and fancy from visiting archaeologists. One could not help liking this affable extrovert who, true to tradition, flashed frequent smiles at the ladies over his shoulder. The

United States had not sapped his pride in his native Yucatan, and his remarks proved that he had been prepared for Mr. Quigly's questions, which must have been asked by many other tourists. Swarthy and pock-marked, he had glittering jet eyes, a small silky moustache, and a grin so good-natured that it might well have advertised toothpaste.

Our road led through interminable henequen plantations and Fred gave us an instructive lecture on that monotonous plant, the sisal-hemp or *Agave sisalense*, whose fibres had brought prosperity to Yucatan in those good old days which were now condemned as evil. The leaves began to produce fibre six years after planting and continued to produce it for another decade. Fred quoted the number of bales exported annually to the United States and the statistics sounded impressive. Mr. Quigly kept repeating: 'You don't mean to say! Well, that's mighty interesting! We live and we learn!'

The women wore attentive expressions but their thoughts were elsewhere. They had flown in from Guatemala and were wondering what they were going to see and do next at Chichen-Itzá: both were expecting something more than ruins. Their tour had been planned in Cleveland, where the Quiglys and Miss Dingeldein happened to reside, though they had never met before this last lap of their journey.

The Quiglys were strict Methodists, abstainers from alcohol and nicotine, as they informed me with a fervour that belonged to the last century, since my person reminded them, somewhat to my surprise, of a Methodist preacher of their acquaintance.

'No sir, I've never had a drop of liquor in the house,' said the husband.

'You're forgetting the brandy-flask, Pop,' said his spouse.

'That don't count. It's for medicinal purposes.'

'Isn't that true of all liquor?' Fred interposed.

'I guess strychnine is reckoned the same as medicine by some folks,' riposted Mr. Quigly. Yet one would have sworn that the old boy was a boozer, with his moist yellowish eye and mottled bottle-nose.

Miss Dingeldein asserted her independence by lighting one Lucky Strike after another, which the breeze wafted towards Mrs. Quigly until she had a fit of coughing.

Within half an hour since leaving the white city of Merida these strangers had treated me to chunks of their biographies. Miss Dingeldein might have been hard to place had she not informed me that she was a trained nurse. Her last case had been a rich widow suffering from melancholia. 'Gee, I nearly went nuts. She never spoke, just made signs, and for six months I had to guess what she wanted to say and keep her company. She wasn't interested in anything but food and I had to sit opposite her while she munched and crunched and swallowed, pointing out new dishes on the menu when her mouth was full, knowing all the while that I'd have to give her an enema later. At first I tried to make conversation—it looked so queer to be sitting together without exchanging a word—but as she never listened, I brought a book to meals. I was offered a big dividend by her trustee if I'd stay with her, but I told him flat if I did I wouldn't be held responsible for my actions. I can tell you I needed this vacation pretty badly. But Guatemala wasn't the right spot for me, no sirree! I couldn't find many to talk to there either. . . .'

'What I enjoyed most about Guatemala', said Mrs. Quigly, 'was the Indians. When I think what a lot I've changed in my short lifetime and they've never changed in all these thousands of years! Though they kid the priests into believing that they're Christians, they go on worshipping the same old idols. You daren't step into their churches for they'd chase you out mighty quick. They're determined to keep their voodoo to themselves.'

'What people see in those Indians I can't figure out,' said Miss Dingeldein. 'I've no use for animals I can't talk to. Talk to a dog and there's a chance he'll understand you, but not those aboriginals. Atitlán gave me the jitters. Nothing to do, nowhere to go, lousy roads, only the Indians and the lake to look at. The Indians meant nothing to me and I got sick of staring at that goddamned sheet of water. There was one American living in the place but she was so bored she was downright anti-social.'

'How come she settled there?'

'She had married a Guatemalan against her folks' wishes and she had hell to pay for it. She could still make herself attractive but she just doesn't care. Why not open up a cute little store for those colourful embroideries, I asked her. That's the one thing the Indians *can* do. She declared she simply despised them. She does nothing but stare at the lake and twiddle her thumbs. I guess she'll go nuts too.'

'Why doesn't she go home to the States?' asked Mrs. Quigly.

'She has a two-year-old boy, and by the law of Guatemala she cannot take him away. All the laws of the country are in favour of the male. If they divorce, the husband keeps the kid.'

'How feudal. You're disappointing me in Guatemala. Personally, I enjoyed it as much as a movie. I guess ignorance is bliss.'

'At least you got one whale of a kick out of all those Indians you snapped,' said Mr. Quigly, 'so don't start telling me you're sorry now. The trip was your idea.'

'I never said I was sorry. You didn't hear me right, Pop. Do you know, before I left Cleveland I was beginning to worry about myself. I didn't seem to get a kick out of anything and that wasn't like me. I had always got lots of kicks out of life, even out of daily chores like cooking and sewing. Suddenly I realized I was getting them no longer. Everything looked the same and tasted the same. The world seemed flat as a pancake instead of round. There's a kind of comfort in feeling that the world *is* round, isn't there? It's so stimulating to wake up in the morning and realize that you're spinning in space. . . . Then Pop decided that both of us were ripe for a real vacation. My first new kick was those Indians: it was like reading Fenimore Cooper when I was at high school. I used to spend hours in the native markets taking all the pictures I could. Some were shy as rabbits.'

'I guess you've used up all your coloured film, Mrs. Quigly. You should have saved some for the ruins.'

'Oh, I've plenty left for those. Mercy! Whatever's that?' Fred slowed down for a long and deliberate reptile to cross the road.

'An iguana, ma'am. Its meat just melts in the mouth.' Fred

licked his lips with a pale pink tongue and gave Miss Dingeldein
a special leer. From that moment Miss Dingeldein seemed hypnotized: she could not take her eyes off our conductor.

'I'd never screw up the courage to taste one of those big
lizards,' said Mrs. Quigly, 'but I'm dying to snap one. Please
stop the car when you see another coming.'

'You'll find plenty more of them at Chichen-Itzá.'

'Well, that's something for me to look forward to. I'm not so
hot on the ruins, those were Mr. Quigly's part of the programme:
he wants to educate me. But I'll soon be a ruin myself. I guess
more women feel that way than men. Are there any markets
around the hotel where I can snap colourful natives?'

'Only a few small villages, ma'am. We're steering straight for
the jungle.'

The word jungle had the effect of a distant drum on Fred's
audience, the jungle so remote from anything they had experienced, a prehistoric womb peopled with dim sinister foetuses.
The women looked wistful in the deepening twilight and Miss
Dingeldein took quicker puffs at her cigarette. 'I feel kinda nervous at the prospect,' she said, 'yet nobody could call me a
sissy. I've assisted at major surgical operations without turning a
hair.'

'You'll find every modern convenience at Mayaland Lodge.
Each room has a shower and a private porch with rocking-chairs.
If you're scared of bugs there are mosquito nets.' Fred's voice
was reassuring.

'I'm not scared of the bugs. I'm scared of myself, what the
jungle may do to me.'

She would not have said this, I thought, in the clear light of
morning. The road became bumpier every minute. The new one,
as Fred explained, had not been completed. Pungent whiffs of
a strange vegetation struck one's nostrils; phosphorescent eyes
peered out of the bushes; unfamiliar hootings filled the air as
we jogged along the solitary road. Conversation languished; my
companions showed signs of fatigue. The glowing lantern of the
moon had risen. A great pyramid was looming on our left. '*El*

Castillo,' said Fred, 'one of the finest jewels of Maya architecture.' He stopped the car for us to admire it in the moonlight.

After the long drive between henequen plantations the height and massiveness of this structure made it as impressive as a modern skyscraper, perhaps even more so. Its builders had never known Egypt, yet here was the same principle, the same idea of a monumental structure.

'Gee whiz, are they all that high?' asked Mr. Quigly.

'No, that is the highest and it is supposed to have occupied the centre of the ancient city. I guess you must be mathematically minded to appreciate its details. The number of platforms, for instance, equals the number of months in the Maya year, eighteen to be exact. And the steps add up to three hundred and sixty-five, the number of days in the Maya year . . . "

'Do we have to climb all those doggone steps?' Mr. Quigly queried anxiously.

'That's up to you, mister. As it's the highest building you get the best view from the top.'

'Well, you say the word, Fred. You're the band leader,' said Miss Dingeldein.

'I'm only the licensed guide,' Fred answered. 'I'm here to carry out your wishes.'

Miss Dingeldein seized his hand and beamed at him: 'You're my leader, remember that, Fred. I'll follow you anywheres you say.'

'Thank you, Miss Dingeldein. I wish all the ladies were like you. It would make my life much easier.'

'I meant it, Fred.' She gave his hand a squeeze.

'We shall see,' he answered quizzically. 'We Latins are apt to be sceptical.'

'That doesn't sound exactly kind, and you look so kind, Fred. Doesn't he, folks?'

Her query was embarrassing. To answer 'Yes' in chorus would sound silly.

Miss Dingeldein had a talent for sudden intimacy. Already she had hoisted her relation to the guide on to a sentimental perch.

She was humming a self-satisfied tune as we returned to the dusty motor.

At Mayaland Lodge I decided to dine alone and wander among the ruins afterwards. They were only a short distance down the road. The moon was propitious, varnishing the scattered buildings with phosphorescent silver. The other monuments were allied in style to the so-called *Castillo*, clean in outline, austere, cubistic. The ancient inhabitants would have approved of Le Corbusier's plans for vertical garden cities, of his dwellings raised above the ground on concrete piles, with plenty of space for stadiums and parks between them. Here the space between rectangular blocks was occupied by a highway to the sacred pool and the lofty enclosure of the ball-court where ritual games had been played.

Was the Maya way of life so different after all? Is not football a ritual in England, baseball in America, and *pelota* in Spain? Millions follow these games from near and from afar, in the press, on television, and over the radio. If the losers survive quite a few would like to kill them. In this ball-court, long deserted, the subtle acoustics conjured visions of desperate contests. A Maya boy was shouting and clapping his hands, and the echoes, enlarged and many times multiplied, were eerily mocking amid the waves of silence that engulfed them. In the old days the captain of the losing team would forfeit his head, as a bas-relief testified. The ball had to be sent through a stone ring set high in the wall, a feat which looked almost impossible since it had to be propelled from the player's hip or shoulder. The lad shouted again and again, and his cries returned in a sepulchral parody.

A lean black dog was following me, stopping now and then as at sight of a ghost or to growl at something beyond my range of vision. It seemed to be the guardian of the place and I felt it wished to speak to me. It wagged its tail in friendly fashion. A phrase of Gertrude Stein occurred to me: 'Needs be needs be needs be near.' The black dog needed to be near.

Most ruins look better by night, like aged beauties whose faces have been lifted and restored by plastic surgeons. They sleep in the daytime and waken after sunset. Now these were wide awake, ready for another ball-game, and I was glad to see them in a conscious state, aware of their original purpose even if no game were played. On the morrow they would close their stony eyes.

Miss Dingeldein was sitting on the hotel veranda, smoking and fanning herself with a newspaper. She had attracted a regiment of flying insects, apart from which she sat alone facing the moon-lit garden of rocks and shrubs.

'Hello stranger!' she called to me. 'Where have you been hiding? Come over and make yourself sociable. It isn't bed-time yet for the worldly-wise.'

I mentioned that I had been on a preliminary prowl.

'Aren't you a heel!' she exclaimed. 'Why didn't you take me along? The Quiglys went off to bye-byes and I've been dying for human company.'

'I felt sure that Fred would look after you.'

'The poor guy was pretty well pooped after the long hot drive with so many questions to answer. He seems real friendly but I can't quite make him out. Do you think he's square? Maybe he acts the same with everybody, just laying on that famous dago charm. Reminds me of an article I once read, "Latins are lousy lovers". There might be some truth in it though I thought it sour grapes at the time. The Yanks are fine specimens physically, but they've a lot to learn about loving. They're not basically inter-ested in the technique—I mean the men. I guess that's why so many of their wives cross the Atlantic. I forgot to ask if you're married.'

'A very indiscreet question. Do I look it?'

'You might have been divorced a couple of times.'

'Thanks for the compliment. As a matter of fact I am single.'

'At your age? Then you've no use for women. Do you hate 'em as much as I do?'

'Perhaps I love them indiscriminately. But I'd rather not talk about myself. You're far more interesting. May I offer you a drink?'

'If it's to keep you company, but you don't have to stand on ceremony with me. I'm only a trained nurse. You don't really like me, do you? I've always been too frank.'

'Your candour is refreshing, and I happen to be thirsty.'

'Well this funny place certainly does do something to a person. Or perhaps it's you. I could open my heart to you, spill out my secrets. You're cosy, that's what you are. You ought to be a psycho-analyst.'

Miss Dingeldein ordered lager, but she allowed it to grow tepid while she discoursed in an even voice. It was like an interior monologue. I deduced that having nursed too many patients she had reached a stage where she needed some nursing herself. This could be done by listening patiently to her random reminiscences.

Her profession was favourable to intimacies, yet these had failed to develop. Men were pathetically helpless in those pools of sickness between the rivers of office life. The toughest of them were apt to melt in gratitude for little attentions. Most of them wanted to be mothered, but a modern wife had other occupations. A nurse could contribute more than any doctor to their recovery if she took the trouble: she wielded extraordinary power in the sickroom. Miss Dingeldein could have married several of her patients but she declared that marriage in those circumstances did not appeal to her: it might be taking advantage of mere physical weakness. Perhaps she was kinky: she wished to be loved for her own sake 'as a woman pure and simple'—not that she was especially pure or even simple, if I knew what she meant. She had made others happy, and now it was her turn. Outside of her profession, however, her relations with men had never got beyond the pally stage.

'I don't know why I've been telling you all this,' she added, 'it's an admission of failure.'

'We all have such moods occasionally. I'm sure yours will pass tomorrow at the ruins.'

'I hope you're correct. I don't want to go to bed but there's nothing else to do. Nighty-night!'

Fred assembled us bright and early. The Quiglys were costumed as for a tiger hunt in the wilds of Africa, with pith helmets,

parasols, alpenstocks and cameras for their weapons. Miss Dingeldein wore a turban and scarlet slacks. She greeted me casually
considering her recent confidences, and switched her whole
attention to our guide.

Fred took his duties seriously. He was determined to make us
appreciate the achievements of his long-forgotten ancestors. Miss
Dingeldein drew her feet out of her Mexican sandals and twiddled
her painted toe-nails as he held forth on the rise and fall of the
Maya Empire.

'You're the perfect professor this morning,' she remarked, after
Fred had explained the connection of Chichen-Itzá, meaning
'mouth of the wells of the Itzás', and the *cenotes* or natural wells,
which had made Yucatan habitable in the absence of running
water. 'Who were the Itzás? It's a funny kind of name, like a
lap-dog's: "I've a cute little Itza whose name is Ritza"'.

'I'm coming to that,' said Fred with a frown that would brook
no frivolity. And come to it he did, telling us about Kukulcan or
'Quetzal-snake', who led the Itzá people to this locality between
A.D. 968 and 987, until Miss Dingeldein was cowed. Mrs. Quigly
was busy with her camera, running off into nooks and corners,
while her husband stood mopping the sweat off his brow. As we
climbed the precipitous stairs to the House of the Tigers, Fred
asked us to notice the serpent balustrade. 'I think it is generally
agreed that the serpent is a phallic emblem,' he asserted. 'You'll
find it everywhere at Chichen-Itzá. Look at these serpent columns
and their big round threatening heads. There can be no doubt of
their human origin even though it has been idealized.'

'You're telling me,' Miss Dingeldein muttered.

'Later on I'll take you to a phallic temple where the carving is
more realistic. The ladies needn't come if they don't want to.
Archaeology can't take account of private prejudices. The facts of
life have to be squarely faced.'

'As a professional nurse,' said Miss Dingeldein, 'I agree.'

'I don't think Mrs. Quigly ought to see it,' Mr. Quigly objected.
'Such things are for men only.'

'Don't be selfish,' said Miss Dingeldein.

'Why shouldn't I see it, honey?' Mrs. Quigly gently protested. 'We've had our silver wedding.'

'He talks as if we were a couple of old sissies,' Miss Dingeldein
spluttered indignantly. 'Pay no attention to him. He's mediaeval.'

'Who asked for your opinion?' exclaimed Mr. Quigly out of
the corner of his mouth.

'We women should stand up for our rights.'

'Or lie down for them,' said Fred with a chuckle.

The frescoes in the House of Tigers were protected by a
respectable penumbra; their details required exceptionally sharp
eyesight. Fred drew our attention to a scene representing circum-
cision while Mr. Quigly stood guard over his wife and shooed her
into the background. Fred warmed to the theme as if, in Miss
Dingeldein's words, he had been a practising surgeon. There
were also dim scenes of combat, and a painted raft which evoked
the legend of an early migration. At the foot of this temple was a
lower chamber with sculptured columns, one depicting a skull's
head with bulging breasts and arms.

'Those people couldn't have had clean minds,' said Mr.
Quigly. 'I reckon that was why they came to grief. It should serve
as an object lesson to our decadent modern society.'

'The Maya Empire vanished, it is true,' answered Fred, 'but
the people have survived it and the language is still spoken all
over Yucatan. V.D. was unknown till it was introduced from
outside. Sexologists would find nothing to do here.'

In spite of Miss Dingeldein's facetious interruptions Fred
remained the resolute cicerone, spicing his lecture with anecdotes
to hold our attention. It was a praiseworthy effort, for Mr.
Quigly was concerned with the moral problems of paganism, Mrs.
Quigly with her camera, and Miss Dingeldein with flirtatious
badinage. His patience was crowned with success when he led us
towards the sacred well.

No fragmentary relic this, but a sheer drop in the limestone
with a huge diameter. Peering over the perpendicular edge into
the stagnant water some eighty feet below, it was easy to imagine

the sensations of the victims before they were hurled in as offerings to relentless gods. In the stillness of the heat-hazed morning you could almost hear their terrified shrieks and splashings. Pilgrims had brought their valued treasures and these were hurled in too. The depths of the pool were carpeted with jewels and skeletons.

Fred described the ancient ceremonies as if he had seen them: how the chieftains fasted sixty days without raising their eyes, not even to glance at the women who brought them snacks, and then at break of day how the loveliest of the girls who had been chosen for sacrifice were thrown headlong into the cenote from the platform where he was standing, to implore the gods for a bumper harvest and other practical benefits.

Miss Dingeldein uttered a little scream and clung to the narrator. 'Shall I throw you in?' he asked jestingly.

Either his words had frightened her or she felt dizzy, for she was swaying dangerously near the edge of the pool. Fred had to jerk her back with all his strength so that they almost toppled over together. Miss Dingeldein had turned very pale. 'Hold me tight,' she murmured. 'I feel ready to faint.' Fred had to clutch her in his arms. The poor fellow was unprepared for this contingency: evidently he had learnt nothing from the Hollywood films. Miss Dingeldein shut her eyes and I thought I detected the flicker of a smile on her lips. Fred lowered her gently on to a patch of grass, from which, perhaps in dull contrast to his muscular arms, she contrived to pull herself together.

'Oh dear, I've been a sissy. Forgive me, Fred, I don't know what came over me. Looking down into the water and thinking of all the things that had happened right here I felt I was one of the victims. You scared me, Fred, honest you did, when you said you would pitch me in. Your eyes were so fierce I believed it.'

Fred made light of the incident but Miss Dingeldein was determined to dramatize it. 'I never realized before that I was psychic,' she said. 'I felt absolutely like one of those Maya girls.'

'Do you remember what you had to ask the gods for?'

'I've forgotten everything except an overwhelming sensation of dread. Please take me away.'

The Quiglys, who had been hunting for a photographic post of vantage, came bustling up for the latest information.

'My, and we missed it all! You'd have certainly slipped into that pool hadn't Fred been hanging around. Mr. Quigly was a champion swimmer at college but those days are over. Heart trouble, so he couldn't have helped you, neither could I. And you don't swim, how come?'

'I guess I was under-privileged.'

'Fred, you deserve a medal for life-saving. She'd have sunk like a stone. Now we'd better go home and relax. We've seen and done about enough for one morning. How are you feeling, Miss Dingeldein?'

'Give me your arm, Fred. Thank you, I'm beginning to feel better—a little muzzy though, like a medium after the séance. It was a genuine psychic experience.'

'It must have been thrilling,' Mrs. Quigly remarked. 'I'm sorry to have missed it. That's the fault of my Kodak. You must tell me all about it. How did it happen?'

'She'd better forget it,' said Mr. Quigly.

'Then tell me later on, dear,' whispered his spouse, 'Mr. Quigly disapproves of spiritualism.'

'I suspect Fred is my control,' said Miss Dingeldein. 'I would never have had this experience without him.'

'We Catholics don't believe in such things,' said Fred.

'That makes no difference. We can all be agents of supernatural powers. I saw you distinctly as a high priest of the Mayas.'

'If I was one you would not be here. I'd have pushed you in.'

'I guess you're one of those split personalities but I love you just the same.' She snuggled up to his shoulder.

'Well, I've never been called that before.'

Fred was slightly bewildered. Some of the tourists he had catered for had been eccentric, demanding supernumerary entertainment, special diets or emotions he had been unable to provide. He was ready to meet reasonable requests half-way: it was his job to see that his clients made the most of their tour. But Miss Dingeldein's behaviour bothered him. She leaned against him too heavily and gazed at him too hungrily. Moreover she was too old for such antics. He was uncertain how to cope with her, so he tried to maintain an even keel between chivalry and chaff. He had a wife in Merida about half Miss Dingeldein's age.

Casually Fred referred to his children on the drive back to Mayaland Lodge. 'My little daughter loves the sacred well,' he said. 'We often picnic there. And my boy's ambition is to dive to the bottom. He knows it has never been fully explored, and like many boys he dreams of hidden treasure.'

'I shouldn't trust any child near it until a strong railing is put up,' said Mrs. Quigly.

'Especially after Miss Dingeldein's experience,' added her husband. 'And she's no kid.'

'Why didn't you tell me you had children, Fred? Are they anything like you?' Miss Dingeldein really meant: 'Why didn't you tell me you had a wife?'

'Fortunately they have their mother's looks.'

'I never thought of you as the father of a family. You don't produce that impression.' She sounded reproachful, as if she had been deceived.

'It's quite normal in our country. Most of us marry young.'

Miss Dingeldein burst into tears.

'For the love of Mike,' exclaimed Fred. 'What's the matter now?'

After she had sobbed awhile she bit her lip and stammered through her tears: 'You meant that for me. I'm disappointed in you, Fred. I've had lots of chances to marry but I preferred to keep my independence.'

'I assure you no offence was intended. If you think it was, you had better find another guide. I am sorry not to have given satisfaction.'

'It's you or nobody. I don't like changing horses in midstream and I paid for this tour in advance.'

'I will see that you are refunded.'

'Hey, don't let's argue,' pleaded Mr. Quigly, 'it's much too hot. I'm dripping and I guess Miss Dingeldein's no cooler than I am. And she's been seeing things no decent lady ought to, married or single. No wonder she's upset. But we're all good friends and it would be a shame to break up the bunch. I invite you all to join me in a coke. Shake hands, you two, and no more arguments.'

Fred and Miss Dingeldein shook hands half-heartedly. Fred's expression was surly and Miss Dingeldein's defiant. Without the latter's co-operation we did not find much to say. The Coca-Colas steamed in our hands and Mr. Quigly distributed saline tablets manufactured by his own firm to revive us. It was decided that we should spend the afternoon at our leisure and continue our tour of the ruins on the morrow. But Mrs. Quigly would not rest until she had snapped an iguana, even if it was to employ her whole afternoon.

'I'll cool off under a shower and lie down,' said Miss Dingeldein. 'I need to think things over. This morning's experience has given me a new angle on myself. Maybe I should have been a medium instead of a nurse. I've a premonition that Maya spirits are after me and that I may be receiving a meaningful message. I must visit that well again.'

'I sincerely hope not,' said Fred.

Miss Dingeldein brightened. 'Don't be sore, sweetie. You're not responsible for me.'

'So long as you're here I must be to a certain extent.'

'You keep an eye on her, Fred,' said Mr. Quigly. 'This has been an unusually interesting morning and we owe it entirely to our wonderful guide. We mustn't blame him if the old Mayas had dirty minds.'

We dispersed to our separate lodgings, and I sat on my porch to con an official publication about the ruins we had inspected. The writer was a specialist on the subject, but he was so prosaic that he failed to grip my attention. So little of the atmosphere had got into his pages that by altering the names it might have been about any other 'archaeological terrain'. The spade had done its work but words were a different matter.

An iguana was sprawling across the path below me like animated driftwood from a prehistoric age. I was about to summon Mrs. Quigly when the Chinese gardener caused it to scurry under a boulder. He had cultivated these few acres of reclaimed wilderness until they had begun to suggest a Chinese pattern, making use of rocks that would have defeated other gardeners. These had no sculptural quality as in China, but he had trained a few plants to upholster them as it were .He loitered by the irises, wrinkled in a contemplative smile: his paternal pride in their petals of purple silk gave him an air of wisdom. I was admiring his achievement when the sight of Miss Dingeldein made me retreat like the iguana.

The trained nurse off duty must have compounded her differences with Fred during the afternoon, for she was dining with him in conspicuous tête-à-tête and gales of laughter reached me from their table. Gales of laughter reached me later when I strolled among the resurrected ruins, where Fred had accompanied Miss Dingeldein with his guitar. '*Besame, besame mucho*,' throbbed his robust tenor, which I took as a friendly warning to keep out of their way.

'That means kiss me, doesn't it?' asked a familiar voice. 'Go right ahead.'

The song proceeded crescendo, '*Como se fuera esta noche la ultima vez*'—'As if this night were the last time.' It was a plangent tune, which the acoustics of the ball-court parodied by over-emphasis. Whether it was followed by osculations I never discovered. The guitar might have been taken as a convenient chaperon, yet Miss Dingeldein was capable of smashing it if it hampered her designs. And Fred was remarkably good-natured: one felt sure that he would let her down gently.

Next morning all of us save Mr. Quigly climbed the steep narrow stairs of the great pyramid of El Castillo. Mrs. Quigly puffed and panted in the rear with her camera and I gave her a helping hand. Her Kodak, as she said, was 'a banner with the strange device, Excelsior!' Miss Dingeldein, surprisingly fleet of foot, was first to reach the room at the summit. Once planted there she shouted down: 'Come on, you sissies!'

There were two serpent columns at its entrance and a few blurred carvings of unknown dignitaries; otherwise it was bare. Beneath it lay a similar structure of an earlier period with a hall of offerings which contained a sculptured Chacmool or rain-god, and a chamber of sacrifices guarded by a stone tiger painted red, with inlaid eyes and spots of jade. Fred promised to show us this as a crowning treat. In the meantime he explained the pyramid's connection with sun worship and the solar year, entering into minute mathematical details—the fifty-two years of the Maya-Toltec cycle, the three hundred and sixty-five days of their year, the eighteen months of twenty days each and five extra days set apart as unfortunate under the name Uayeb, so that I felt as addled as Mrs. Quigly appeared, shaking her head and saying with a sigh: 'It's just too bad Mr. Quigly couldn't make this climb on account of his heart. He's got a wonderful head for figures and I can scarcely add two and two together.'

'I'm with you there,' I said. 'It's by no means certain that two and two make four. One of the Rothschilds said, "Two and two make twenty-two."'

Miss Dingeldein was humming '*Besame mucho*' with one arm clasping a serpent pillar, her eyes focused on some interior vision, for they were neither looking at us nor at the view.

Unperturbed, Fred pointed out the scattered monuments in store for us, the circular 'Snail' or astronomical observatory of the Mayas, the Tomb of the High Priest, the House of the Deer, and an adjacent 'Nunnery' where vestal virgins were trained to minister to the Sacred Fire. Whoever allowed herself to be seduced was condemned to death without mercy, he added. Miss Dingeldein emitted a whistle by way of comment.

It was not easy to identify the dead grey piles among the untidy clumps of vegetation with Fred's lively descriptions of what they had been originally. Most of them had kept their secrets in spite of the probings of archaeological detectives. The names attached to them were often misleading. They dotted the horizon like puzzles waiting to be solved. The conglomeration was as alien to European culture as the Maya words pronounced by Fred, words that crackled and fizzled in one's ears: 'Pop, Uo, Zip, Zodz, Zeec, Xul, Yaxkin . . .'

'I hope I'm not boring you,' said Fred.

'I wouldn't have missed this for the world,' Mrs. Quigly assured him. 'I never expected any ruin to give me such a kick. When I get home I'll let my friends have it.'

'I'm glad you feel that way. I remember another lady saying to me, "Why travel so far and waste so much dough simply to wear yourself out?" '

'Oh I'm never tired when I get really bitten. But Mr. Quigly has to be careful on account of his heart.'

I began to wonder at Miss Dingeldein's silence, which was unusually prolonged. She had removed her sandals and was walking along the outer platform barefoot. Gazing at the panorama, we too fell silent. Fred seemed to have talked himself out. He had subsided into melancholy after his statistical ebullience. Perhaps his Maya blood was reasserting itself and he was brooding on what his people had lost for ever. His eyes were as inscrutable as balls of obsidian: he resembled another Chacmool waiting for rain. The clicking of Mrs. Quigley's camera was the only sound above the tropical stillness.

'Well, I guess it's time for us to be inching along,' said Mrs. Quigly. 'Mr. Quigly must be awful discouraged sitting all alone down there. Where's Miss Dingeldein? Oh, there you are! Have you seen enough, dear?'

'You folks forget about me; I'm staying right here.'

'What else is there to stay for?'

'I'm here on a special assignment. I've the Sacred Fire to look after.'

She said this in a matter-of-fact voice, as if she were busy with a patient. None of us could help laughing, for Miss Dingeldein in the role of a vestal virgin was incongruous, to say the least. 'Hadn't you better wear your shoes?' Fred suggested.

'Remember the spiritual, "When I get to Heav'n goin' to put on my shoes, goin' to walk all over God's Heav'n."'

For answer she flung one sandal after another to the bottom of the pyramid.

'Whatever did you do that for?' Mrs. Quigly quavered in alarm, as if she feared that Miss Dingeldein's clothes would follow.

'Good-bye to life's illusions!' Miss Dingeldein retorted gaily.

Fred gave a nervous twist to his moustache. He had paled through his swarthy complexion. 'I advise you to join us. It will soon be too hot for more sightseeing,' he observed, 'and the rest of the party are anxious to move on.'

'Yeah, the mercury's rising and Mr. Quigly's waving his hat at us. I'm afraid he'll catch sunstroke. Don't make us wait too long, dear. We appreciate your company and there's more sights for us all to see.'

'Run along then and make it snappy. You'll have plenty to tell your friends when you get back home.'

'We'll call for you later,' said Fred. 'We're going on foot so you can relax in the car.'

'Don't waste your time. I've got the Sacred Fire.'

'Why not join us now and return in the cool of the evening to watch the sunset,' Fred tried to coax her. 'That's also a sacred fire. You'll get a wonderful view.'

'You can't kid me. I belong right here. I've my mission.'

'We'll be missing you. On our last morning at Chichen-Itzá it's a shame to break up the bunch,' pleaded Mrs. Quigly.

Concluding that further argument was superfluous, we descended the precipitous stairs. As another group of tourists were on their way up, Fred consigned the care of Miss Dingeldein to a colleague who was guiding them.

Mr. Quigly grumbled: 'I thought you were never coming down. I might just as well have sat on the hotel porch. At least I'd have had a chair to sit on. The car is like an oven.'

'It was Miss Dingeldein's fault. Some fool notion has got into her brain. She declares she's a vestal virgin and won't come down.'

'That woman burns me, honest,' Fred confessed. 'She seemed O.K. last night but she acted funny at the pool and she's acting funny now and I don't like any part of it.'

'I reckon she's old enough to look after herself,' growled Mr. Quigly.

We resumed our tour with less buoyancy than we had begun it. The heat grew so oppressive that all movement was a strain, and the ruins seemed to crumble more and more as we stumbled on. At the Akab Dzib, or House of Dark Writing, Fred pointed out a stone lintel with hieroglyphic inscriptions which nobody had been able to decipher, and some scarlet stains which turned out to be impressions of severed human hands. According to Fred these were symbols of the gods who had been invoked there. To my eye they appeared quite recent, but in certain surroundings a mere smear may be fraught with mystery. 'Celestial' though the hands were reputed to be, they had a crude, murderous aspect. 'Perhaps it's as well we left Miss Dingeldein behind,' I said, 'since she has become so susceptible.'

'You mean screwy,' said Mr. Quigly. 'I wouldn't recommend that woman as a nurse—not to my best enemy.'

'Do you think we shall find her hysterical on the summit of the Castillo?'

'I don't know what to think,' Fred muttered grimly. 'I've a hunch that we shouldn't have left her.'

'I'm all set for another round of Cokes,' said Mr. Quigly. 'You've got a swell show here, Fred, but Chichen-Itzá would never do as a health resort. The way back to the car seems as long as the way to Tipperary.'

A small crowd had gathered at the foot of the Castillo, as if something spectacular had occurred or was occurring. Fred quickened his pace and we followed. In complete silence the crowd was staring at the staircase of the main façade. I was reminded of a rapt assembly in front of a church at Assisi where a statue of the Blessed Virgin was said to have spread both arms in a gesture of benediction.

'Well, what's happened?' exclaimed Mr. Quigly. 'I can see nothing that wasn't here before.'

Somewhat officiously he elbowed his way towards Fred, who was conferring with his colleague in a troubled undertone.

A boy was sluicing the balustrade with water from a pail.

'It must be something psychic,' said Mrs. Quigly.

'What's the dope, Fred?'

In reply Fred made the sign of the cross: 'May the soul of Miss Dingeldein rest in peace!'

Mrs. Quigly dropped her camera and clung to her husband.

'Why, you don't mean to say—!'

But there was no more to be said—at any rate for the moment. The vestal had taken a dive into the void.

THE OPERATION

'As long as you go to Professor Nagler you will never need a surgical operation.'

More than one of Aubrey Vernon's friends had assured him of this as an infallible axiom. An operation was a luxury which so eminent an actor could ill afford. Apart from which he had a gnawing horror of the knife since one of his kidneys had been removed instead of a little stone.

'The whole organ was diseased: you will be better off without it,' his surgeon had blithely explained. 'Nature can be wonderfully economical. The remaining kidney will do the job of two.'

While Aubrey had become reconciled to his loss he resented the deep cleft and surrounding bulge which marred the symmetry of his athletic figure.

He had enjoyed a preliminary decade as a matinée idol in the role of ever-fresh juvenile lead. His stage kisses, infinitely protracted, were in a subliminal class of their own: they would have won the first prize at any competition. Husbands and wives, bachelors and spinsters, craned their necks and wriggled in their seats at the climax when these occurred. The spell they cast was due to a subtle blend of technique and physique, for Aubrey was too self-absorbed to lose his head over a woman. He only indulged in fugitive affairs for the sake of publicity. And all the girls he was advertised with were eager to collaborate. They basked in his glamour and married rich stockbrokers.

The highbrow critics who had praised his competence and good looks with patronizing condescension discovered that Aubrey was an actor of the first rank when in a spirit of bravado he had daubed and furrowed his features beyond recognition and recited the role of Lear in a flowing beard. Overnight he became a leading Shakespearian actor. Othello, Hamlet, Macbeth—he had tackled them all with versatile mastery, and he diversified these with the heroes of Ibsen, Shaw, Sheridan, and a few Restoration revivals, but he never approved of Wilde. He remained a box-office magnet. Foreign visitors to London made a point of seeing him as one of the living sights. Nor were they disappointed: he gave them what they had been led to expect and even more.

In daily life Aubrey Vernon was just a jolly good fellow with tastes conspicuously athletic. The biggest room in his flat was a small gymnasium where he punched a bag and practised shadow-boxing besides weight-lifting and skipping over a rope. He was affluent but far too generous to amass a fortune.

In his theatrical make-up he could still play the role of juvenile lead—or couldn't he? Critically he examined his features in the shaving mirror. His cheek-bones had a hectic flush and his eyes were faintly bloodshot. As he twitched up an eyelid he could hear the rapid pumping of his heart. Perhaps he should follow the advice of Derek and Mona and submit to a medical check-up. But it seemed absurd to endure a series of tiresome tests when one wasn't definitely ailing. Another round of golf at Samaden banished such neurotic fancies. In his bath, however, he noticed a little swelling below the groin. Gently, then less gently, he pressed and massaged it. Since he changed his clothes as often as if he were engaged on a film set he had ample opportunity to inspect its steady growth. Even when fully dressed he was conscious of this teasing protuberance: his hand explored it through a trouser pocket while he sat in the hotel bar with Derek and Mona. Not that it itched or ached, but its presence made him nervous. Perhaps he had strained himself weight-lifting: he suspected a hernia.

'What's up, old boy?' asked Derek. 'You look out of sorts. Take a tip from me and consult Professor Nagler. All of us over-forties need a periodical check-up.'

Aubrey grinned, knowing that Derek was rounding sixty.

'Everybody recommends Professor Nagler as a miracle worker,' he answered wearily.

'That's precisely what he is.' Derek reeled off an imposing list of patients whom the Professor had cured of diseases which had eluded other diagnosticians. He went on to describe a mysterious malady of his own. 'I swear by Professor Nagler. He's expensive, mind you, but he's worth every golden guinea. I regard him as my life insurance. So does Mona. Don't you, darling?'

Perversely, Aubrey conceived a prejudice: the more he heard of the Professor's magic, the more sceptical he grew. But the swelling continued to bother him and when he returned to London it was still aggressively there, decidedly bigger. Rather in the spirit of a gambler he suddenly exclaimed: 'Why not?'

Over the telephone Professor Nagler's secretary sounded coldly supercilious. 'I'm afraid the Professor is entirely booked up for the next month. If the case is urgent we might squeeze you in between his other appointments. Let me see. What about Thursday fortnight at twelve-fifteen? That is the best I can do for you.'

Aubrey was too famous a figure to appreciate being squeezed in anywhere, yet he gruffly assented. 'Put me down for Thursday fortnight.'

'Sorry, I didn't catch the surname. Will you be so good as to repeat it?'

Aubrey articulated the popular syllables with a defiant *hauteur*.

The secretary caught her breath. 'How exciting! If you leave your private number the Professor may be able to fix you up a date next week. I'll have a word with him. Bye-bye.'

Next week, by special arrangement, Aubrey was ushered, after a long bleak session with *The Times*, into Professor Nagler's huge consulting-room. Small probing eyes behind gold-rimmed spectacles twinkled at him with perfunctory benevolence and a Central European accent invited him to take the chair opposite the monumental desk where the Professor sat beside a telephone.

'It is a pleasure and a privilege to meet you, Mr. Vernon. My wife, my children, my secretary have admired you in many plays and films, but I—alas—am generally too tired after my day's toil to enjoy the theatre. But I would not exchange my profession for any other. It is my joy to heal the suffering.'

Professor Nagler was most communicative about himself. While he talked he scrutinized his new patient and made copious notes while listening to his heart-beats and taking his blood pressure. The examination was thorough.

'I am happy to tell you that for a man of your age you are in excellent condition. Your liver is wonderful, your heart is splendid, and there is nothing wrong with your kidney. Your blood pressure is low but that is better than high. A course of my injections will increase your animal energy. Let us begin right away.'

As for the swelling, the professor assured him that it was not due to a hernia, it was merely a symptom of sluggish circulation. 'I'll give you my lamp treatment to tone up the system. I will also prescribe an ointment for local application. I am satisfied with your prostate and your urine is beautifully clear. You have nothing to worry about.'

Aubrey was exhilarated by this consultation. Twice a week he repaired cheerfully to Professor Nagler's consulting-room to lower his trousers for an injection and recline under a mysterious lamp. Gradually the swelling subsided, and he had to admit that he felt more relaxed. In cold and foggy weather he found himself looking forward to Professor Nagler's treatment with something like a drug addict's anticipation. The injections stung but they were stimulating, as if they contained a pharmaceutical equivalent of dry champagne; and the rays of the lamp penetrated his belly with comforting warmth. In the meantime the Professor soliloquized about his prodigious achievements, past and present.

'Mine is basically a religious vocation,' he asserted. 'I rescue my patients from the brutal surgeon. Did you see that tall aristocratic gentleman when you stepped out of the lift? He is a retired admiral, eighty-six years old. You would never guess it, would you? Since he visits me regularly he grows younger every year. It was Lord Levy who sent him after giving him up as a hopeless case. "I can do nothing more for him," he told me. "You are the only person in London who may solve this particular problem." And now he is as pink as a baby and as straight as a statue.'

The Duchess of Tonbridge was another of the Professor's triumphs and her name cropped up incessantly in his conversation. 'I cured her in twenty-four hours,' said the Professor complacently. 'Are you comfortable? Just turn over a little more to the right, please, and undo more trouser buttons. *Mein Gott*, that is an ugly scar. It is a pity you did not come to me before they stole your kidney.'

Simultaneously the telephone rang. The Professor became flustered: he raced towards the receiver. 'Tell her Graciousness I'll be ready to receive her in two ticks,' he stammered into the instrument while Aubrey was buttoning his flies.

'A beautiful lady is the Duchess, a veritable *grande dame*, and so considerate, so grateful for all I have done for her. Every year she sends me grouse and pheasants from her estate. For Easter she gave me a Fabergé egg in gold and enamel, and for Christmas this magnificent pocket book.' He flourished a shagreen wallet with a glittering monogram as he bowed Aubrey out of the room. He always bowed like a courtier. While the door was flung open Aubrey could hear his effusive greeting: 'Good morning, your Graciousness. You bring me the sunshine. You are looking marvellous. It is my best reward.'

The Professor's antics would have been considered grotesque on the stage but they fascinated Aubrey for that very reason. He could hardly restrain himself from parodying his idiosyncrasies. The diction reminded him of Svengali in *Trilby*. What fun he could extract from that role! But all the highbrow critics would be down on him like a ton of bricks. Supposing he offered it to one of the 'new wave' dramatists to rewrite? Tickled at the notion of what Beckett or Harold Pinter would do to *Trilby*, he studied the doctor's mannerisms with renewed interest. Nagler had an accomplished pupil in his secretary Miss Kunkel, whose foreign accent made the grossest flattery acceptable to the English. If a distinguished patient were kept waiting, she entertained him with saccharine compliments and titbits from her personal gossip column. Her mantelpiece was crammed with photographs of celebrities dedicated to the miracle worker.

'I hope we may add yours to our collection,' she remarked pointedly to Aubrey. 'If you don't mind my saying so, you're ever so much handsomer than your photos.'

Though Aubrey had been forewarned, the eventual day of reckoning came as a shock. 'For a supreme artist like you I make extra-ordinary terms but I must beg you to keep this a secret between ourselves. I shall deduct fifteen per cent.' Even after the deduction his fee was fantastic. Moreover the Professor requested to be paid in five-pound notes. While explaining this indelicate transaction his manner became abrupt, the amiable twinkle became a hostile glare, as if he expected a protest. A grizzled gangster peered through the mask of benevolence. The metamorphosis was so sudden that Aubrey felt embarrassed. He would fork out the five-pound notes but he would not return thereafter.

Preoccupied with a new production of *Love for Love*, Aubrey soon forgot his resentment. He needed some other restorative after so many Faiths and Troths and Sirrahs. Derek invited him for a Mediterranean cruise but that was out of the question. Derek also gave him Professor Nagler's kindest regards: 'The old boy says it is high time you paid him another visit.'

Mesmerized like Trilby, Aubrey telephoned Miss Kunkel for an appointment with the Professor. 'We were expecting a call from you,' she replied. 'Professor Nagler had already scheduled you for a refresher course.'

And so the treatments continued. The doctor informed him that he was paler than he ought to be. 'But your colour will soon return,' he said cheerfully, patting his back. 'Your liver is still wonderful. While you are under my care you will keep your youthfulness. You will be able to play Peter Pan. Why don't you?'

Aubrey explained that this was a feminine role, but the doctor insisted that a male should interpret it, slim and athletic like Aubrey.

'This time I have given you a new Swedish preparation: it is twice as strong as your previous injections but it is not yet available in England. As it is only produced in small quantities it is difficult to procure. Therefore it is costly, but health is far too important to count up the pennies, is it not?'

If only they *were* pennies, thought Aubrey, delivering a larger packet of five-pound notes which the doctor counted with a rapt expression. On his slightly stunned way out he was inveigled into Miss Kunkel's snuggery. She demanded his photograph—'Cecil Beaton's is the one I love best, and please don't forget to sign it. Your signature is so artistic it adds to the beauty as well as the value of such a souvenir.'

By accident or by design his old friend Derek had the next appointment. 'Good for you!' he exclaimed. 'I'm glad to see you've taken my advice.'

Derek was so opulent that he could afford Professor Nagler whereas, in spite of his nominal deductions, his fees burnt a considerable hole in Aubrey's pocket. But his injections were an effective pick-me-up and Aubrey required every ounce of energy he could muster for his continental tour: Paris next month, then Berlin, Rome and Venice, in a hectic repertory of costume plays from Shakespeare to Sheridan.

It was after a thunderous ovation in Paris that Aubrey felt the return of his swelling below the groin. Next morning he succeeded in telephoning to Professor Nagler, who assured him that it was innocuous: a little of the ointment he had already prescribed and some vitamin complex tablets would cause it to disappear. 'Forget about it, dear Mr. Vernon. Nobody else can see it and it does not hurt you, so why do you worry? As soon as your tour is over please pay me a visit. I have a new Bulgarian tonic which I am reserving for you. The Duchess says it works like magic. Her gratitude is truly touching.'

Within a week the swelling had subsided, but in Rome it cropped up again in a far more sensitive spot. Frantically busy with performances, rehearsals and interviews, Aubrey had no leisure for introspection. He applied the Professor's ointment and swallowed his tablets as he tanned his face and torso under a sun-

lamp before posing with a tennis racket for his photograph. Off
the stage he loved to stress his manliness: he took pains to create
a popular image that was athletic rather than theatrical. In this
frame of mind the swelling was most irksome. The Professor's
ointment had lost its efficacy: instead of soothing it caused an
inflammation. Alarmed by its angry hue, Aubrey decided to
consult a doctor recommended by his Italian impresario. The
Italians take virility seriously and Aubrey's swelling was near the
main source.

The Roman doctor shook Aubrey's hand limply like a guest at
a funeral and in hesitant vocables interpreted the significance of
the X-ray. 'I regret to say it is graver than I had suspected. It is
not a hernia and it is not malignant—not yet—but it is likely to
become so unless . . . unless you have a little operation. The
sooner the better. It should not be painful—no more than the
removal of an appendix—so you can set your mind at rest. I
advise you not to postpone it. You said it became noticeable two
years ago. It should have been dealt with then.'

Aubrey gasped. 'An operation plumb in the middle of my tour!
I can't break contracts. The whole company depends on me: I *am*
the company.'

Aubrey was youthfully ambitious as well as conscientious, and
the applause of several capitals meant even more to him than his
health. He would sooner expire on the stage than in his bed. The
operation could wait. In the meantime he recruited his strength
with the aid of extra vitamins and champagne.

His tour was a series of spectacular triumphs. But off the stage
he looked harassed. The swelling invisible to others was only too
palpable to himself. His hands could not help touching it. The
Italian doctor's warning kept him awake at night. Was it possible
that the infallible Nagler had made a mistake? He still cherished
a vague hope that the Professor would save him from an operation.

Nagler did not keep him waiting as long as usual for an appointment. He congratulated him on his triumphant tour but remarked
that he was looking sallow. 'But the roses will return to your

cheeks since you have come to me. My Bulgarian serum is miraculous. The Duchess was telling me . . .'

'The swelling has come back,' Aubrey interrupted him. 'I'm afraid it is something serious.'

'Please do not exaggerate. If it had been serious I should have been the first person to tell you so.'

Aubrey had brought his X-ray, which he now produced with a dramatic flourish. 'What about this?' he exclaimed.

Nagler pursed his lips and shook his head. 'I am not persuaded of its authenticity.'

He examined it, however, with a gradual change of expression, scornful at first, then perplexed, but without his customary smile of complacency. He also examined the swelling. 'This is different from the oedema you mistook for a hernia. It is in a different place altogether,' he pronounced. 'There is no connection between the two.'

It was the first time Aubrey detected a certain uncertainty in the Professor's manner. Nagler mopped his brow: he was visibly embarrassed. 'I am well known for my opposition to surgery, but in your case I fear it will be necessary. Against all my principles I must advise you to undergo an operation.'

Aubrey grew hot and cold as he listened to the oracle.

'Fortunately the operation is simple, easy and practically pain-less. A mild indisposition, a period of rest, and you will return to your rapturous public a new-made man. I'll put you in touch with Mr. Flanagan, the only surgeon I can recommend.'

'I'll have to think it over. I'm not at all keen on being cut open yet. The swelling may not be what it seems. You admit that it has no connection with its predecessor. How can that be?'

The Professor smiled wanly but his words were blunt. 'I am sorry, dear Mr. Vernon, but I refuse to be responsible for future developments unless you accept my advice.'

'I have my theatrical commitments. I can't throw them over suddenly like that.'

The Professor's injection smarted more than usual and the lamp failed to warm his interior. Aubrey had been chilled to the marrow: he was shivering when the Professor helped him into his coat.

'Please let me know your decision as soon as possible. Mr. Flanagan is always in demand and the rooms of the Mayfair Clinic are as booked up as the stalls of your theatre.'

Miss Kunkel was prattling to the Duchess of Tonbridge outside the door. She gave Aubrey an elaborate wink, or was it an illusion?

Actors tend to be superstitious and Aubrey fell back on fortune-tellers when he could not make up his mind. Madam Isis was so frequently consulted by the members of his company that he dubbed her the *vivandière*. Though she was also regarded as a figure of fun she extracted surprising and sensational news from a commonplace pack of cards. These were mainly concerned with love affairs and she never minced her words about the gender. 'I'm sorry to say this time it's not a girl. A rich old man will make you very happy. You'll be left a lot of money in his will,' and so forth and so on. Her predictions had often been verified.

'The awe-inspiring Aubrey!' she croaked, never moving from her green-baize table under the Egyptian lamp. 'What brings you to my den? I can guess the answer but the cards will soon confirm it. Or would you prefer me to gaze into the crystal?'

'The cards will do nicely, thank you. I'm sure they're sufficient for the purpose.'

'They have never failed me in my long career.' Madam Isis cut the pack and asked him to cut again. According to the card which turned up she delivered her verdict.

'Something's the matter with your health. Exactly what that is does not appear, but it is in the lower region below the belt and I'm sorry to say it needs a drastic remedy.'

'Go on. What do you mean by drastic?'

'A surgical operation. Cut again. You will soon recover but somehow you'll be changed.'

'What do you mean by that?'

Madam Isis put a finger to her withered lips. 'Hush. Cut

again. Bless us, the Queen of Hearts!' She began to titter. 'Well, I never. Changed into a queen!'

'Stuff and nonsense. What next?'

'I can't help what the cards blurt out. It often sounds like nonsense but there's plenty of sense underneath. Well, one thing's pretty clear at any rate. You're to have an operation below the belt. If you want further details I can consult the crystal but it'll cost you another guinea. You have no idea, my dear, how crystal-gazing takes it out of one. It always leaves me with a splitting headache.'

'I'll spare you that, Madam Isis.'

'Mind you follow the cards. They have never let me down.'

'I wish they had better news for me. This is hardly encouraging.'

'I have a second pack. Like to take another chance? Sometimes what doesn't come out of the first pack will come out of the second.'

'One's quite enough for the present, thank you kindly.'

'The benison of Ancient Egypt goes with you.'

The fortune-teller was more persuasive than the physician. Aubrey tossed a coin: 'Heads I do, tails I don't.' And heads it was. He took his X-rays to Mr. Flanagan the surgeon. That clinched it.

Mr. Flanagan was breezy, even optimistic. 'It's a straight case of the stitch in time, Mr. Vernon. You've been neglecting yourself.'

'Far from it. I've been under special treatment for a couple of years.'

'What sort of treatment may I ask?'

'Professor Nagler's injections, rays and ointments.'

Mr. Flanagan chuckled. 'It's lucky you came to me: I'll put you right. The Mayfair Clinic is crammed just now but I'll try to smuggle you into St. Asaph's.'

'How long will the business take?'

'You must allow for a fortnight bar complications. The trouble with those fashionable treatments is that they tend to conceal the virus. It goes underground as it were, to pop out in some other part of the organism. That is just what has happened to you.'

'Am I likely to have complications?'

'As you're not married I don't foresee any.'

'What has marriage to do with it?'

Mr. Flanagan looked faintly embarrassed. 'Your sexual potency might be affected for a while. I don't expect it will be in your case, Mr. Vernon, not if you have the operation soon.'

The fee was discussed: it was quite modest compared with the Professor's.

Aubrey had to sign an ominous document of submission for admission to St. Asaph's, but he was able to drop the stage name by which he had won celebrity. Nobody had heard of Percy Pringle since his school days in Tasmania. He spread the rumour that he was flying to Bermuda for a rest. This was plausible after his continental tour.

His room in the hospital overlooked an inner courtyard where white-clad figures flitted like ghosts in a churchyard. Consequently it was peaceful as well as austere. Though he felt more depressed than ill his temperature was taken frequently and he was given a diet of liquids and Epsom salts for two days running. He had to pose for more X-rays in a sombre cellar to which he was escorted in his dressing-gown by a limping attendant.

He was never allowed to enjoy solitude for more than half an hour at a time. A nurse would pop in to offer him tea or medicine as soon as he dozed off with fatigue and under-nourishment. The nurses were chirpily cheerful. 'Tomorrow morning at six o'clock you'll take a nice hot bath. Complete abstinence after midnight I'm afraid—not even a glass of water. At eight o'clock the anaesthetist will be calling. He's sure to give you a heavenly sensation.'

The sister on night duty, a hockey-playing type, surprised him by turning on the radio. 'It'll soon be over. I can see that you're as brave as a lion. Let me give you a soothing sedative. Would you prefer hot milk, tea or cocoa to send it down? Nighty-night, Mr. Pringle.'

Throughout the night there was a constant ringing of bells and pattering of feet down the corridor. The walls seemed to be made of cardboard, for the whimpering and moaning of a woman next door was distressingly audible. 'Nurse, nurse, nurse! Oh dear, oh dear, oh dee-eear! I can't stand this pain. God help me. Help!'

The moaning died down but the misery of it haunted him and he tossed and turned restlessly before the sleeping-draught stole over his jaded limbs. He was fast asleep when he was roused for his six o'clock bath. His swelling resembled a plover's egg since the surrounding area had been cropped. Would a scar be any improvement? His mouth was so dry when the anaesthetist called that he longed for forbidden water: he could hardly articulate.

The pricking of a needle dispatched him into prompt oblivion. When he opened his eyes it was evening. His right arm was stretched out rigid under what seemed an inverted jam-jar half full of liquid which slowly, very slowly, dripped through a winding tube into his veins.

'Do you fancy a drop of tea?' said the nurse.

His efforts at speech were cramped by catarrh: he coughed and it was as if his intestines were being wrenched, but he could only grip his belly, a bulge of bandages, with his left hand as he stifled an agonized groan. All the nurses on duty peeped in to see how he was doing, and he was aware of dozens of eyes peering through the glass partition in the door, winking and twinkling eyes. He seemed to hear smothered giggles down the corridor— seemed, for he could not be certain of anything in his actual state.

The sister on night duty bustled in as from a game of hockey. 'Congratulations, so the worst is over and done with. Doesn't he look splendid considering what he's been through?'

He woke up blinking while she rearranged his pillows.

'Do you know who you remind me of? Aubrey Vernon. You're a good deal older of course, but you've got his features.'

'That's not my name,' Aubrey protested feebly.

'I know, Mr. Pringle, but somehow you remind me. Oddly enough the matron told me that Professor Nagler has been pestering her on the phone to speak to Aubrey Vernon, insisting that he's a patient of Mr. Flanagan. It's a queer coincidence, isn't it?'

'Very strange. Who is Professor Nagler?'

'He's the hospital headache, one of those fashionable private practitioners. Mr. Flanagan can't stand him.'

Aubrey shut his eyes and yawned. 'Forgive me, sister, I can hardly keep awake.'

'Happy dreams!'

The nights and the days melted into each other without any apparent distinction. Mr. Flanagan came in at curious hours to examine the wound, followed by the staff nurse and an auxiliary with a rattling trolley piled with paraphernalia. Aubrey turned away when they changed his dressing and gritted his teeth when they ripped off the Elastoplast like another layer of skin. He suffered dumbly.

Mr. Flanagan made the V-sign. 'You're doing well, very well indeed. We'll soon have you running around with your plastic bag pinned to your dressing-gown. I hope you're getting used to that ingenious contrivance: you needn't feel shy about it. Get him up before dinner, nurse. And let him take a bath tomorrow, a good soak for twenty minutes.'

Sleep was the only pleasure left, but uninterrupted slumber is the rarest of luxuries in a hospital where the patient is constantly roused under one pretext or another. Somehow Nagler had discovered his real name and rung up the matron to enquire about his condition. That wise woman had replied that he was doing very comfortably, thank you.

Fortunately St. Asaph's Hospital was a very long way from Harley Street.

When his private nurses were no longer required Aubrey saw more of the regular staff, a rich variety of preponderantly cheerful women who took turns in dressing his wound. He had not the courage to look at the mutilated area until a nurse whose mischievous eyes always seemed to be mocking him remarked: 'Why not face up to it? You'll jolly well have to when you take your bath. For a wound of that size, it's neat and rather pretty. Reminds me of the petal of an azalea.'

Aubrey gathered the strength to look. He shuddered at what he saw, and fell back on his pile of pillows with a stifled cry. He only had one kidney and now—oh horror piled on horror!—he only had one . . . He could not bring himself to pronounce the word for this gland, so essential a part of his virility. He did not speak for several days, and he only ate and drank because he was threatened with the drip machine.

'Come, come, be a man!' Mr. Flanagan exhorted him.

At last Aubrey spoke: 'But I don't *feel* a man—not after what you've done to me.'

'You'll manage to rub along just the same on one, that I can promise you.'

He who had been justly proud of his physique and endowment with all the manly attributes felt profoundly desecrated and un-clean. When he tried to explain this the surgeon remarked: 'You've been lucky. Had you not come to me in the nick of time you'd have lost the other one. When you're fitted with a truss nobody will be any the wiser.'

'Not even my girl friends?'

Mr. Flanagan was taken aback. 'You needn't make love with the light on. Just pull the sheet over you.'

Aubrey uttered a shrill cackle (what had happened to his voice?) and Mr. Flanagan was even more disconcerted when he confessed: 'I always make love with the light on.'

Aubrey sank into a lethargy from which he was roused by the tittering of nurses. They were giggling at him, he imagined. No doubt they nicknamed him 'One Ball Pringle'. Luckily they had no inkling of his identity. The secret must be kept at all costs: he had asked the surgeon to take every precaution. In the meantime he decided to grow a beard, but the stubble was stubbornly static and his voice assumed a squeaky timbre as if he were entering a second puberty. This made him exceedingly nervous since it was not due to a chill. Plumb in the middle of a sentence—'Sister, would you kindly hand me the—bottle?'—crack, squeak, it was almost high falsetto.

'What has got into your whistle?' asked the nurse with the

mischievous eyes. 'Sounds as if you had swallowed a fishbone. Open your mouth and let me see. I wish you'd have a shave. I'm not an expert with a razor but I'm ready to have a try if you won't send for the barber.'

'On one condition,' said Aubrey.

'And what might that be?' the nurse challenged him.

'That you kiss me on the lips.'

'Where do you think you are, Mr. Pringle? Perhaps when you've had a clean shave I might oblige, but not when I'm on duty.'

The monkey had suddenly turned prim. She handed him the bottle with an air of genteel distaste.

'Be a good girl and kiss me,' he repeated.

'Mr. Pringle, I'm surprised at you—a man of your age. You're old enough to be my father.'

Did she think him so old? He glanced at his mirror and was appalled by the ravages of the last few weeks—were they weeks or months?—pouches under his eyes, wrinkles at the corners, a drooping, sagging mouth. Even in the role of Shylock he had never appeared so squalidly unappetizing. Nobody could have recognized Aubrey Vernon. He was thoroughly disguised.

Against his will a porter wheeled him to the bathroom down the corridor and stood by him when he doffed the white shirt open at the back, which was the hospital substitute for pyjamas, and helped him into the steaming tub.

'You needn't stay,' he said.

The porter declared that he had to obey instructions. 'Many's the patient that has fainted away right here in this bathroom. And if you was to act silly I'd be the one to get into hot water.'

'But there's a bell above the bath. You can wait outside the door.'

'No time to press the button when the fainting spell comes over you all of a sudden. I've seen it happen more than once. That's why I'm supposed to be here.'

Aubrey could still boast of a broad chest and slender hips; his legs had the muscular calves that had thrilled Victorian damsels.

But oh, the solitary pouch! He quailed at the sight of it though the wound was bandaged.

'Stop staring at me, man!' he shouted hysterically.

'Lord help me, sir, I'm not staring.'

'You are, you devil, you are!'

'What is there to stare at?' he sniggered.

Whereupon Aubrey lost his temper and splashed him with hot water.

'Look here, you behave yourself. I'll complain to the matron.'

'So shall I. Get the hell out of here.'

But the man defiantly stood his ground. 'I'm doing my job. You'll need me to dry you with the towel.'

And in fact the hot bath weakened him and it was not easy to pull himself up and climb out of the water in which blood from his wound formed brilliant circles of red smoke. The porter piloted him into a chair and wheeled him in a daze back to his room.

'Did you enjoy a lovely soak?' enquired the staff nurse with professional brightness.

'It was sheer Turkish Delight,' he replied ironically. 'But I wish you had kept me company instead of that perambulating moron.'

'I'm afraid I have more serious cases on my hands. Now that you're on the mend you must learn to shift for yourself.'

The ache of his mutilation was more mental than physical. He was allowed to leave the hospital before it had healed. The nurses had lost interest in him. The woman next door had died.

Aubrey muffled his face like a Bedouin and crept furtively out of the vast impersonal building.

He had sent a telegram to Mrs. Frost, his female factotum, advising her that he had shortened his holiday and that he hoped she would prepare the flat for his arrival and order a fish supper from Prunier's round the corner, specifying that he yearned for oysters. He explained that the long air journey had worn him out.

'My word, you don't have to tell me that. You look completely done in, dear. So don't you start opening your love letters now. Early bed for you tonight, Master Aubrey!'

A mountain of correspondence was stacked on his desk.

'Poor Miss Loelia's been fretting herself sick about you, telephoning all day and every day. She complained that you hopped off without a word or giving her your address. How could you be so cruel to that sweet innocent? And she's really and truly fond of you—no play-acting about her!'

'But I'm a play-actor, Mrs. Frost. You ought to know that by now.'

The telephone tinkled. 'Would you mind answering it for me? Pretend I'm still in Bermuda.'

'O.K., dear. It's bound to be Miss Loelia again. She worships the ground you tread on, poor lamb. I hate to disappoint her.'

'Tell her I'll be home in a fortnight.'

Mr. Flanagan had exhorted him to take things easy for the next six months but Aubrey was too attached to his profession not to plunge into the study of new parts. Surrounded by photographs of himself in all the pinnacles of his career, he forgot his recent ordeal until it was time to bathe: even then, wrapped in a towel as in a toga, he postured and strutted in front of his pier-glass, declaiming the speeches of Caesar and Mark Antony. If his face was haggard his figure had become more slender in compensation, for he had lost much weight. He applied his Romeo make-up and wore his Renaissance wig. The effect was so rejuvenating that he skipped for joy and blew kisses at his own reflection. Suddenly he thought: 'I'm making an ass of myself. If anyone could see me now, what would he say?' Yet he could not help it, he grew unaccountably skittish. Hand on hip he minced away from the mirror with delicate steps and when he reclined on the sofa he toyed with the oblong cushion with the fancy tassels, hugging and embracing it as if it were—whom? Not Loelia certainly. It was as if an amorous siren had taken possession of him and he longed to be gripped and held by two vigorous arms. No doubt it was a passing whim.

Alone, except for the photographs lining the walls, Aubrey

wondered if he had any individual being apart from his public appearances: without a packed auditorium he felt curiously limp and empty. His whole life had been lived in public: his most memorable love scenes, all those showers of burning kisses on lips and hands and arms, had had no parallel off the stage except as a form of rehearsal. What was Loelia to him or any of her predecessors but a microcosm of all the females in his audience? He practised his stage business on her: according to her reactions he could discover whether it was effective or not. She would recoil from some embraces with a shudder; to others she would surrender swooningly. He scrapped the former and elaborated the latter, playing variations on them like a composer. And Loelia never guessed. He was the Aubrey of many scattered hearts; he had created protean images of himself; but the real Aubrey, born Percy Pringle, who was he? Since his operation he did not feel sure that he could repeat his former triumphs. His nerves had been exacerbated during his period in hospital.

He had an impulse to shout for no particular reason and when he shouted the sound was so shrill that he noticed something strange had happened to his voice. It was disconcerting and totally unlike his Shakespearian recordings—the cry of some outraged prima donna. Consciously lowering his vocal chords from an inflated chest he repeated a speech from *Coriolanus*, but the strain involved made it false and artificial. It might be due to his recent operation: perhaps it was premature to plunge into Shakespeare. *Cyrano de Bergerac* had been mastered when he invited Loelia to dinner. He would take her to 'Chez Tonton', regardless of the press photographers who would snap them in intimate colloquy. He was feeling ready for some advance publicity, in preparation for which he plucked his eyebrows, applied cream and powder to his face after a close shave with the latest invention in razor blades, and sprayed himself with a masculine essence called 'Polo.'

Loelia flung her arms about his neck and in the hungry kiss that ensued she bit his lip until it bled while he crushed her bosom and clutched the small of her bare back. Breathless they tumbled on the sofa.

'Darling, this won't do. We'll be too dishevelled to dine in public,' he gasped, when she unbuttoned his jacket. 'Let's save our ecstasies for later on.'

'No, now! I can't wait another moment. I must have a morsel of Aubrey before dinner. Don't I deserve it, you magnificent beast?'

He let her fumble through his clothes with frantic fingers and lolled passively until she touched his truss. This made him jump, for that part of him was curiously sensitive.

'Do control yourself, my pet. "Chez Tonton" is always crowded and Louis won't reserve the table if we arrive too late. I'm famished. Aren't you, dear?'

'How can you talk of food at such a moment? You men are so materialistic.'

Gently he withdrew from her to button his shirt and adjust his necktie.

'Chez Tonton' was packed. The stage celebrities of London were on display at separate tables, ranging from Noël Coward to Terence Rattigan. Many of them greeted Aubrey and continued to watch him obliquely. Their sharp eyes could not fail to detect a difference in him as he followed Loelia with a nervous glide instead of his self-confident 'Here I am' swagger.

Aubrey was acutely conscious of the eyes observing him. Prior to his operation he might have been pleased and flattered, but now he wondered if they had noticed any change. He wriggled in his chair and remained *distrait* throughout the meal while Loelia prattled on between mouthfuls of smoked salmon and braised sweetbread.

'Isn't that Laurence Olivier behind those blue goggles? I love this place. It makes me feel like a celebrity too.'

She clasped his hand and gazed tenderly into his nostrils while a press photographer clicked his camera close by. From Loelia's point of view Aubrey had not changed a whit. Not so far. She saw him as he had been before his operation. But his nervousness increased as the evening wore on: his eyes blinked incessantly, his mouth and nose twitched like a rabbit's, and his feet tapped restlessly under the table. Should he or shouldn't he put his amorous powers to the test? Was it too soon? He remembered Mr. Flanagan's assurance that all would be plain sailing under the sheets.

Loelia mistook his tapping for fond dalliance: she pressed one foot upon his until it pinched and he withdrew it. Late to arrive, they were later to leave the restaurant. Derek appeared from nowhere and joined them for a liqueur. 'Congratulations on your recovery. I've been hearing all about it from the Professor.'

Aubrey nudged him to make him change the subject but Derek was either obtuse or wantonly malicious. 'By the looks of you nobody would guess what you'd been through,' he went on.

Aubrey tried again to stop him with winks and signs, but he rattled on like a train. 'Have you decided where to convalesce? Don't believe the surgeons: it takes a whole year to recover from such a butchery. Why not join Mona and me in St. Moritz?'

'An operation!' Loelia exclaimed. 'And you never breathed a word about it to little me! Aubrey, you're incorrigible. I thought something odd must have happened. You're definitely a great deal thinner.'

'Oh dear, have I dropped a brick?' asked Derek naïvely.

'I'm afraid you have. Loelia wasn't intended to know.'

'Sorry, old boy. I thought everybody knew you'd been under the knife.'

Loelia had never seen Aubrey in such a temper. His hand trembled so violently while pouring a glass of water that he slopped it over the tablecloth. His face was livid.

Aubrey's hand was still shaking when he signed the bill. 'Let's go home,' said Loelia. 'You look tired and upset.'

'I'm merely exasperated by Derek. Let's go to that night club you mentioned.'

'Dewdrop's' was even more crowded than 'Chez Tonton', but a table was found for Aubrey and Loelia in the space reserved for performing artists. Though he was obliged to pay for champagne Aubrey drank Vichy water with a couple of vitamin pills.

Drat it, there was Derek again. 'It's a wee world,' he remarked

sententiously. 'What a funny spot you have chosen to convalesce in. Mind if I join in? So many queers in the offing that a
lone wolf feels kind of lost.'

'Aubrey has never seen Dewdrop. The point about Dewdrop
is that he's square in private life, happily married with a large
family in Dorking.'

'I suspect that's hooey,' said Derek. 'No man with such mannerisms could possibly be normal. His mother must have dressed
him up as a girl soon after his birth. I'll bet you he's been doing it
all his life.'

'And I'll bet you I could do the same stunts just as well,' said
Aubrey.

'O.K. I'll take you on for fifty quid.'

'You'll be the loser, *chéri*,' Aubrey retorted in a strident voice.

Derek guffawed uncomfortably. He had been drinking steadily
since dinner and his glazed eyes were glued to Loelia's bosom,
whose pearly whiteness became more pronounced in the penumbra. Her scent was aphrodisiac in this atmosphere. He drew his
knee closer to hers and she did not resist. She too was flushed
with food and wine and a vague sensuality. Parties were simmer-
ing and mellowing at every table; conversations were growing
more incoherent on the tiptoe of expectation.

Dewdrop was shrewd enough to keep the audience waiting until his *aficionados* began to fidget, shuffle and shout: 'Dewdrop!
We want our precious Dewdrop!' Waiters whizzed to and fro
with napkin-corseted bottles.

There was a crescendo of clapping when an angular girl in a
close-fitting garment of rippling gold and a huge ostrich-feather
fan willowed across the clearing under the spotlight and waved
the fan flirtatiously at the audience. 'You perfect dears, each and
every one of you,' she gushed. 'I'm in the mood for love and I
hope it's mutual. Good evening, boys and girls—I mean good
morning! Not so much noise in that ingle-nook, please, if you
want to hear your Dewdrop. Hush over yonder! Now I've
guessed what you want me to warble: "Down in the forest something stirred".'

After a burst of applause there was breathless silence. To begin with Dewdrop emulated the dusky tones of Miss Dietrich with eyelids incredibly languid and parted hungry lips, then he proceeded to render the ballad in the wailing manner of Piaf and the jauntiness of Miss Gracie Fields. The late-night sophisticates bellowed 'Encore!'

Aubrey borrowed Loelia's lipstick, powder and pocket mirror, and after a lightning transformation of his face he grabbed her mink coat and minced towards Dewdrop's microphone. 'Make room for me, dear,' he muttered. Before Dewdrop had time to object he crooned a different version of the song in which the forest and the bird had become suggestively Freudian.

Outraged at first, the audience rocked and fell off their seats with ribald laughter, while Dewdrop bashfully spread his ostrich feathers in front of his false bosom and tried desperately to recapture attention with startled cluckings.

Derek and Loelia drew closer together in their astonishment. 'He must be demented,' said Derek. 'This will do him no end of harm if it gets into the newspapers.'

But the audience, which was peculiar to night clubs, failed to recognize the interloper in the mink coat who slithered back to his table in the penumbra.

'I fancied I was all alone in the great big world,' cooed the Dewdrop, 'and lo and behold I've found a kindred spirit. Isn't she ravishing?'

Before Dewdrop could drag Aubrey back to the microphone Derek gripped his arm and growled: 'Let's be off. I don't like being made conspicuous. Enough's as good as a feast.' Aubrey was smuggled away from the scene of his meteoric début as a transvestite.

'What on earth made you do it?' asked Loelia, indignant and hurt.

Aubrey seemed dazed: he did not know what to reply. He could not explain the impulse which had driven him to compete with Dewdrop.

'Well, you've won your bet,' snapped Derek. 'I'll write you out a cheque.'

'I thought you were a better loser,' said Aubrey.

Loelia sat between Aubrey and Derek in the latter's Rolls, which gave Derek a chance to pursue the pressure of her knee. She refused Aubrey's invitation to join him 'for a nightcap': it was getting late and she was feeling sleepy.

Aubrey protested 'Surely not,' but he was inwardly relieved, for his impromptu performance at Dewdrop's had left him exhausted. However, he was unable to sleep, perhaps because he had been over-excited. Was he developing a bosom? He ran his fingers over his nipples and it seemed as if twin mounds were bubbling under his touch. He anointed them with cream, quivering with an unaccustomed thrill in his crêpe de chine pyjamas. For a while he wriggled like a restless débutante itching for a Hercules to clasp her in hairy arms. A fabulous career flickered before his dreamy eyes: he would become another person. He must send himself some orchids in the morning.

But in the morning he was appalled by the recollection of last night's lapse. The pictures on the wall were solemn reminders that he was the most admired figure on the English stage. It would be better to retire from the stage altogether than to destroy the public image he had created, to whose power of magnetism a shelf of bound press-cuttings and a cabinet crammed with fan-mail were ample testimony.

Loelia, who had spent the rest of the night, or rather the early hours of the morning, in Derek's bed, rang up shamefacedly to enquire after Aubrey's health.

'I've been anxious about you. You were so unlike yourself. Your act at "Dewdrop's" was eccentric, to say the least. I felt just as embarrassed as Derek.'

'I see. You went to bed with Derek and this is your excuse. I must say it's a lame one. You'll have Mona to cope with now. I don't envy you and I don't want Derek's leavings. Good-bye, Loelia.' He rang off.

He was glad she had ended the affair without putting the

remains of his virility to the test. It had been a convenient solution. Sooner or later she would have discovered that he was merely miming with her. Now he could get back to business.

Within a month *Cyrano de Bergerac* was under rehearsal at the Pearl Theatre. 'We must play it as a surrealistic romance,' he told the bewildered cast. 'Colour and flamboyance will delight the public after so much drabness.'

Flamboyance in scenery and costume was supplied by Sylvester Todd, an international byword for the *dernier cri* in lavishness.

The company thought it was a crazy gamble but under Aubrey's guidance they threw themselves into the spirit of the straightforward plot and complex action. As the grotesque hero with the heart of gold Aubrey pranced through his part like a vocal ballet dancer. His voice ranged from baritone to alto: the odd break in it accentuated, as it were, the monstrosity of his false nose and added such poignancy to his self-sacrifice that there were few dry eyes and many damp handkerchiefs among the snuffling audience. And all the while Aubrey swashbuckled and cut his capers he was challenging his inward sense of degradation with an intensity that made the toughest critics gasp. The play might be tripe but there was a consensus of opinion that it was worth seeing for Aubrey's pyrotechnical performance. He had gambled with heavy stakes and won, as so often before.

The queues before the Pearl Theatre grew larger and more obstructive and the play was assured of an exceptionally long run. Yet behind the scenes the other members of the cast were perplexed by Aubrey's antics. He who had always appeared a paragon of normality had taken to kicking up his legs in a ludicrous can-can on the way to his dressing-room, where he lolled on a sofa crooning to himself so mournfully that those who heard him shuddered with a premonition of disaster. When they looked in for a chat he hid his face in his hands and burst into tears. They feared he was on the verge of a breakdown.

He became even kinkier after the hundredth performance. Instead of his former dignified bows and self-deprecating smiles when he was called before the curtain, he skipped along like a tipsy chorus girl, rolling his eyes and blowing kisses right and left, to the disgusted amazement of his erstwhile admirers. The majority suspected he had taken to the bottle.

One Saturday night he returned alone to 'Dewdrop's'. Nobody recognized him for he was dressed as a merry widow of the nineteen-twenties with a platinum blonde wig, a monocle, and a long jade cigarette-holder. When the sable slipped off his bare shoulders at a table near the demented drummer, the sequins of his black gown glittered like cats' eyes in the semi-darkness.

'Hello there!' shrilled Dewdrop who had spotted him during his preliminary patter. 'Let's welcome the Queen of the Night. Will you be our guest-performer, Ma'am? Boys and girls, let's give her Majesty a big hot hand!'

Aubrey rose and bowed with becoming modesty and Dewdrop curtseyed before ushering the guest with his ostrich fan towards the microphone.

'I'm in one of my magnanimous moods tonight,' said Aubrey, opening his arms as if to clasp the whole audience. Swaying slightly, he ran his fingers along the bulge of his bust and announced: 'I'll sing you a dear old ballad you must have heard in the nursery: "I can't give you anything but love, baby".'

As from a mossy bed with velvety huskiness the voice rose and quivered through the floating screen of cigarette smoke. Those night-clubbers whom the tepid champagne had melted gazed liquid-eyed at their companions when Aubrey wailed out the last words: 'I can't give you anything but love.'

Dewdrop was deeply affected. 'You've wrung my heart,' he whispered, wiping a tear from one eye.

Aubrey was beginning to feel faint. 'Excuse me, dear,' he muttered to Dewdrop. 'I've got the curse coming on. I must go and loosen my stays.'

When the couples returned to rocking and rolling, snapping fingers and stomping feet, it was easy for Aubrey to vanish. He was forced to realize that he did not belong to the sixties.

The crisp early morning air rushed into his lungs refreshingly as he drove home in his Jaguar through the empty streets. Unused to high heels his feet ached intolerably, and the ache spread upwards through his silk-stockinged legs. He asked himself what subconscious urge had lured him to Dewdrop's after what he knew to have been his finest and most strenuous performance in *Cyrano*. For once he had felt his pre-operational self, ready to embark on an affair with a new Loelia. Yet, as if hypnotized by Professor Nagler, he had rigged himself out with borrowed plumes from his theatrical store and applied his cosmetics with consummate artifice before wending his way automatically to the nightclub. The sequel he could hardly remember, he was so tired. 'Too tired to wash the dishes, too tired, too tired,' he hummed as he kicked off his shoes and unzipped his gown. He thought of visiting the Professor in feminine disguise and venting his pent-up spleen. Aware of the Professor's partiality for titles, he decided to call himself Lady Muriel Beckley. Otherwise he would have to wait a month for an appointment.

Miss Kunkel purred over the telephone when he told her in accents of impeccable gentility as Lady Muriel that he longed to consult the marvellous Professor, of whose miracles he had heard so much from bosom friends.

'Next Wednesday, Lady Muriel, at eleven o'clock, the Professor will be free for a consultation. I hope that is convenient for you.'

'Convenient? I shall be enchanted to come at that hour. Allow me to say that I've seldom heard a sweeter voice than yours. It makes me feel better already. Am I speaking to Mrs. Nagler?'

'I'm only Grace Kunkel, the Professor's private secretary.'

'Well, I'm sure you are as charming as your voice and I look forward to meeting you, too. Till Wednesday as ever is, dear Miss Kunkel.'

When he appeared Miss Kunkel failed to see the disguise.

'You're every bit as winsome as your voice!' Aubrey gushed.

'I fear you flatter me,' Miss Kunkel simpered. 'I'll send word to the Professor that you're here. He happens to be engaged at the moment with the Duchess of Tonbridge. She's his favourite patient.'

'Lucky Duchess! In that case I suppose he charges her less than the others. Between ourselves I'm rather nervous about his fees. A little bird told me that they are apt to be astronomical. I should hate to have to sell my family jewels. I'm not nearly as rich as my reputation, you know.'

Miss Kunkel's manner changed. Though she knew nothing whatever about Lady Muriel's reputation she suspected something fishy from her speech. She wished she could warn the Professor about her misgivings. This newcomer had roused her distrust.

'What a fascinating collection of photos you have on the mantelpiece. I don't think Aubrey Vernon's does justice to him. No doubt the Professor makes special terms for theatrical celebrities. They are excellent publicity. So am I as a matter of fact. Cosmeticians have offered me fabulous sums for the use of my picture on their advertisements.'

Miss Kunkel tried to discourage further conversation by blowing her nose.

'I wish I could emit so pure a note,' said Aubrey. 'You must have exceptional nostrils. May I look into them? I'm particularly intrigued by the human trumpet and its possibilities.'

Miss Kunkel concluded that Lady Muriel was unbalanced. She tapped her forehead and winked at Professor Nagler when he escorted his favourite duchess to the lift, but he was too engrossed in his rococo compliments to notice Miss Kunkel's signals.

Aubrey marched straight into the consulting room and occupied the Professor's chair.

'You've kept me waiting an unconscionable time,' he remarked. 'I hope you won't overcharge me for it. As I was telling your secretary with the noisy nostrils, I should be sorry to have to part with the Beckley jewels.'

The Professor contrived a smile but his eyes blazed with

indignation. 'I adore your English sense of humour,' he said. 'May I ask who recommended you to visit me?'

'Oh dozens of people, beginning with my old friends Derek and Mona Mortimer who swear by you. To cut a long story short, Professor, I'm neither man nor woman. I want to be one thing or the other.'

The Professor's smile faded. 'I think you have made a mistake, you have come to the wrong address. You should visit a psychiatrist, Lady Muriel. You are evidently suffering from delusions.'

'Come on, undress me: you will soon find out.' He noted with satisfaction that the Professor was growing panicky.

'I want you to undress me stitch by stitch. Mona declared you had lights on the tips of your fingers. Out with your stethoscope. I'm ready for a thrill.'

'I'm trying to be patient, Lady Muriel.'

'None of your hanky-panky, Professor. I refuse to go until you have examined me properly.' Aubrey prevented him from telephoning. 'You've got the wind up because I told you I wasn't as rich as Derek and Mona. You're afraid you won't be paid in those famous five-pound notes to avoid income tax. You could be struck off the register for that.'

The Professor folded his arms and glared through his spectacles. 'I order you to leave,' he shouted. 'Do so immediately or I shall summon the police.'

Aubrey toyed with a syringe he found on a tray. 'Would you like me to give you an injection?' he enquired, thrusting it towards him.

He pulled the Professor towards the sofa and a tussle ensued, but it was impossible to escape from Aubrey's muscular arms. He gagged him with a handkerchief and fastened him to the sofa with a belt he had brought in his handbag. Then he proceeded to unbutton the Professor's trousers and turn on the lamp, as the Professor had done to him before his operation. 'You are looking a bit off-colour after your bout with the duchess. This lamp should restore your energies. And I'll give you a delicious injection as well. It will sting but the effect is euphoric.'

Aubrey had taken the precaution to lock the door. Miss Kunkel knocked: hearing no reply and presuming that Lady Muriel was on the couch, she announced in a loud voice that Admiral Murchison had been kept waiting beyond the time fixed for his appointment. The Professor was wriggling on the sofa while the lamp was growing hotter.

'Keep quiet, Professor. The magic heat will do you a world of good. Turn more to the right. Once you have been exposed to these rays you will never need an operation, isn't that so?'

The gagged purple face and the plunging feet on the couch seemed to tell a different story. Waving a heavily beringed hand at him, Aubrey cooed: 'Have a good time cooking, Professor!'

Miss Kunkel was too preoccupied by her telephone to notice his exit.

In the waiting-room downstairs Aubrey introduced himself to the solitary old sailor nid-nodding over *The Times*.

'Perhaps you don't remember me. I'm Muriel Beckley,' he said in a mellifluous falsetto. 'Professor Nagler asked me to tell you that he regrets he is too busy to see you today as he has to attend an urgent operation.'

'How annoying, when I might have been dictating my memoirs. But do tell me, where did we meet before? I seem to remember your face but I can't exactly remember the circumstances.'

'It must have been at the Palace garden party. We had such an interesting chat that I have never forgotten it.'

'Of course, of course. How stupid of me.'

'It's the rush hour. Do you mind if I share your taxi? What's your direction?'

'The Athenaeum. I say, now it all comes back to me. You used to know my late wife. Won't you join me for tiffin if you've nothing better to do?'

Aubrey thought it would be a supreme challenge to his art to enter the annexe of the Athenaeum in his present disguise. 'I'd simply love to,' he replied. 'Our meeting again has been a delightful surprise.'

'Your company will cheer me up,' said the Admiral. 'One gets tired of lunching alone.'

He hailed a passing taxi and helped Aubrey to step inside with the gallantry of a more leisurely age. Already the Admiral looked forward to a mild flirtation. He thought Lady Muriel a fine specimen and tried in vain to recollect their former meeting, for he would never admit that his memory could have played him false after so many of Professor Nagler's special treatments.

'A SKETCH, LENT BY MISS TEMPLE'

I HAD decided not to visit the Kelsall Exhibition, for I could anticipate the vast array of conventional models and predict the lack of joy. Several friends accused me of highbrow intolerance and other unsocial tendencies on this account. In spite of their accusations and perhaps because of the unanimous plaudits of the Press (the exhibition was described as epoch-making, an event of paramount importance in the field of modern art) in spite and because of the fact that it was the topic of ubiquitous conversation, my curiosity failed to rise to the occasion. There was a solidity about Kelsall's work combined with a technical mastery that wrested from one a grudging admission of his emphatic pictorial powers.

Kelsall required no posthumous advocate. He had traversed all the stages of celebrity and mundane success. First the appreciation of the esoteric and the deference of the intellectual élite, which he did not hesitate to cast aside. Then, a more paying proposition, the hosannas of cosmopolitan rank and fashion. Before the lucrative middle years of his celibate life the laurels were settled on his brow. They fitted it neatly. By this time Kelsall was firmly propped upon his pedestal: his mere name seemed to bear with it an aura of infallible authority. During his lifetime he had enjoyed precocious recognition, and he had been treated as an Old Master long before his death. This left me cold, for I could derive equal pleasure from the prose of a Macaulay.

The art lovers came and went, expatiating on Kelsall. While the majority maintained he was the last great portrait painter a minority were disposed to bid him good riddance as a purveyor of the 'meretricious element' in art. I agreed with each in turn according to my mood, perceiving that in each lay half a truth.

The processional drums had rolled and their echoes had begun to fade. Everybody had attended the Kelsall Exhibition with the exception, presumably, of myself. The votive offerings had accumulated, and now the flowers before the shrine were wilting and the flames in the candle-sockets were flickering out. A large proportion of those canvases would find their way into public galleries and sale-rooms: they would be seen again, but in an atmosphere less heavily charged with awe and superstition. Others would cross the equator. They would never be quite the same.

The memorial service was nearly over. I was beginning to waver a little, sentimentally. Soon the opportunity would be lost, and I might succumb to regret. But had I not made up my mind irrevocably at the outset? Then I met my old school friend Basler in Jermyn Street, or rather he fell upon me with impetuosity. He was on his way, he informed me, to see the Kelsalls for the last time before setting sail for India. There were almost tears in his eyes and he seemed to be swallowing hard at a lump in his throat. One could discern that for him Kelsall was no ordinary hero. His emotion was so genuine that I found myself walking lamb-like by his side, and before I knew it, across the solemn threshold of Burlington House.

Why had I not trusted my intuition? My worst fears were only too well founded. Room after room of prominent effigies: actors and admirals cheek by jowl, toxicologists and stockbrokers folding their arms beside each other. A hispid much-bemedalled general glared across the hall at one of those 'demned bohemian poet-johnnies'. And oh, the dog-collars and frock-coats, the Churchmen and aldermen, the editors and labour-leaders, their wives and hostesses apart! A panorama truly historical. Basler, having purchased a catalogue, extracted his reading-spectacles from one pocket and a silver pencil from another. Religiously he advanced on the tips of his toes, burying his military moustache first in the catalogue, then in another canvas.

'By Jove,' he exclaimed, stopping before the portrait of Lady Beauvedere, *décolletée* in violet brocade with lace lappets, diamonds, and an enormous tiara, 'Women were Women then!'

The pupils of his eyes dilated behind the gold-rimmed spectacles. 'I could have worshipped that creature. The innocent, entrancing roguery of her! Only Kelsall could have managed the pearly flesh-tint of that bosom.'

For the life of me I could detect no innocent roguery in that over-corseted upholstered dame. I let it pass without challenge as I listened to Basler's raptures, trying to keep pace with his enthusiasm. It was not only art that had brought him here, I concluded. This was for him a suite of drawing-rooms where he could wander at will, bowing and making acquaintances. One expected him to put out his hand and nod a how-do-you-do. When he surveyed a picture from a distance he did so as if he were examining some celebrity. 'Tell me, is that So-and-so? Really? I would love to be introduced.' And I realized that others were doing likewise. I too should have joined in the game: my attitude was mistaken. But the socially inquisitive instincts of Basler were dormant in myself. I walked in his footsteps with a sensation of being undressed before this higher hierarchy, as I adjusted my shoe-laces with a suspicion that my sock-suspenders were falling about my shoes. Such trifles would have been unnoticed in the presence of truly great paintings. I looked about me trying to see with Basler's eyes, but my aversion became more acute. So I turned to recollections of Kelsall the man, of his appearance, his life, his personality.

He had not discovered happiness in popular applause. Bluff, bulky, brawny, bearded, he had the exterior of a Wagnerian *Heldentenor*. Yet he had always lived with his two sisters; no love-affair, indiscretion or escapade, had been held to his debit or credit. For all his lion-like attributes, the brawn and the beard and the carnivorous appetite, Kelsall, by modern standards, was sadly sexless. Tolerant of fame on the easiest terms, he had been modest and self-effacing, dressing quietly and appearing seldom at fashionable assemblies.

On the sole occasion I had met him he had spoken of his agony while attempting to delineate his own features for the Uffizi collection of self-portraits. His devotees admitted it was his feeblest work, wooden and embarrassed in execution, whereas a slap-dash freedom reminiscent of Frans Hals was his leading characteristic when the subject appealed to him. His unwillingness to flatter was often mistaken for arrogance, even for heartless cruelty. . . .

I glanced at my watch. Since Basler seemed disposed to loiter among Kelsall's dowagers we shook hands and parted. Before I could reach the exit, however, I had to pass through innumerable ante-rooms. I had come to the last when I was arrested by the glow of a single canvas.

Mellow lamp-light moulded three-quarters of a visionary face and left the rest in shadow. It lit the entire corner of this room which, despite the flashing diamonds and flowing chasubles, the pomp and whalebone and coronation robes of other inmates, was so dark and dull by comparison. I had stumbled upon this sudden warmth with the sensation of an intruder. A sweet air moved about it, a perfume unmistakable and peculiar to itself. It was intensely private, and this was such a public place! And I had only smelt studio varnish hitherto. It was almost an anachronism here, exposed to what Goncourt called 'the icy admiration of crowds'. I do not know whether it was the light or the shadow that drew me first towards it, but the delicate beauty of the model affected me like an aria of Mozart—*Voi che sapete*. Eyes, mouth, nostrils, eyebrows—the latter arched like the Empress Eugénie's, only thinner and more Chinese—were questioning, alert, in suspense for this fraction of eternity. The thought which had pierced the brain would evaporate in a moment. The features, the supple form, and the personality burning behind them in a steady fire of concentrated feeling would instantly relax in laughter or in tears. Precisely which of these alternatives was immaterial, for we were within another sphere of emotion ready to burst volcanically forth. We were on the perilous brink of a rupture, of something passionate in the girl's temperament which made other emotions puny by comparison. Would the lamp burn itself out, or would it blaze into a roaring bonfire? For the moment it was tense, and I stood floundering among metaphors for the fleeting glamour of youth, all hackneyed and artificial in the lamp-light of that Victorian evening. But were warm evenings very different in spite of electricity? Did the period matter? 'What were the good of weaving cloth with words?'

A breeze from the window had blown aside one strand of hair, and a spray of white lilac lay lightly on the table. They assumed symbolic proportions which made one forget the oppression of neighbouring canvases. It was Manet rather than Kelsall, the Manet of Eve Gonzales; and Kelsall had succeeded in capturing the flush beneath a transparent skin. Who the model had been I did not bother to enquire: she might have been Spanish, an aristocratic Carmen.

Under her spell I retraced my steps, peering at the duchesses and burgomasters to see if I had not been blinkered by prejudice, but in their portraits I could find little trace of the genius that had transpired through the girl in the amber lamp-light. Kelsall had taken his models as he found them, passive in their pretentiousness and posing, 'dressed up to the nines' for the camera man de luxe. Basler was still standing in contemplation of a statuesque lady in a chinchilla jacket. I pretended not to see him, and hurried back to the Carmen in chiaroscuro.

I had vaguely expected it to undergo some alteration during my brief absence. Maybe I had made a romantic fool of myself, reading into the picture qualities that had never been there; or the desire to justify the triumph of this exhibition had shot forth illusionary buds, and out of nothingness had created this unique masterpiece. . . .

But when I returned it seemed more wonderful and I held my breath. Again I gazed my fill on the velvety shadows, on how the tender flesh was modelled beneath them. Even the darkness was luminous and caressing. Here the painter's technique had been dominated and transformed: none of his usual slickness was apparent. Bold it certainly was, and bravely conceived, but so spontaneous that one did not consider the method, and those tricks of trade that jump to the eyes, as the French express it, from so many of his portraits. It left me pondering on his potential achievement, had he been free to paint as the spirit moved him.

To do him justice he had often revolted against his commercial patrons. They had sat or stood for him at their peril. To some he could hardly be civil: he would paralyse them for hours on end in his draughty studio till pins and needles pierced them. Fiercely, with all the armoury of his realism, he would daub them duller than they were, laying on the pigment more thickly to match their thickness out of sheer exasperation. Perhaps his thoughts returned to the girl in the lamp-light; he remembered what might have been, and took a skilled revenge. The majority paid for his name, and he made them pay lavishly. Even the highest bidders were apt to hesitate, but they hoped to invest in immortality—a speculation as costly as it was precarious. Whereas the Carmen must have been a personal friend, possibly something more. One could visualize the scene. A late afternoon in the eighteen-eighties, after the tea-table had been cleared, Kelsall had pulled out a sketch-book and then a canvas, persuading her to keep her most natural pose; and then the same evening after dinner he had begged her to sit for him again. Thus casually, in the midst of a mild flirtation ('Do let me choose a prettier dress!' 'The one you're wearing is perfect.') Kelsall had produced his masterpiece, not in a studio but in a drawing-room, with a background of cosy Victorian furniture and the folds of drawn chintz curtains.

Before leaving Burlington House I examined the ticket attached to the frame, and read: 'A Sketch, 1888. Lent by Miss Temple.'

II

Many months had passed and I had forgotten the Kelsall Exhibition, or rather, I had forgotten the portrait by virtue of which I should have remembered it. I was on a pilgrimage to Assisi when my friends the Masinis invited me to stay with them near Florence. They possessed a charming villa which had formerly been an old

Tuscan farmhouse. Under a sunny terrace the *podere* remained intact with its vines and olives: they had not attempted to convert it into a formal garden. Guido Masini was a sculptor, but I was more interested in his conversation than his art, which was steeped in archaistic mannerisms. His wife spoke English with an affected Italian accent though she had originated in Surrey, interspersing her language copiously with *magari* and *davvero*.

Rose Masini was the specimen of unsuccessful novelist who talked incessantly about her public, the friendly correspondence between her readers and herself, and the importance she attached to their tributes and confidences. The common reader mattered more to her than the craft of fiction, so she believed that one should 'write down' to that reader's level. She wrote lower and lower down, poor dear, and was painfully surprised when her writings were ignored by reviewers. Yet she managed to maintain the airs and graces of a literary lady.

Rose was not without her secret tragedy, and had she been granted a modicum of success she would have been less of a bore. While wishing her better luck I could not help being relieved when, after the heat of the day, she left her husband and myself to cool off on the terrace in the twilight, explaining that *purtroppo* she must put the finishing touches to 'another little causerie for Jack o' Lantern'.

Guido, with a flask of Chianti beside him, would open a discussion on the eternal topic, which was neither politics nor sport, but art. One evening Kelsall's name cropped up.

'A generous-hearted man,' said Guido. 'Fantoni was much indebted to him. Whenever somebody commissioned a portrait from Kelsall he would only accept on condition that the same person agreed to sit for Fantoni, who was hardly known.'

'An eccentric form of philanthropy,' I replied. 'Fantoni was a bogus Impressionist, a confidence-trickster. He imitated Kelsall's slap-dash style, but his dashes and slaps were clumsier, and he tainted his models with his own vulgarity. O'Shaughnessy, the most ethereal of poets, was depicted in a sprawling posture with pince-nez tilting off a purple nose, and the austere Lady Killballock was made to leer like one of Lautrec's strumpets.'

'But his texture was marvellous,' Guido objected. 'Who else could introduce bits of glass into his pigment with such striking effect?'

Guido's defence of Fantoni was eloquent, but it seemed to be prompted by patriotic fervour. He had not seen the portraits referred to, and if he had, he might not have been shocked by the vulgarization of figures who meant nothing to him. Kelsall had never been guilty of such offences, and I recalled the girl in the lamp-light of the 'sketch, lent by Miss Temple'.

'Miss Temple?' he queried. 'That must be our neighbour Priscilla Temple. She was an intimate friend of Kelsall. I've heard her speak of him often. For her he was a god.'

'Who is she, what is she?'

'Oh, just another of those old English maids. They come out here to die.'

His tone was contemptuous and rather cruel, as if he had suffered from their importunities. Perhaps his wife had been in the habit of foisting her exclusive readers upon him, and he preferred models of a younger generation.

'Every year these living antiques are imported from England,' he added viciously, 'but they seem to love Italy, and I have no wish to offend you.'

I retorted that this was another instance of the law of mutual attraction: the antiques were drawn to the antiquity of Florence; and I should be delighted to meet Miss Temple. At least I would go one further than my school friend at the Kelsall Exhibition. He had nodded and bowed to mere canvases, but it would be my privilege to meet Kelsall's loveliest model in the flesh.

Guido was nonplussed. Was I not sufficiently familiar with the species he described? The cheaper *pensions* were packed with them. But I withstood his sneers. 'Never mind, she is responsible for Kelsall's masterpiece.'

'That must have been ages ago. Also I must warn you that she does water-colour drawings. The *Duomo at Sunset, the Campanile at Dawn.*'

As this type of delicate dauber is becoming extinct I persisted in my request. The hardships suffered by some of these amateurs, the extremities of heat and cold in the most unlikely places, setting forth before sunrise with knapsack and campstool, put the hedonistic professionals to shame. This indeed was art for art's sake—if there was any meaning in that slogan.

'As you please,' said Guido, 'you only have to ask her and she'll show them to you, portfolio after portfolio—rhododendrons at Bournemouth, fountains at Tivoli, puppies among the poppies. Well, don't blame me if you're bored!'

Having finished her causerie, Rose waylaid me with a languid smile as I was bedward bound: 'Guido tells me that you're longing to meet our English neighbour. Perhaps I had a premonition of this, for I asked her to dine with us tomorrow. I'm afraid Guido has done his best to prejudice you against her. Pay no attention to him: he will never see anything in a woman unless she'll pose for him in the nude. *Insomma* Priscilla Temple is a Perfect Dear. She used to be a militant suffragette but now she's an ardent theosophist and vegetarian. I'm sure you'll get on like a house on fire. Happy dreams!'

It was late when I reached my bedroom. The distant bells were booming and the near mosquitoes zooming in my ears. I opened the shutters to catch whatever breeze might be. In frail fantastic spirals the fireflies waltzed and pirouetted between the vines and olives; they raced on the grassy slope beneath my window, accompanied by an orchestra of frogs and crickets. The night was diaphanous: I peered across the way.

Just then I heard a voice of singular sweetness singing an aria I had always loved, '*Voi che sapete che cosa è amor.*' Gracefully, lightly, as if it belonged to a firefly, it glided through the Mozartian melody. It was not a young voice: on some of the notes it faded, dying gently from a higher to a lower key, like a sigh towards the end.

The diction and tone were not Italian, and the accompaniment was scarcely audible. But the melody was so subtly rounded that its curves were almost visible. Sung as I heard it tonight, there was an undercurrent of sadness in its smooth and simple modulations. I stood listening in my pyjamas, incapable of motion, and when the hands were taken off the keys—had they been playing a harpsichord, I wondered?—and the voice was stilled, I had a vision of snow under a leaden sky. Then the stars glimmered and the fireflies danced again to the accompaniment of crickets and amorous frogs. I poured myself a glass of water for my throat was dry.

The voice had conveyed to me an emotion poignant, desolate, akin to despair. I watched the dim light from the window whence the music had been wafted, trying to peer behind it, but it was soon extinguished and the house was left in darkness. For all my straining I had caught no glimpse of the singer.

Mechanically I propelled my limbs into bed, with '*Voi che sapete*' echoing through my brain. I could not sleep for the spell of that music was not broken, the mysterious desolation of its phrases lingered in my ears.

As I lay awake the pale features of Kelsall's portrait moved out of the canvas in the lamp-light, and the arched black eyes looked up at me. I recognized them instantly, and the proud bearing, tense and slender, and the strand of hair blown by the breeze. But this time the hair was streaked with white and the face was worn with wrinkles. The voice had surely been Priscilla Temple's.

The withered lips tried to smile, but in that heroic attempt there was such anguish that I turned my face to the pillow.

Pondering on my previous night's experience, I found it difficult to account for over my morning coffee in placid sunshine, and it puzzled me to realize how strangely moved I had been. Perhaps it had been due to the Tuscan Midsummer Magic which Vernon Lee had evoked, now prolonged into September. Certainly there had been magic in the air.

All the same I was determined never to meet Miss Temple. I would find some excuse and apologize to the Masinis for my departure. They were surprised and slightly upset, but Rose compensated for Guido's want of tact in pressing me to stay, and said she 'quite understood'.

I wonder if she did understand? Looking back on the incident, I am not sure that I do.

ARABY

NIGHT and day the swimming pool glimmered in the centre of the sub-tropical garden, now a transparent cerulean, now viridescent, a vast rectangular eye all-seeing and reflecting.

At night few ventured to plunge into it, though now and then in the hottest weather some sleepless eccentric, or a festive party flushed with wine and youth, might cool their ardours in its caressing depth, chasing and ducking and splashing each other across its illuminated expanse. In the daytime it was filled not only with long-haired adolescents of indeterminate sex but with paunchy middle-aged folk and even with withered old bipeds who forgot their age when they jumped into it or ruffled the water with tentative toes, laughing, spluttering, cackling and shouting, paddling and advancing with deliberate strokes or floating on their backs and gazing at the cloudless sky.

Here it was eternal June. They had come from lands far away to escape the severity of a northern winter, and made the utmost of their hibernation.

Before eight in the morning Abdul, the swarthy guardian of the pool, raked its bottom with a long pole attached to a brush which he dragged to and fro while he crooned a monotonous ditty. Already, in spite of a nip in the air, the bellyflops of the first bathers resounded like falling bombs. Proud of their pluck, they rubbed themselves vigorously with towels: some of them rubbed each other. The sun rose rapidly higher. Soon it would be blazing. In the meantime Abdul arranged chairs of various sizes and dimensions in social groups and dropped mats and cushions beside the small tables where coffee would be served. Gently he helped an old dame on crutches into a chaise-longue and lit her cigarette with a courtly bow; he fetched rubber swans and paddles for the children; he fed the family of monkeys in their cage who were so much livelier than those other mammals. For the majority would merely sprawl around the pool till sunset, occasionally shifting a leg or an arm, anointing their limbs, covering their heads with kerchiefs, sucking the regenerative rays through every pore and admiring the changing surface of their skins, the transitions from salmon pink to golden brown. Nothing else mattered but this: to lie neither asleep nor awake fully facing the sun, and when they began to simmer in rivulets of sweat, to turn over and roast their spines and flabby buttocks. Eyes closed or protected by dark glasses, the mind grew deliciously blank. Personalities melted into abstract anatomies, surrendering their wills to an impersonal Eros, too languid to move more than a few inches. Let others run and dive and kick up the silvery spray, they reclined as in a hospital, drugged by the sun. Time ceased to count though their wrist-watches ticked on. Some couples lay side by side never exchanging a word. Words meant so little under this thermal eiderdown which gradually reduced them to— what? Something that forgot about reading and writing, goods and gadgets, perplexities and cares, technology and telephones.

Thirst introduced a delightful sensation to dry mouths and tongues, for it could always be promptly assuaged. Towards mid-day a regiment of waiters in snowy white uniforms brought them iced drinks like liquid melodies. The most energetic—those who had been in and out of the pool all morning—had worked up a voracious appetite. Saliva began to trickle, their lips were moistened, their Adam's apples twitched. A buffet luncheon awaited them with savoury whiffs under an awning. They stood scrutinizing the copious viands spread out on a trolley with a glass cover. Some were tempted to taste a specimen of every dish on display; others struggled against temptation for the sake of their figures. Plastic trays with neat compartments were loaded and reloaded. Plump matrons bursting from bikinis carried them carefully across the lawn to the scattered tables under striped umbrellas. Late comers tripped distractedly through the grass seeking a vacancy with tense near-sighted expressions. A radio transmitted fluffy thé-dansant music while they chewed and swallowed, belched and wiped their mouths. Their jaws were more active than the waiters, who seemed dazed by the profusion of soft white flesh.

All the rooms faced the garden, the pool, and the sea beyond it; each contained a private balcony. Lionel sat writing at this observation post whence he could survey every detail of the scene below.

So far he had seen little outside the hotel, though he had arrived with a serious purpose: to steep himself in local colour for a travel book. Looking down from his notes, the sight of so many ungainly bodies lolling and gambolling beside the water's edge repelled him, for his mood was prepared for more spiritual sensations. But he could not help smiling at the gesticulations of a woman whose false teeth had slipped out while gnawing a leg of chicken. Surely that tum-ti-tum tune from the radio was dear old *Tea for Two*.

From the distance hidden by a grove of palm trees a stentorian voice repeated a morose refrain. Nobody paid the slightest attention to it, but Lionel realized that it was the call to prayer. All forms of worship appealed to his aesthetic sense regardless of the divinity to whom they might be directed, and he was irritated by the patter of ping-pong balls, the radio tunes, and the continual cavortings of bodies in the pool. Perhaps it was a mistake to stay in this ultra-modern hotel instead of some native caravanserai, but since his hiking days were over he was accustomed to European standards of comfort. Native inns were notoriously noisy and none too clean. At least the hotel was quiet after midnight. As it provided every convenience for tourists: a bank, a boutique, a beauty parlour, Sauna baths, hairdressers, masseurs and manicurists, as well as its luxurious 'Garden of Eden', few visitors were inclined to stray from its premises. The mediaeval city was within walking distance, but it did not exist for the votaries of the pool.

Despite its amenities the hotel affected Lionel with a pang of claustrophobia. He longed to breathe a more exotic air, to stretch his legs on truly indigenous soil. Why waste such a valuable opportunity?

'Won't you be taking a guide, sir?' the hotel porter queried. But Lionel did not want to be told what to see and how to look at it. He was eager to form his own impressions. A guide, however useful, would cram him with ready-made comments and interfere with his vision.

Outside the hotel entrance Lionel was buttonholed by half a dozen oily individuals who proposed to show him everything and more. They clung to him and when he expressed his indifference they whispered incomprehensible suggestions in his ear. He had considerable difficulty in shrugging them off. One stout fellow remarked with a malevolent grin: 'You think you know better but you will regret your obstinacy.'

After these he had to run the gauntlet of horse-cab and taxi-drivers who followed him with more incomprehensible suggestions in brisk competition with each other. Their language sounded like expectoration and they did not look trustworthy. He quickened his pace under the crumbling outer wall of the city. All the length of the road creatures muffled in ragged blankets squatted singly and in groups. Some stretched out their gnarled paws towards him automatically.

Lionel passed a forest of cheap bicycles, a yard of ramshackle buses daubed in garish colours, and a few dismal cafés whose occupants looked as if they were waiting for death. Horns honked and donkeys brayed beside ruminative camels: all were hurrying in the same direction. Magnificent black eyes peered at him from ravaged faces. Skins varied from sallow to polished ebony; clothes from woollen blankets to vague western attire, sweaters and ubiquitous blue jeans; headgear from tarbooshes to skull-caps and battered Panamas. The women were shawled and veiled in brighter hues; they huddled together like sheep. Thus far they were too intent on their own affairs to give Lionel more than a glance, but the glance was none too friendly. A confused strepitation of voices and thumping of drums grew louder as he approached the famous square. It was not strictly a square but a straggling fair-ground. He approached it with a beating heart.

Here was ample material for his first chapter. He gasped at the frenzied vitality of it all. It presented a formidable challenge to his descriptive powers. He would pour the animal excitement of the scene into his purplest prose. . . . How could those tourists waste their holiday at a swimming pool when there was this fascinating phantasmagoria round the corner? He was glad he had refused a guide. Here he could wander with the throng and concentrate.

At first he could not help feeling rather self-conscious. His false air of being at ease could hoodwink nobody. He had become an anachronism, an intruder into a bygone ageless age. The aromas that greeted his nostrils were atavistic, as if they were wafted from some tribal camp in the Old Testament. Most of the people round him were dusty nomads from the desert beyond the mountains and they had wild wondering fatalistic expressions. The desert was in their eyes and in the clothes they wore. They reeked of solitary tents, of goats and camels. This was their Piccadilly Circus. Spellbound for hours they watched the jugglers, buffoons, charlatans, acrobats performing in circles all over this vast area, and for them Lionel was part of the show though he had come with the same intent.

A troupe of male dancers were leaping and twirling frantically to the crescendo rhythm of tambourines: backwards and forwards, jig-jig-jig, crouching to leap even higher, it was a brainless exercise in perpetual motion, or could it be ecstasy, the last remnant of some dancing dervishes? Lionel decided in favour of ecstasy: these black boys garbed in white must be temple acolytes. A strenuous form of spiritual abstraction, very salutary no doubt. He was a little too old for it personally, but he would recommend it for English teenagers—keep them out of mischief. Amazing how rapidly they twirled, just like tops. Then one of them caught his eye, stopped twirling, and rushed towards Lionel for payment. Lionel produced a coin but no, it was not enough, and the dancer gesticulated for more. Lionel dropped additional coins into his grubby hand and the other spectators laughed. None of them had contributed a penny.

Pursued by a rabble of urchins, Lionel joined a bigger circle surrounding a snake charmer who was extracting a huge black cobra from a leather bag. It was a dramatic moment. The magician chanted a mysterious litany while he tickled the snake with a wand, swaying his long hair from side to side and foaming at the mouth. The cobra swayed more slowly in unison inflating its flat head. Again Lionel was reminded of the Old Testament, how the serpent 'was more subtil than any beast of the field which the Lord God had made'. Poor beast, pathetically reduced to the role of public entertainer! It behaved with great dignity in the circumstances. Seeing Lionel, the magician attempted to wind it round his neck, but the serpent slithered away through the frightened audience. 'Baksheesh, baksheesh!' the magician called after his retreating figure, and the urchins repeated the cry. Like a swarm of wasps they buzzed around him and he began to wish that he had taken a guide for self-protection. By scattering money he merely attracted others.

Beggars pressed up against him, advertising their hideous deformities; they tugged at his jacket and grabbed his feet and would not let him go. Gnats, flies, mosquitoes, black beetles. 'Keep your temper, old man!' he adjured himself. 'All men are brothers.' But his charitable instincts were strained as he elbowed his way towards a less teeming hinterland of rickety booths and open-air kitchens, where cauldrons of steaming broth, chunks of grilled meat on sticks, fried locusts, salted fish, little bowls of peppery sauces, round loaves of bread and mounds of rancid butter and clotted honey, attracted the hungry, including a group of bearded westerners disguised as natives. An urchin pointed at them and said 'Hippies'. Hashish was cheap and abundant in the market yet they did not look happy over their meal.

Lionel shuddered when a huge head attached to an armless and legless trunk was wheeled beside him; a dwarf turned somersaults; a leper thrust out a stump from his bundle of rags. Their persistence had begun to exasperate him. He cuffed an urchin who had kicked a mangy dog and the urchin shouted obscenities in English. Where had he learnt them? Such language was as sickening as the beggars' sores. The effluvia of putrid smells became oppressive.

Seeking a refuge from the glare and blare, Lionel made for an arch between mud brick houses. He found himself in an alley like a winding corridor between rows of coffin-like stores. If he imagined this would be quieter he was soon disillusioned. There were streams of people shuffling in both directions with tinkling bicycles and overloaded donkeys: he was jostled and swept along towards a broader alley where the merchandise resembled a flamboyant herbaceous border until one examined it in detail: gaudy textiles and rugs, gleaming daggers and leatherwork, cannabis among the canna lilies. As soon as he halted he was urged to come in and buy. 'Hi, step inside, sir!' 'Hello, Mister, what is your special desire? I have carpets of every size for every sex of feet.' Others assured him: 'No obligation to buy. Only come in and look. Let me pour you fragrant tea.' One pulled him by the arm, another by the coat, another whistled. Their voices were wheedling, bullying, cajoling. 'Come back, come back. I have many more wonders to show, beautiful objects for ladies as well as gents. This is Aladdin's Cave.' 'Another day,' said Lionel, 'another time.' He pretended not to understand, to be deaf, to have an engagement elsewhere, but they shouted after him while idlers collected to watch the fun like jinns of the desert, malignant sprites on the prowl for unwary travellers. Some offered themselves as guides to tombs and wombs; others merely offered themselves '*pour faire l'amour*'.

Lionel shook his head sadly. The air he breathed was infested with corruption. Overcome by weariness, his temples throbbing, his eyes blinking, walking around in cirlces, he fancied he was lost in a maze when suddenly, as from a tunnel, he came out again into the open square. The black boys were still desperately twirling; the story-teller was still elaborating his complicated narrative for a dwindling audience; but many of the performers had departed in a floating haze of dust which mingled with the acrid smoke of cooking offal. It was as if a barbaric camp were breaking up, the tents were being folded and mongrel dogs were rooting among the garbage. Again the stentorian voice from a minaret called the population to prayer. This time Lionel heard it with a different emotion. A factory siren would have been more effective.

Thirsty, footsore and coated with dust, Lionel tottered into a shabby café facing the square. Having ordered some mint tea he proceeded to scribble a few notes while the images were fresh in his mind's eye. Even in this dark corner he was not left in peace for a fat man waddled up to him and asked in French: 'Do you require a guide, sir? I am an experienced guide with a diploma.'

'Please leave me alone.'

'I beg you to be careful, sir. Not nice people here, not correct. But with me you are always safe.'

'Some other time. Can't you see that I'm trying to write?'

The man plumped himself down beside him and continued doggedly: 'I will take you to a nicer place, more correct, with a fine choice of maidens for your entertainment.'

Lionel offered him a cigarette in the hope of silencing him while his pencil raced on under the hot impulse of memory.

'Voluptuous virgins, hygienic and not expensive,' his oily neighbour confided in a cloud of garlic. 'Real bargains in human flesh!'

The salient episodes of his excursion recorded, Lionel replaced the notebook in his pocket and fumbled for his wallet to pay for the tea he had not touched. He fumbled in vain; it was gone. He searched the floor in case it had slipped out, but it must have been filched in the tumult or even here. The interloper guessed what had happened. 'Permit me to settle with the waiter,' he said with an unctuous air of triumph. 'Tomorrow I will call at your hotel to show you the famous tombs, and perhaps a few girls who deserve to be famous. There are also young boys who are not to be despised. Is Monsieur a voyeur by any chance? I can arrange many exciting combinations.'

Defeated and depressed, Lionel muttered: 'That's enough. Of course I shall repay you. You know my address?'

The fat man grinned with all his yellow tusks. 'I saw you at the hotel entrance where I volunteered my services. You rebuffed me most unkindly but my nature is forgiving. Pray accept my visiting card.' He escorted Lionel to a battered taxicab. 'Tombs tomorrow,' he repeated merrily.

Lionel lost no time in slipping down to the swimming pool. For once it was empty, a large lamplit aquamarine in the surrounding penumbra. He threw himself into the water with a loud splash and revelled in the sensation of melting like a piece of soap. After his sweltering afternoon in the city he felt purified body and soul. He was not quite alone, for a slim white girl was drying herself under an oleander bush. Combing her copper-gold hair, she looked so clean and civilized that he longed to embrace her, but he merely smiled and she returned his smile.

'Isn't it bliss?' she remarked. 'I've been here since lunchtime and I simply hate to go indoors and dress.'

The patter of ping-pong balls no longer vexed him, and the laughter of the players was oddly exhilarating. The mild melodies from the unseen radio, carefree and optimistic, were soothing to his nerves. Though he could not pretend to be musical he recognized his old friend *Tea for Two*.

On his way to dinner he stopped at the cage of monkeys, who thrust out their paws gibbering like the urchins in the market. He handed them the pages of his notebook. Grabbing them eagerly, they tore his memoranda to shreds.

'O THOU I'

As too often happened Lucy telephoned while Hilary was soaking in the bathroom. Dripping over the carpet, his wet hand grasped the slippery receiver and Lucy's quavering voice apologized for disturbing him so early, but Lady Twilight was giving an intimate luncheon for the ex-Queen of Iberia and she was hoping for Hilary's support. Her Majesty had expressed a keen desire to meet him again as she had greatly enjoyed his conversation.

Vexed by the trickle of water down his spine and the damp towel dangling from his loins while Tim was laughing at him from the tousled bed, Hilary was tempted to shout: 'Go to Hades!' But as usual he surrendered to the pathos of Lucy's plea. Lady Twilight might scold her for failing to catch him in time. So he merely said: 'Thank you, I'll come with pleasure. Give Lady Twilight my love.'

There had been a period when his pleasure was genuine. Everyone who knew Lady Twilight agreed that she was one of the last of lavish Edwardian hostesses. Formerly she would prescribe the topics of conversation in advance. Guests would find these inscribed on slips of paper beside their plates. Birth control, the progress of biology, ecology, comparative religion, and so forth. Unfortunately none took these seriously. They digressed into trivial topics, and Lady Twilight concluded that while birth could be controlled conversation could not. However, it had been a praiseworthy effort. The food and wine were invariably superlative, but the titles of the guests promised more than they could fulfil: Hilary's Proustian expectations were disappointed.

It was the personality of the hostess that continued to whet his curiosity. Was she an inspired mystic or a worldling? Her comments on people and places were as often silly as they were profound. She said she could only bear to read philosophy: in fact it was read to her by Lucy as the print tired her eyes and she refused to wear glasses. Lucy confided to Hilary that Lady Twilight would often fall asleep while she read to her, but as soon as she stopped Lady Twilight would murmur 'Go on, I'm listening,' and fall asleep again. She never referred to her patroness by her Christian name.

'All wisdom comes from India,' Lady Twilight was fond of repeating. 'Our philosophers are puerile after theirs. Purely puerile.' She made exceptions for Pythagoras and Plotinus. Nevertheless, in the spirit of Margaret Fuller's 'I accept the universe', she had chosen to settle in Monte Carlo. Since houses were too much bother she kept a permanent suite at the Hotel Splendide. 'It may not be the right milieu for my aura but it has its compensations,' she explained. This was one of the paradoxes of her life. Doubtless the methods of meditation that purify the soul may be practised anywhere, but Monte Carlo did not seem conducive to that sort of exercise. Perhaps it was owing to her meditations that Lady Twilight had achieved a certain timelessness. Clocks were anathema to her, the sound of their ticking was torture. Nobody could guess her age. She had a rosy complexion with abundant silvery hair and her smooth doll-like features expressed little but benevolence. There was never a hair out of place, and it was entirely her own dressed regularly by her sullen maid. 'I have to put up with Odile because she's the only person who can keep my hair in order, but she can be a terrible trial,' she said with a sigh. In her clothes she showed an excessive tidiness though she despised the latest fashion. Her diction was as distinct as her memory was vague.

Lucy was her living memorandum and timepiece. 'Where are we dining tonight? What was the book Monseigneur recommended to me? Who was that dreamy young man we met at Aspasia's?' Lucy remembered everything and helped her to decide what to wear. Her voice was plaintively genteel and her eyes were slightly blurred, as if on the verge of tears. In spite of Lady Twilight's vagueness hers was the stronger will.

Their disparity of age—Lucy at least twenty years younger—was scarcely noticeable. Lucy had faded steadily throughout the years of their association while Lady Twilight remained placidly static. Some were inclined to pity her, but she had made her choice early in life. Several men had proposed to her when she was governess to Daphne, Lady Twilight's adopted daughter, and later when she had been promoted to secretary-companion she nearly married a nice young doctor. 'If you leave me you'll only get a wedding present,' Lady Twilight told her. 'But if you stay on you'll get more than a comfortable annuity. Every year I'll increase your legacy.' After much heart-searching the nice young doctor was dumped.

Did Lucy repine? Her hurt hesitant manner suggested it as well as a tendency to pout when she fell silent. Since Lady Twilight would go nowhere without her she had fewer matrimonial opportunities. Lady Twilight's friends complained of this imposition. Whereas an extra man might be convenient an extra woman with an aggrieved expression was *de trop*. It was supposed that she insisted on accompanying Her Ladyship to parties and that she made scenes when she was not invited. Though she never appeared to enjoy herself she made a meticulous scrutiny of all the guests. What they wore, whether they looked older or younger or had had their faces lifted—there was little that she failed to observe on the material side, and she regaled Lady Twilight with a detailed inventory while Odile was brushing her hair.

Lucy had made herself indispensable and her efficiency had helped to foster Lady Twilight's vagueness. 'What was that pregnant saying from one of the Upanishads I wanted Hilary to hear?' she asked. 'Something about honey and thunder. In Western literature it would be blood and thunder. We can never get away from blood.'

Lucy looked puzzled, but only for a moment. In the flat voice of a schoolgirl reciting a poem without understanding the words she replied: 'Thunder is the honey of all beings; all beings the honey of thunder.'

'Thank you, Lucy. And it goes on: "The bright eternal Self that is in thunder, the bright eternal Self that lives in the voice, are one and the same" . . .'

Lady Twilight's voice was low and honeyed: it contained no hint of thunder. 'It is a wonderful saying, quite as profound as any in the Old Testament. And so poetical.'

Hilary listened in amazement. Supposing he called his next novel *The Honey of Thunder*? It was not a bad title though the aphorism remained obscure. But obscurity was modish nowadays. Personally he regarded thunder as a great big bore. He had to admit that he understood the Bible better. 'I fear you are a sophist,' he quizzed.

'I am merely sophisticated, like you dear Hilary. I distrust the commonplace. Truth can't be reached by argument, only by meditation.'

Such statements were hard to reconcile with Lady Twilight's penchant for social tittle-tattle. She could talk of an Indian guru with greater fervour than of the Grand Duchess Gaby, but if she had to vote between the two the Grand Duchess would have won. For Lady Twilight harboured a dark secret: she had been born in Idaho, and her career had been an effort to obliterate that fact. So successfully had she studied elocution in London and Paris that her original accent had evaporated. Her languid lisping English was sprinkled with French clichés of 1890 vintage.

By her marriage to an English peer she had adapted herself to insular customs and prejudices. Though she bought her clothes in Paris she considered it bad form to look *chic*. She had evolved a style of her own, distinguished without smartness, of clinging gowns with ample bodices, and she adhered to it with minor variations after Lord Twilight's death. She had no cause to regret Lord Twilight, of whose unlimited extravagance she spoke with a tolerant smile.

Her conspicuous fortune had been inherited from Clarence Billings, a bachelor uncle to whom Lord Twilight had been indebted. Billings had struck a bargain with the penurious peer: he would cancel the debt if he married his nice Delphine. Lord Twilight, a sexagenarian profligate with a paunch and bloodshot eyes, accepted the gentleman's agreement with alacrity, and Delphine was won over by his title and the mortgaged manor which sounded grander than it was. She was grateful to the uncle who had introduced her to Europe, but it had been embarrassing to be mistaken for his mistress. It was no hardship to exchange one old bachelor for another when she gained a coronet and financial independence by the transaction. And the hair that was her pride and glory had always hankered after a diamond tiara.

Albeit her income was in trust Lord Twilight squandered all of it he could lay his hands on, for he was an inveterate gambler with a passion for horse-racing. He made no pretence to love his American bride who treated him as a comic anachronism. With other women he flirted, but this seldom went beyond a pinch and a kiss. He was no match for the combination of Delphine and Lucy, who by gradual degrees kept him under petticoat control, supervising his diet and sending him early to bed. Occasionally he played truant and spent a night on the tiles. He returned so exhausted that he eventually succumbed to a stroke. His widow, accompanied by Lucy and little Daphne, set forth on a series of cruises round the world. For many years they alternated steamers with hotels while Twilight Manor was sold and demolished. Lucy enjoyed the kaleidoscopic variety of scene but Daphne became listless as she grew up without a fixed abode: she missed the dogs and stables of her bucolic childhood.

The more Lady Twilight saw the more she wished to see. In India she announced: 'I think we shall find our true selves here. Why go further?' She had met a wandering guru with hypnotic eyes who told her that she was ripe for illumination. He gave her introductions to famous swamis all over India. She visited their ashrams for weeks at a time and practised meditation under their guidance with unflagging enthusiasm. In scorching heat Lucy and Daphne trailed after her. Each city seemed more desiccated than the last, shuttered against the sun, but in some places their rooms overlooked a garden where tropical vegetation slumbered in the steamy air and only the birds were energetic, chattering and fluttering among the dense foliage like messengers of the gods with happy news. Unable to share Lady Twilight's exaltation, Lucy and Daphne ransacked the bazaars for bright saris and bric-à-brac. Daphne ridiculed the yogis and complained of everything else. Lady Twilight taxed her with ingratitude and advised her to master her mind. But Daphne refused to join her breathing exercises.

When the heat became intolerable the trio sailed for Japan, to which Lady Twilight was drawn by her interest in Zen Buddhism. The fascination of Zen was all the more powerful because nobody could explain it in intelligible words. 'Language only leads one astray,' said Lady Twilight. Which did not prevent her from reading, or making Lucy read to her, abstruse tracts which helped her to soar to higher spheres. Closing her eyes, she wallowed in prescriptions for attaining a state of complete wakefulness. In the meantime Daphne slipped out of the hotel with a brawny Canadian tennis champion she had met in the swimming pool. Her absences were not perceived until she announced that she wanted to marry him. The fiancé reminded Lady Twilight unpleasantly of the sophomores she had waltzed with in Idaho. 'I'm surprised that Daphne hasn't better taste after all you've done for her,' said Lucy.

'It must be chemical,' Lady Twilight decided. 'One shouldn't interfere with natural chemistry. Daphne's old enough to know her mind, what there is of it. How old is she?' 'Eighteen.' 'Better early than late. She may not find another tennis champion.'

Unfortunately few Japanese spoke English as fluently as the Indians of Lady Twilight's acquaintance. Even her interpreter-guide was taciturn and she was perplexed by his pronunciation. He presented her to several Buddhist monks but their intercourse did not progress beyond formal bows and smiles. The charm of their quaintness soon wore off. When she questioned them about conscious Samadhi and Tureeya, the Self and the One, they were as flummoxed as an Anglican parson would have been. The mass of Buddhist literature she had collected helped to fill the human gap and she was gratified to learn about an escape from the intellect, never realizing that this was quite natural to her. In the case of Zen Buddhism, however, it was precipitated by shock, which might be produced artificially by the teacher. Many curious examples were described, and they were more physical than mental. For instance a young monk remarked to his Abbot: 'I have noticed that when anybody has asked about Nirvana you merely raise your right hand and lower it again, and now when I am asked I answer in the same way.' The Abbot seized his hand and cut off a finger. The young monk ran away screaming, then stopped and looked back. The Abbot raised his hand and lowered it, and at that moment the young monk attained the supreme joy.

Lady Twilight punctuated this anecdote with a startled exclamation. 'Perhaps that dear old abbot who invited us to his temple will do the same to me. I can't say that I fancy the idea. I think I could attain the supreme joy without losing one of my fingers. Which reminds me I need a manicure.'

'There's a manicurist in the hotel, a sweet little Japanese girl.'

Lady Twilight examined her slender hands with complacency. 'That story about the finger has discouraged me. I'm not sure that I really care about Zen Buddhism. Let us return to India.'

Daphne eloped to Canada with her fiancé, leaving a rude note for Lady Twilight, who shrugged her shoulders and wished her luck in Toronto. After another hectic tour of ashrams even India palled. A retired civil servant in Madras introduced her to Sufism but she was not in a receptive mood for it. One Sufi saying impressed her, however: she repeated it till she learnt it by heart. 'I went from God to God, until they cried from me in me, "O Thou I".'

Lucy was inwardly relieved when she decided that they had wandered far enough. Flies, insects of all kinds—she saw and heard them buzzing everywhere, even when they were not present. She blew and beat the air automatically. It had become an obsession which only the ocean could cure. Lady Twilight's friends the Graingers had invited her to Monte Carlo. Why not join their yacht at Naples as they had suggested?

Passages were booked from Bombay. While Lucy paid the bills and tipped the regiment of servants Lady Twilight sat with her sullen maid among piles of luggage in the lounge. 'O Thou I', she murmured with an ecstatic expression. She would have the words engraved on her writing paper.

In Naples she nearly lost Lucy to a receptionist at the hotel. Since the Grainger yacht was not quite ready their stay was prolonged by a week. The receptionist Carmine took Lucy out boating in the bay after Lady Twilight had retired to meditate. The morning before their departure she announced that he had proposed to her. This was not true, but she had imagined that a night of such voluptuous embraces could only lead to marriage.

'Don't let me spoil a romance,' said Lady Twilight with a benevolent smile. 'Remember you're older than Daphne, and a hotel clerk's salary . . . well, please consider it. Have you met his parents? You may find yourself married to his whole family and you don't even speak the language. Stay on by all means, but nothing will stop me from sailing tomorrow. We are dining with the Graingers.'

Carmine was not free to take Lucy out that night though she had sent him word of her imminent departure. He swore he had a business engagement which might affect his future. 'But I must leave tomorrow,' she wailed, 'and I don't know when or where we shall meet again. Try to postpone it. Do I mean so little to you?' Lucy swallowed her tears.

'Be reasonable, *cara*. You promised me a souvenir of our evenings together,' and kissing her hand he unclasped her gold Rolex. Slipping it over his own small wrist, he said gaily: 'It might have been made for me!'

Lucy was less happy about it. 'You should give me a memento in exchange,' she suggested. 'The coral horn on your chain would look better on my bracelet.'

'This was given me by my blessed mamma, God rest her soul.

I couldn't part with it. But I'll get you one just like it, against the Evil Eye.'

'Well, at least you might give me a photo.'

He fished some snapshots from his battered wallet: himself sunbathing on the rocks of Capri. The hairy limbs gleamed with oil, and the grinning face might have belonged to any gigolo with bulges in the appropriate places. Lucy examined each critically and selected the bulgiest. He scribbled *'Baci, baci, baci'* and signed Carmine on the back. An elderly dandy in a purple blazer waddled towards him with a whiff of Chanel and drawled: 'Are you ready?' Carmine was too flustered to introduce him to Lucy. 'Bye-bye,' he whispered guiltily.

Simultaneously Lady Twilight appeared from behind a potted palm.

'Is everything packed? The Graingers are waiting for us in the car.'

On the terrace of the open-air restaurant Lucy caught sight of Carmine with his purple companion: they were holding hands. 'What's the matter, dear?' Lady Twilight asked her as she burst into tears.

'A touch of hay fever,' she answered, blowing her nose. 'I suspect it's a local allergy,' said Lady Twilight. 'You've never had hay fever before. The yacht will soon cure it.'

A group of strolling singers bellowing *Funiculì funiculà* diverted the Graingers' attention. 'There's nothing like the good old songs,' said Sir Eric. 'Takes one back a bit, eh Norah?'

'You're thinking of the days before you met me,' Lady Grainger retorted.

The corpulent owner of the restaurant proposed that the ladies touch the massive horn dangling from his waistcoat for luck. Again the tears sprang to Lucy's eyes. Not far away Carmine was showing his snapshots to his flashy friend but he was too self-absorbed to notice her. And to think that only last night . . . The glint of her gold Rolex on his wrist made her angrier with herself than with him.

Later, when Lady Twilight asked: 'Are you coming with us

or would you prefer to stay?' she replied: 'I wouldn't dream of letting you sail without me.' But she could not banish the memory of those hot wet kisses redolent of garlic. During her routine reading of extracts from Buddhist lore Lady Twilight interposed: 'Louder, dear, I can hardly hear you.' Lucy's voice had sunk to a whimper when she came to:

> 'As rain breaks in upon an ill-thatched hut,
> So passion breaks in upon the untrained mind.'

'Perhaps you ought to rest. You are not looking well. The sea air will bring back the colour to your cheeks.'

'I'm scared of being seasick.'

'Take two of my tablets. What a depressing subject before bedtime. Go on reading and you'll forget it. That bit about the bee.'

> 'As the bee—injuring not
> The flower, its colour, or scent—
> Flies away, taking the nectar;
> So let the wise man dwell upon the earth.'

'Let's dream of bees—always on the wing like us. Speaking for myself I'm full of Indian nectar. You too, dear, I hope.' Lucy had felt full of Neapolitan nectar. Alas, it had turned rancid.

Should she have made a final assignation with Carmine? She boarded the Grainger yacht with a heavy heart. The crew were certainly handsome. 'Quite a male beauty chorus,' Lady Twilight observed. 'I wonder if Sir Eric has other tastes. The way poor Norah has let her figure go I wouldn't be surprised. His love of yachting looks like an alibi.'

They were joined by the vivacious Hilary who had flown from Ischia by helicopter. One could rely on him to keep the ball rolling. His effect on the Graingers was rejuvenating. The cruise was cloudless, cool and calm: the peacock glitter of the Mediterranean was barely flecked with silvery caps of foam. Lady Twilight seldom left her deck-chair where Lucy read to her about Buddha's thirteen lives. The others played chess or ping-pong.

At every port of call the whole party except Hilary were entertained by some prominent local magnate. Hilary's excuse was that he had to finish writing a novel.

'What is your subject, if I'm not being indiscreet?' Lady Twilight enquired.

'It's madly avant-garde. I've done nothing like it yet. No plot, no development of character, but lots of fornication and schizophrenia.'

'It's bound to be a best-seller,' said Sir Eric, 'though not in my line.'

'Nor in mine I fear,' said Lady Twilight. Hilary looked so decorative, she thought, in his daffodil yellow pullover. It was a pity he had that morbid urge to write. She had hoped he would marry Daphne, who had been impervious to his charm. Even Lucy criticized his excessive attention to old ladies. It was unnatural, she maintained.

Back in Monte Carlo the traditional frivolities resumed their sway. As the Bhavagad-Gita says, only those need renounce worldly actions who are still inwardly attached thereto. The uncertainty of what Lady Twilight would do or where she would go next kept Lucy on the *qui vive*. Her gargantuan luncheon parties were the only certainty. 'Often I wake up in the night with a sense of dread and realize it's because I'm giving a luncheon,' Lady Twilight told Hilary. 'Why do I go on doing it I wonder? I've come to the conclusion that it's expected of me. Lucy loves telephoning and making the arrangements. Actually they bore me to distraction. One should eat alone, a little at a time, whenever one feels like it.'

Those who saw her in the front row at concerts imagined that she was musical but in fact she was amused by the grimaces of the singers. It was one of Lucy's most arduous duties to quieten her while the rest of the audience darted furious glances in her direction. Once her laughter became so uncontrollable that she had to leave in the middle of the concert with a handkerchief pressed to her mouth. Whether contraltos were funnier than sopranos was indeed a very moot point. She was convulsed by the plump prima donnas who tried to imitate birds, accompanied by flute and piano. 'Debussy sends me in stitches,' she said. 'Mélisande being dragged by the hair moaning "*Je ne suis pas heureuse ici*".' Lucy, who had to sit beside her amid indignant protests, was more confused than amused.

'Without Lucy and my meditations I'd suffer from a sense of emptiness. What was Professor Spandril's expression for it, dear?'

'A nothingness neurosis, Lady Twilight.'

'Precisely. One of the major problems of the modern world. Lord Twilight suffered from it, so did silly Daphne. Lord Twilight took refuge in gambling—at my expense. As for Daphne, she's been a disappointment. We haven't heard from her once since her marriage.'

Lady Twilight unbosomed herself to Hilary while waiting for the ex-Queen of Iberia, who always arrived on the dot, a little breathless, kissing the ladies who curtseyed to her and helping them most graciously to rise. She never said much but she added an aureole of distinction as she led the vanguard towards the dining-room. Like Lady Twilight she ate nothing but fruit and vegetables with a glass of milk, which confused the waiters but did not prevent the others from gormandizing.

Lucy looked harassed throughout the feast, her eyes roving round the table and fixing Lady Twilight's when called upon for a name or anecdote that had slipped her memory. Wine glasses were filled and refilled and the guests tucked in with gusto, though many had brought pills to swallow furtively. Hilary was the only guest under fifty and for once he felt his talents were wasted. His neighbours were too intent on their plates to appreciate his whimsical saga of the Grainger yacht. Lady Twilight looked so dazed she was hardly there. She's in one of her trances, thought Hilary, 'O Thou I'. Professor Spandril diagnosed a nothingness neurosis. 'The food's below par,' he complained. 'And the menu's always the same. As Lucy does the ordering we might give her a few hints for non-vegetarians.'

'Others don't seem to share your opinion,' said Hilary. 'Just think of the starving peasants who'd envy us even the rolls.'

'I'm afraid that wouldn't help to feed them.'

'But it's as well to remember the starving now and then, especially when one's surrounded by querulous gluttons. Eat and be thankful, say I. Don't you feel guilty about leaving so much on your plate?'

'You should set up as a Hyde Park orator.'

'And you should be sent to Biafra.'

The professor helped himself to a double portion of strawberries and *crème double* with a shrug of defiance.

Lady Twilight gazed at her guests without seeing or hearing them. For the first time Hilary noticed that she was registering fatigue. Evidently her thoughts were very far away. 'It was even duller than usual,' she remarked to him later. 'And it was gallant of you to help me out. I was never a motherly person but you make me regret I have no son. Poor Daphne was always inconsiderate. I have to blame myself for adopting her: it was a sentimental mistake.'

Lucy whispered something in her ear. 'Don't we all live too much in the moment?' Lady Twilight continued. 'We don't give enough thought to eternity, for which this is a mere rehearsal. Now Lucy reminds me that I ought to be lying down. Please do me a favour and disperse the stragglers. Royalty is so considerate, the first to come and the first to go. But Professor Spandril will stay all afternoon, the victim of his nothingness neurosis.'

'I've recommended a trip to Nigeria.'

'A brilliant solution. Au revoir, dear boy.'

She disappeared in a cloud of floating scarves.

II

Lucy had lived so long with Lady Twilight that she mistook her spells of dizziness for increasing vagueness. She alone knew the date of her birth, and vagueness at such an advanced age seemed normal. Though she was too stately to be described as senile, the biology or psychology of aging might have had something to do with it. She remembered half an incident but Lucy had to supply the other half. Nevertheless she remained very much in the centre of her own picture.

Apart from a refusal to consider herself old, a horror of hypodermic syringes prevented her from experimenting with methods of rejuvenation recommended by the Archduchess Gaby, who greatly enjoyed her annual course of treatment in Switzerland. Professor Spandril often popped behind the Iron Curtain for similar reasons, not that he was an advertisement for perennial youth. Lady Twilight was faithful to her breathing exercises, but latterly the yogic postures had become too much of a strain with the exception of Siddhāsana, 'My Master's Favourite', which only involved folding the legs, stretching the arms and resting them on her knees. No doubt she owed her regal poise to this, for while even the Archduchess and the Professor stooped Lady Twilight remained erect whether sitting or standing. Yes, she had worn well, but she longed to loosen her social ties. How little she really cared for the people she invited. Why did she continue to invite them? For Lucy's sake, she decided. Lucy took pride in her high standard of hospitality and kept a scrap-book of her guests, Royal Highnesses, statesmen, diplomats, financiers, and titled personages whose names were printed in the social columns. As long as anyone in Monte Carlo could remember her luncheons had lived up to the Splendide's reputation. Year after year and week after week, she officiated at the same table in a bower of fragrant roses and carnations. But her intervals of silence grew longer, her smile became more vacant. She confused the identities of her queens and princesses, perplexed Monseigneur by asking him if he was still satisfied with his injections behind the Iron Curtain, and puzzled Professor Spandril by questioning him about his mission to Biafra. To the ex-Queen of Iberia she spoke incessantly of haemophilia, declaring that it could be eradicated by banning bullfights. 'The bull is sacred to Siva,' she told her, proposing a pious pilgrimage to Hindu shrines. 'I'm afraid it would be too hot for me,' said Her Majesty. 'I suffer from exaggerated blood pressure.' 'It's due to those bullfights,' Lady Twilight replied, to the Queen's discomfiture. 'You should take a dip in the Ganges, Ma'am.'

Hilary suspected that her vagueness was often calculated. 'I lost my old self in India and haven't found a new one here,' she told him. 'My heart's in the Himalayas.'

After a luncheon in honour of the Archduchess Gaby she complained of giddiness to Lucy, who unobtrusively helped her to lie down in the ante-room. 'Don't worry, dear, it will pass. Run back to the guests and order more liqueurs. Nobody will notice my absence.'

Lady Twilight closed her eyes, murmuring 'O Thou I.'

It must have been a quick and painless death. Hilary was astonished to learn that Lady Twilight was ninety-six. She had instructed Lucy to give a farewell luncheon after her cremation. The guests were specified and Hilary was included among them. Dom Pérignon of the finest vintage was to be served throughout and Lucy was to read her favourite passages of Oriental wisdom with the coffee.

The funeral guests chattered as if their hostess were still with them. Many realized this was the last occasion they would assemble in such outmoded luxury, and they sighed as much over their second helpings as over their absent hostess. Lucy alone could hardly swallow as she gazed round the sumptuous table, dreading the moment when she would have to read those mystical aphorisms she had read so often to Lady Twilight. They meant little enough to her; they would mean even less to the present company. She wondered why Lady Twilight had persisted in feeding them all these years. They condoled with her in a perfunctory way, unaware that she was the chief beneficiary of Lady Twilight's will. Their condescension made her bite her lip. 'Remember the years of freedom ahead of you,' they said. 'You deserve to enjoy them after your years of bondage.' She protested that this had been the life she had chosen. They looked sceptical. 'At least you were spared a long-drawn agony. Lady Twilight was able to keep going to the last gasp. A happy release indeed!'

'Happy for her perhaps, but not for me. Nobody was ever kinder, more generous, more . . .' In a flood of tears she hid her flaccid face. Hilary urged her to sip some champagne. Even so she collapsed when she had to read: 'Thunder is the honey of all beings; all beings the honey of thunder . . .' Hilary came to her rescue and read a selection from the Upanishads intermingled with Buddhist Beatitudes. A reference to abstinence from strong liquor caused no embarrassment to those who were swilling old Armagnac from huge bell glasses. One of them hiccuped and said 'Pardon me', but the recital was impressively oracular and exotic in these meretricious surroundings. Many were mysteriously edified and broke into applause. Dabbing her eyes, Lucy said: 'Thank you. I'm sure Lady Twilight was listening. I could feel her presence.'

Lucy stayed on at the Splendide until she found a spacious apartment with balconies facing the sea. As Lady Twilight's friends could expect no more free meals they forgot her existence. How mercenary, how mean they had proved to be since the glory had departed! The funeral wreaths had been disappointingly meagre: the biggest had been sent by the hotel management.

It was dismal to eat alone in the gaudy restaurant. Lucy felt horribly self-conscious under the pitying eyes of the waiters. How was she to make new friends? Apart from Lady Twilight she had never formed a real intimacy since her childhood. Lady Twilight had frozen her up. She caught a glimpse of herself in a gilded mirror and was shocked by the drabness of her appearance, so unlike her abstract idea of it.

Odile had called her a *cafard*—a cockroach. Of all those who had bitten the hand that had fed them none had been more odious than Lady Twilight's maid. Instead of helping to dress her for the cremation she said: 'I can't bear the sight of a corpse. Anyhow it's not my job. All that hair's worth money though: it would make a handsome wig. Somebody should cut it off before she's sent to the oven.' She had immediately claimed Lady Twilight's personal effects including her furs and jewels. Since she had already received a princely pension Lucy was firm with her.

She allowed her to take the fabulous collection of clothes, but only one mink coat. When Odile started screaming at her, Lucy said calmly: 'Remember you're not speaking to her Ladyship. who was far too patient with your tantrums.'

'I'm speaking to the nursery maid who wormed her way into Milady's confidence and bled her like a leech.'

'The sooner you go the better. Back to Belgium! Hand over those pearls at once!'

In the ensuing tussle the string broke, the pearls were scattered, and Lucy threatened to summon the police.

'This isn't the last you'll hear of me,' the harridan shouted. 'I'll bring an action against you.'

It took Lucy several weeks to settle in her new apartment, a few minutes' walk from the Splendide. The cream-coloured drawing-room was dominated by a piano, but for whom should she play? And to whom should she show her albums of photographs and the relics of her travels in the Far East? Again she was forced to realize that she had no friends. For old sake's sake she wandered back to the Splendide for a cup of tea. The sandwiches were wafer-thin: the music was fat and full-skirted, Lehar and all the Strausses. The head waiter, accustomed to seeing her with Lady Twilight, told her how much he missed *une véritable grande dame*. She tried to look as if she were waiting for somebody. The regular clients who knew her by sight were careful to avoid the table where she sat so demurely. Like an actress without a role she could only be herself, but unconsciously she had assumed a few of Lady Twilight's mannerisms—an air of vagueness and a dreamy smile. She smiled at the familiar strains of *The Merry Widow* to which she had waltzed in her girlhood—how long ago!

A sinuous figure approached her and said: 'I refuse to be cut by you. May I sit down?'

Lucy's eyes, still blurred with youthful memories, stared at the intruder in blank bewilderment. Then it dawned upon her: Hilary Bevis. 'Oh, you've grown a beard. No wonder I failed to recognize you. If you don't mind my saying so, it's an improvement.'

'Just as I was about to shave it off. Perhaps I'll keep it. And how are you? Long time no see.'

He drew up a chair and finished the sandwiches. 'I've been working so hard I'm famished.'

Lucy ordered more tea. 'Another naughty novel?'

'I've given up writing. My readers were too exclusive. No, I've opened a gift-shop, the *Dernier Cri*, very sparkling, very trendy. Come and inspect it. And if you have anything twee to dispose of, I'm your customer. Lady Twilight must have left a lot of art nouveau litter.'

'All Lady Twilight's relics are sacred to me. I'm parting with nothing.'

'Maybe the *Dernier Cri* will make you change your mind. You'll see something you like better. So you've decided to linger in Monte?'

Lucy explained that its associations had endeared it to her; besides, where else was she to go? She spoke bitterly of the way she had been dropped by Lady Twilight's sycophants, for whom she had ordered countless meals in the past. Only two or three had sent her letters of condolence. She could mention several who had begged her for loans which were never repaid. 'I was their reluctant go-between. They came snivelling to me. One blushes for them,' she added. 'Of course many expected to be remembered in her will. I'm glad I persuaded her to forget them. As you know, I was responsible for all her social engagements and I had the right of veto.' But her own nephews and nieces in Bournemouth were just as bad. She had paid for their education and set them up in business, but with growing prosperity they had ceased to send her Christmas cards. So she might as well stay put. The Riviera was prettier than Bournemouth and Monte was wholesome enough—outside the Casino. The average resident lived to a ripe old age . . . like Lady Twilight.

'I hope you don't put me in the sycophant class,' said Hilary.

'Lady Twilight had a special fondness for you. And your wreath was the loveliest. She would have been touched.'

'I could do with a cocktail, couldn't you? Let's go over to the terrace and enjoy the view. Perhaps we'll see the Graingers. Their yacht's in the offing.'

The other women were so garishly clad that Lucy was conspicuous in her widow's weeds, like a provincial Frenchwoman who had strayed into an English herbaceous border.

'You ought to do something about your make-up,' Hilary remarked. 'Lips more pronounced, bee-stung, blue on the eyelids, hair loosened and lacquered. Stick to austerity in dress. Restraint should be the keynote except for the bosom.'

No man had ever talked to her like this. Lucy was subtly flattered. 'Oh, I'm past praying for. I was always the ugly duckling.'

'Nonsense, you don't exploit your individuality. Mere prettiness is old hat. With a little trouble you could be striking. Let me take you in hand.'

Lucy became light-headed after a couple of White Ladies. Unaccustomed to cocktails, she behaved like a giggly girl while Hilary prattled about his gift-shop, his capricious customers, and the oddities they bought. 'If you bring me any you'll get commissions on their purchases.'

'But I tell you I've been dropped by the parish. I suppose they suppose I'm poor.' She added with a chuckle: 'Sucks to them! I'm quite an heiress.'

Hilary pricked up his ears. 'Another White Lady? Well, if you've nothing better to do, why not join me for a *bouillabaisse* at Villefranche?'

It was a thrill to drive like the wind in Hilary's open sports car, for Lady Twilight had always insisted on crawling. Hilary seemed to know everyone at the cosy restaurant near the waterfront.

Though it was crowded to capacity an extra table was juggled in for Monsieur Hilaire, as the *patronne* called him. The cheeky young waiters in flowery shirts and the tightest of blue jeans shimmied to and fro flashing their eyes as if they were part of a cabaret show. This was the first time they had seen Hilary with a woman, and Lucy in her mourning struck a discordant note. '*Dis donc, chéri, t'as changé de goût ce soir?'* said the cheekiest, who shook hands before taking his order.

Lucy noticed the familiarity with surprise. 'It's a sweet little place. So bohemian.'

'I'm glad you like it. A slight change from the Splendide. The cooking's aggressively local. Now you have joined my parish.'

She had often yearned to penetrate such popular resorts but it had not been possible with Lady Twilight, who did not mind where she ate in India and Japan but would only set foot in grand restaurants on the Riviera. After a momentary shrinking at the spectacle of so many unbuttoned and uncorseted parties masticating and swallowing with noisy relish, she was fascinated by the general animation, the effluvia of pungent dishes. E. M. Forster's message, so often quoted by Lady Twilight, 'Only connect,' assumed a realistic significance. Here she was connecting with people who had been beyond her ken. What friendly young waiters. Lady Twilight, who admired the Hindu caste system, would have been outraged by their familiarity but Lucy had always been democratic at heart. The *vin rosé* was making her tipsy and Hilary continued to replenish her glass as soon as she emptied it. In this carefree atmosphere she forgot to feel overdressed. There was an abundance of bare flesh, plump arms and legs both hairy and smooth, contrasting with a trim group of American sailors with crew-cuts and frank faces. Two sauntered over and greeted Hilary, who introduced them to Lucy as Al and Pete and offered them drinks. They patted Hilary on the back. 'Oh, boy, it's good to see you. The night's still young.'

Lucy's presence put them at ease though her dingy black perplexed them. When she retired to powder her nose Pete said she reminded him of the schoolmarm who had been his first lay: cool on the surface but hot underneath, and a real lady. This emboldened him to play footy-footy with her under the table. Hilary observed her growing gaiety with interest. This was a different Lucy with the twinkle of adventure in her eye. 'Pete has taken a fancy to you,' he told her. 'I'm almost jealous.'

The copious libations of *vin rosé* had flushed her cheeks and her lower lip had a sensual quiver, so that when Pete grasped her hand she let it lie passively in his, palm to adhesive palm. The contact quickened her pulse. She felt suddenly emancipated from her past, stepping into a garden of spontaneous friendship. She became more articulate, licking her lips and flickering her eyes at Pete who, simple soul, responded eagerly. 'My honey, my peach,' he murmured. 'I can hardly wait to eat you.'

When Hilary proposed that they all drive back to his flat Lucy raised no objection though there was scarcely room in his car. She agreed to sit on Pete's knee with Al between them. It was a tight squeeze but it was a sensation not wholly uncomfortable to perch on so sinewy a seat. While swerving on the hairpin bends she held on to him like a child on the scenic railway, elated by the rapid motion but afraid of falling out.

By the time they reached Hilary's flat she had pins and needles. 'I'd better leave you boys,' she said with atavistic shyness. 'It's getting late.'

'Another little drink won't do us any harm,' said Hilary, turning on the gramophone. Lucy found herself dancing with Pete as she had never danced before. How slim and flexible he was, snapping his fingers to the rhythm and twirling around her, drawing her towards him without actually touching, as in a ballet of courtship. He continued to call her Baby though he could have been her son. The lights were discreetly dim and she began to feel drowsy. 'Let me fix you a gin fizz,' said Pete.

'And how's our débutante?' asked Hilary.

'Enjoying myself,' said Lucy. 'I believe I must be squiffy.'

'Why not? You need to relax.'

She had always thought of Hilary as a cold-blooded highbrow, and it was a surprise to discover that he could be so human and sympathetic. Evidently he was popular with the sailors, who were really very sweet. The way Al put his arm round his shoulder reminded her of Whitman's poems in *Calamus* which she had read to Lady Twilight: in particular one about the love of comrades. Lady Twilight had cherished Walt Whitman for his muscular mysticism.

After dancing a while Hilary vanished with Al but Lucy was oblivious in Pete's sturdy arms, her whole mouth devoured by his. 'Tonight you belong to me, Baby,' he whispered, and she let him undress her on the divan, trembling all over in a fever of excitement, nibbling her breasts and earlobes and flinging his arms about her hips, crushing her body against his. She melted and sighed for pleasure. 'O Thou I'—how much she had missed in life! She must start at once to make up for it.

This was far tenderer and purer than her fleeting experience with Carmine, who cared more for his own body than for hers. Perhaps it was as well that he could not stay the whole night, for he was insatiable and she had begun to feel her age. For a split second his frenzied plunging had made her feel ridiculous, aware that she was not the baby he repeatedly invoked. But there was no play-acting as with Carmine. She had surrendered to positive desire, and it had been delicious to be desired so strenuously.

She was partly dressed when Hilary returned with Al. 'I hope we're not interrupting . . . Everything okay? I've got to drive the boys back to their ship. Another little drink for the road?'

Lucy hastily readjusted her blouse. Having scattered her pollen she felt light as air.

'You've been simply adorable, Pete. We must meet again. Here's my phone number.' Pete, meet, repeat: the words clicked like billiard balls in her brain.

'Sure,' he said warmly, 'sure. I sure hate to leave you, Baby. You've made me feel real good.'

'Your first gift from my gift shop,' said Hilary with a chuckle. 'Ring me up in the morning.'

She walked home humming one of the tunes she had heard on Hilary's gramophone, 'Lucy in the sky with diamonds'. And at last she thought she understood the meaning of 'Thunder is the honey of all beings; all beings the honey of thunder.'

ANTICLIMAX

THE girls had been so hungry that they were ready for anything that would bring them a little nourishment. Except hard black bread, mealy potatoes, leathery cabbage and dry carrots, nearly all the food they could obtain was *ersatz*, and barely sufficient to stay their rumbling stomachs. A baked apple and a few dried raisins provided an occasional treat. Beer had become scarce. Several bottles of sparkling Moselle had been hoarded for the day of victory, and these were still unopened in spite of strong gusts of temptation.

Last winter had been the longest and cruellest they could remember, incessantly bombed under a freezing temperature. But youth may still furnish its own fuel to a certain degree. Though often faint from undernourishment the girls could wangle a few titbits here and there from military friends, the uniquely privileged. Spring had softened the air but there was no other sign of it in the city, remote from the farmyards, fields and orchards of their infancy, the fruit trees they could climb, the streams in which they could paddle, the cows peacefully grazing. Oh for a glass of foaming fresh milk! It did not bear thinking of . . .

Most of the familiar landmarks, the streets and shops they had taken for granted, had been reduced to rubble. As half the population lived underground like troglodytes the girls were lucky to have a roof over their heads. Thecla maintained that this miraculous exemption was due to the intercession of her patron saint, to whom she prayed often albeit she was no nun. In fact Thecla was the most voluptuous member of the small feminine community and the most demonstrative, slender and olive-skinned with smouldering speckled eyes. Her mother had been Milanese. The other girls were more nonchalant and phlegmatic, but all of them tried to make the best of a miserable situation and create a home away from homes that had ceased to exist. They had nowhere else to go, and no news of what was happening outside. Their radio had broken down, anyhow they had long ceased to trust it. Lies and rumours, rumours and lies, then a sinister buzzing and crackling and fizzling out. Without electricity, telephone, running water, or any of the normal amenities of modern existence they contrived to keep relatively clean and outwardly cheerful, sharing soap and towels, taking turns to cook and do the laundry. Their rooms were poky but the beds and bolsters that monopolized them were soft and feathery with gaudy counterpanes. Frilly lampshades of preposterous shape, dolls and golliwogs and absurd knick-knacks, imparted an atmosphere of spurious cosiness. After the beds looking-glasses were the most prominent fixtures, enabling the girls to scrutinize and embellish themselves, study new gestures and poses in sitting and reclining, wriggling their arms and legs and twiddling their pink toes. Mirrors were stimulants to erotic ecstasy, especially for the patrons who liked to see their embraces doubled and magnified even when they were far from flattering. Yes, mirrors were supremely important. They adorned and lengthened the smallest rooms, they multiplied the cuckoo clocks and paper flowers. The cupboards contained an amazing variety of garments, strings of beads, imitation pearls, picture hats, feather boas, muffs, leather jackets, false leopard skin coats and chiffon scarves for gala evenings. There was barely space for so many bits and pieces of fancy dress, apart from the slippers, shoes and high-heeled boots for fetishists. The framed oleographs on the walls represented babies (though this was no place for babies to be born), pussycats and puppydogs, views of vertiginous Gothic castles and Heidelberg in aniline moonlight.

The front parlour boasted a gramophone with a pile of scratchy records—Viennese waltzes and languorous Hungarian czardas for those inclined to dance—and another pile of old illustrated magazines much tattered and stained, but even so relics of a civilization that seemed to have been destroyed together with illusions of national glory.

The differences between the girls were more physical than mental. On the whole they were easily amused. They loved to giggle and play pranks, and they shared whatever fun came their way. Like sisters they protected each other. But they had had few visitors lately. The war had left them in an artificial vacuum.

Bertha was the most boyish with her neat bobbed hair, small bust, athletic figure and inseparable riding crop; Greta was the most girlish with her flaxen hair in plaits and pear-shaped breasts; Lotte, over thirty, had enormous hips and lips, pouting and wistful, she spoke in baby language with a lisp, rolling porcelain blue eyes; Helga was the most piquante with her tiny upturned nose, greenish eyes, and an orange tinge to her fluffed-up hair bound with scarlet ribbon: her freckles invariably bewitched the oldest clients. The remaining blondes were less definite but they formed a feline and frolicsome chorus when they bounced into the parlour kicking up their heels in a can-can to display their splendid legs.

Since the bombing had stopped they looked forward to welcoming visitors, never mind of what nationality. Their Leader having let them down they could not afford a stubborn patriotism. In spite of Lotte's tearful protests they tore up his photographs and emblems and put up a little red flag above the front entrance. Theirs was one of the very few houses still standing in the district. When brothels had been banned it had flourished surreptitiously as a discreet house of assignation. Several of the girls had influential patrons, and some had part-time jobs in cinemas and clubs. The owner's brother had been a Gauleiter but he had disappeared in Russia. It was no longer necessary to camouflage its real status.

For the time being everything seemed paralysed. It was a long, long wait and the girls killed boredom with card-games and telling each other's fortune. Helga had an uncanny talent for reading hands: the life-lines, love-lines, lines of health and wealth—she could tell which was which and weave enthralling romances about them on the spot. Not that this required any original flight of imagination for they all dreamt dreams of plushy opulence, of sables and diamonds and fashion parades at the Opera, though some would have been content to settle down with a solid bourgeois husband and lots of babies like those in the framed oleographs. Such pastimes took their minds off the gnawing emptiness inside them. They had not even cigarettes to fill that emptiness with illusive warmth and soothe their jumpy nerves.

They tried to look over and above the ruins around them. In relays the girls had staggered with buckets of water from a distant pump since the nearest had been buried under bomb craters. They had to use it with economy as well as the substitute soap which never bubbled when they washed themselves. Oh for the halcyon days of running water, of rivers and lakes in which they could splash and swim! Surely they must soon return, now that the war was over. Greta glistened like a Rhine maiden as she sluiced her creamy neck and arms and let the water dribble between her massive breasts. The impulsive Bertha couldn't help kissing the shiny button of her nose. She was tempted to go further and tickle her under the armpits, but this would lead to one of those romps that wasted energy and conservation of energy was essential. So they rubbed themselves and gargled, rinsed their mouths and sprayed themselves with the last drops of scent that remained and applied the last of their cosmetics, for their cheeks and lips were too pale. All soldiers were partial to pink cheeks and carmine lips.

Ulrike, the oldest of the family except for 'Grandma' who was bedridden in the upstairs attic, wore her blue glass ear-rings to match her blue hair and fluttered her false eyelashes, ogling her reflection in her cracked hand-mirror, sprinkled with the powder that flaked off her puffy jowl. She was surprised that she was no thinner after months of semi-starvation, but plumpness had its advocates and advantages. All made themselves as winsome as they could be in anticipation of the visits that were bound to come soon—pray Heaven soon.

The prospect was thrilling but also frightening. It was reported that Russian troops had entered the city. The girls would have preferred English or Americans, white or black. In their experience all soldiers were basically similar, with crude and quickly satisfied desires, and they were apt to be liberal with chocolates and cigarettes if not with money. If they were sozzled so much the better: they soon fell asleep and they were less exacting in bed. But those Russians—nobody knew much about them except that they were barbaric. Of course everybody had heard of the Cossacks, those wild horsemen of the steppes, but didn't they belong to a bygone age? The assumption that they were savages presented a certain challenge. The girls had plenty of initiative and even lions could be tamed. No doubt they too were simple and undemanding, rough children of the soil, more muscle than mind, with broad grins and an elementary sense of humour. Laughter would be an easy substitute for language, and the girls were proficient at parlour games in the course of which they were bound to pick up fragments of Russian speech. Their prefabricated images were varnished with sentimental romance.

While discussing the invaders they tingled perversely at the thought of yielding to their fierce embraces, but even more at the thought of the victuals they might bring. At least their officers should be well provided with goodies. Perhaps they would bring some beer or their native vodka. Greta had the improbable notion that they might bring caviar, which 'was tasty but hardly substantial, besides it made you thirsty'. Better tins of corned-beef or something you could put your teeth into, said Bertha. Talking of food their mouths began to water. Christmas goose, duck stuffed with apples, tender *kalbsfleisch*, smoked eels, many kinds of delicatessen—all the appetizing dishes they had devoured before the war, and their savoury odours, the sheer bliss of frying fat, the aroma of genuine coffee, were conjured so vividly that Lotte implored them to change the subject. It was too tantalizing, and she was less hopeful than the others for she suffered from toothache, a shrinkage of the gums, and no dentist was available. In her opinion fresh bread and butter would be the quintessence of luxury. She examined her tongue: it was a furry white and her saliva was slightly sour. However, she rouged her cheeks, a dab on her chin and earlobes, and smeared a touch of blue over each heavy eyelid. There now, she already looked better though she was feeling winded . . .

Thecla suggested that the soldiers might bring balalaikas. 'Let's have some music,' said Greta suddenly. 'We haven't danced for days, or is it weeks?' 'Not that we had cause to, but perhaps we ought to get back into practice,' said Thecla. So couples whirled again to the waltzes scraped out of the gramophone, but they were soon dizzy and out of breath. Limply they collapsed among the faded cushions of the big divan. Thecla became kittenish and caressing though her mouth and lips were dry. Lotte burst into tears for no particular reason unless from fatigue. 'Don't let's mope, dear,' said Ulrike, shaking her ear-rings at her with a comical grimace. '*Über allen Gipfeln ist Ruh*. We must all act coolly and calmly and forget our troubles. When the lads arrive greet them with smiles and kisses. I've been longer without a man's kiss than any of you. I'm even in the mood for a beard though I prefer them clean shaven.' The boyish Bertha gave her a hearty hug, and the others showered kisses on her by way of compensation. 'Now I'm all mussed up,' she panted, freeing herself from their impetuous endearments. 'And I've got no more make-up. *Gott im Himmel* I must look a scarecrow! Which reminds me, I ought to see Grandma.'

Old Frau Wegener up in the attic had been temporarily forgotten by the girls who flitted about chattering and whistling like birds in an aviary. They needed nourishment more than she, and she deprived herself willingly for their sake, keeping barely alive on pap and cups of hot water flavoured with slices of apple or onion. Weaker and weaker she lay without hope of recovery. The girls were wonderfully considerate, but it was useless to pretend that such a life was worth living at her age. Crippled with rheumatism, racked with sciatica, she felt superfluous and longed for death. Why had she been spared by the bombs? The house belonged to her and she had managed it efficiently as long as she could move about. But now she could do little enough even for herself. She was conscious of becoming a burden and she tried to be as light a burden as possible. Though unable to kneel she prayed incessantly in a cramped position with her eyes closed, yet watching a film, as it were, of angels with melodious harps and golden wings. The angels assumed the features of her girls, with Bertha, Lotte and Greta leading the choir. Her mind wandered away to her distant childhood when the Fatherland was on top of the world. What was happening downstairs concerned her less than to find a position in bed where her bones would stop aching. Alas, she was one big ache. Dimly she heard the nostalgic waltzes from the gramophone and hoped that the girls were having a bit of fun. The nights were worse than the days and they seemed eternal. Surely that was Greta laughing so shrilly. Maybe some visitor had called . . .

Thecla peeped round the door and asked: 'Are you all right, Grannie? Is there anything I can do for you?' 'No thank you, my love. The bedpan's empty. I'll soon be dead and ready for the dustheap.' 'You mustn't say such things, Grannie. Now that the war is over we'll be getting more food in and you will recover your strength. The boys will come home and life will return to normal.' 'Life!' the old woman muttered bitterly to herself. She could only think of death. Had the gas oven functioned she would put her head in it. She had worshipped the Führer: for her he was the Superman in whom she had absolute faith. Like the Kaiser before him he had been betrayed. Judases everywhere. Her hatred of the enemy was intense enough to heat her blood, and she dreaded the Russians more than the rest of them. 'Dear God, let me die,' she prayed. 'I don't want to see those devils. Spare my poor girls!' Patting Thecla's cheek, she said: 'You will need all your courage now.' She had urged them to escape but most of them had originated in other towns and villages cut off by rail and road: those who had not been estranged from parents and relations had lost contact with them since the war. One or two had talked of suicide but that was nonsense. When they spoke of killing themselves she said: 'Kill me first!' She was far too weak to argue with them. Fortunately they possessed the resilience of youth and they could be tough in dealing with the opposite sex. They decided it was safer and more sensible to cling together and form a united front.

'I'm beginning to wonder if they'll ever turn up,' said Greta with a sigh as another dejected day of iron rations dragged on. 'If they don't, we'll have to run out and catch them. We must be brazen and seize the initiative. This waiting wears me out.'

A grey drizzle was falling steadily on the debris outside. The house was ominously silent except for the pattering raindrops, so that when the front door was bashed open the thud of heavy boots combined with the barking of baritones resounded like claps of thunder. The girls shivered in momentary panic and darted for their liveliest kimonos. Ulrike stepped boldly forward and drew aside the plush curtain over the parlour door, her mouth contorted into a smirk of welcome. The others seated themselves in attitudes intended to be graceful, preparing to smile too.

The five boisterous intruders shuffled in somewhat unsteadily as if they had been drinking, and one of them clutched the curtain for support. They were dishevelled and unshaven with coarsely carved wooden features. Their filthy tunics were open at the neck and they stank of rank sweat, stale cheese and alcohol. For what seemed at least ten minutes they paused blinking as if stunned by an unexpected vision. Like yokels they stood with gaping jaws but they made no movement towards the girls who winked invitingly and bared their bosoms to encourage them. Instead they examined the furnishings, removed the cuckoo clock and shook it like a money-box, picked up the ashtrays and knick-knacks and dropped them on the floor. Not one of them smiled. Their high cheek-boned, slit-eyed masks were grim as they uttered their unintelligible jargon. The girls did not know what to make of this behaviour. Not one of the boors responded to their liquid glances, to the soft white curves of their flesh palpitating under semi-transparent kimonos, parted like their lips for kisses they failed to receive. Only the word 'beer' was comprehensible. Evidently they wanted booze. The girls shook their heads with negative gestures and opened a cupboard of empty bottles. Greta drew the youngest and least repulsive of them towards the divan but he gave her arm such a wrench that she cried out. The other girls whispered in confabulation. Should they fetch their precious Moselle from its hiding place to mollify them? By no means, said Ulrike, since the boors had brought nothing with them, not even cigarettes. 'Balalaika?' she repeated with sudden inspiration, putting a record on the gramophone, remembering that Russians were reputed to be famous dancers. Bertha, Lotte and Helga approached each man in turn but they were roughly shaken off.

The men were after something else. Apparently the lack of drink had angered them. They paid no attention to the music, and when the girls began a strip-tease as a last resort they were equally indifferent to the charms displayed before them. Ulrike was rewarded for her persistence with a humiliating wallop on the bottom. She was about to hit back but she was not quick enough with her fist and the Slavs marched out of the parlour. From room to room they clattered, opening all the cupboards and drawers and sweeping out their contents. Beads, hats, dresses and footgear were flung out pell-mell in heaps on to the floor. The pluckier girls attempted to grapple with them but their shins were kicked and they limped howling to the nearest couch. Stolidly the Tartars continued their search under cushions and pillows which they ripped open when nothing was found but feathers and stuffing. Lamps were shattered, chairs overturned, and in the kitchen, where they could find neither food nor drink, they smashed all the crockery and threw pots and pans out of the window. The wailing chorus of wenches made no more impression on the brutes than their pleading bodies, if anything it stimulated their destructive mania. One grabbed Greta's wristwatch: in her struggle to save it the glass and hands were crushed. Another tore the heart-shaped locket from Thecla's neck, and another thrust a horny hand between Helga's legs to see if she were hiding anything of value there. She wriggled and whimpered under the pressure of his sharp claws and there was a sharp rent in her kimono.

Maybe the Moselle might have appeased them but it was now too late. The barbarians were running amok. After breaking more vases and crunching the fragments with their boots they stood like gorillas with arms akimbo, eyes bulging, considering what to smash next. They filled their pockets with the bracelets and necklaces of false pearls; they would have torn off Ulrike's ear-rings if she had not removed them herself. All the girls had to surrender their trinkets and ornaments. Those who resisted had their toes trodden on. Of watches and clocks the men made a clean sweep. Then they started cracking the gramophone records.

In her upstairs attic old Frau Wegener heard the hubbub and cowered under her blanket. Usually she could rely on the girls to look after themselves and each other but there were limits. It sounded as if babel were let loose with the banging and slamming of doors, the crashing of crockery, the creaking and squeaking of furniture, the stamping and shuffling of hobnailed boots and the cacophony of voices. The cries of the girls were pitiful as they made strenuous efforts to invoke compassion, but the Tartars were immune to pity. To prevent them from doing further damage they linked arms and blocked the staircase. As the tricks of their trade had been ineffectual they thrashed out with the whips and canes reserved for flagellants. Even so they were no match for the maddened boors who, as in a football scrum, plunged headlong into their midriffs like battering rams. Obstructed by the girls clinging to their heels, all five staggered slowly up the stairs towards the attic.

There was a synchronized howl of exultation when they reached Frau Wegener's bedroom and flung the door open. The old woman sat up and screamed '*Heraus!*' while the men surrounded her chuckling. At last they had found what they were seeking. With frantic lust they ripped off the blanket. Each in turn lowered his breeches and fell on top of her, pulling up her nightgown and nuzzling into her withered breasts. '*Heil Hitler!*' she moaned. Raped repeatedly, her shrieks gave way to a prolonged whimpering, gulping, gasping, a choking sound and then silence.

Whistling and singing, the five victors strutted down the stairs. According to an ancient superstition they had gained strength and power from this anomalous consummation. They felt revitalized in consequence. As they passed the terrified girls huddled together in the parlour they collected their loot and spat contemptuously in their direction. The rain drowned their voices and footsteps once they had marched out into the rubble. Ulrike burst into a hysterical fit of laughter which Thecla smothered with both hands for fear that the beasts might hear it and return. Then timidly she crept upstairs to visit Grannie's corpse.

A MONOPOLIST

ONE of the witches in Macbeth: that was my first impression. Though he did not croak 'Double, double, toil and trouble', these words condensed his career in hospital.

The paramount aim of Mr. Hutchins seemed to consist in giving endless trouble: he expected all to toil for him, and at the double.

Jaundiced eyes, the right pupil more protuberant than the left, lolled from deep sockets in the waggling skull over which the grey-green skin of a desiccated reptile was drawn in sagging folds. But more than a witch, he was a devotee of diseases in general and of his own in particular. He was as proud of his long catalogue of operations as if he had performed them instead of being performed upon; no detail of their saga, even to the tint of his urine, was too trivial to be retold, and each version grew more polished in the telling. But his epilogue seldom varied: 'It was a bad show. The nails were practically in my coffin. I was almost a goner that time. Guts pulled me through, sheer guts. That comes of being British.'

Nobody was allowed to have suffered more acutely than Mr. Hutchins. That he had survived was a miracle for which he monopolized the credit, and he wished all to marvel at the hero. But his audience was limited to visitors and new patients. Most of the time, propped against a back-rest, he would stare vacantly beyond me as towards an invisible horizon, and occasionally he broke into snatches of old song, such as: 'At Trinity Church I met my doom—Now we live in a top back room.'

I had been condemned to lie in the opposite bed, so there was no escape from his moronic stare and from his crushing bouts of monologue. Between us was a table piled with boxes of case-histories, temperature charts nailed to boards and writing paraphernalia. Eventually this table attained a symbolic significance. Sometimes it served as a protective screen, but when I was thus reprieved from Mr. Hutchins's scrutiny, he would ask for the table to be cleared—'as I can't see the Flight Lieutenant.' When I expostulated that I was no thing of beauty and in any case desired to bury my head in a book, he remarked: 'Never mind, I wish to see you all the same.'

It was difficult enough to concentrate amid the continuous coming and going of sisters and orderlies in that small crammed surgical ward, but being gaped at by those insistent eyes as I turned the pages, it soon became impossible.

'What have you found to read?' he would interpose. 'You look mighty interested.'

Hutchins cared little for any book which he could not describe as 'a rattling good yarn'. I lent him a novel by Virginia Woolf but he objected that it was all double Dutch to him. 'I'm afraid we'll never see eye to eye about literature,' he remarked after I had expounded its merits. None the less as an opening gambit he would generally ask what I was reading. I think it gave him a malicious pleasure to interrupt. 'You read far too much,' he was also fond of saying; 'you're ruining your eyesight.'

His English was the clumsy dialect of club convention in India, but his diction was more precise than the norm. While he talked one felt that he was repressing a tendency to sing-song and at the same time to gesticulate with his claws. He professed to have spent his youth in Norfolk, and though fond of referring to boating on the Broads, his recollection of definite places in that county was extremely hazy. When I mentioned Fakenham and East Dereham he thought they were in Yorkshire.

To Indians he was rabidly allergic. The appearance of the sweeper, a spectral figure with timorous pleading eyes and a straggling moustache, was a signal for ever-renewed storms of violent abuse both in English and Hindustani. That overworked personification of humility paid no attention, however, and as if deaf and dumb continued with his job. Mr. Hutchins would keep it up as long as the sweeper remained in the ward. The melancholy barber who circulated with a little pewter pot and his left wrist ringed with a heavy coil of lather; the newspaper vendor, in cricket blazer and turban, his pink shirt-tails hanging modishly well below the blazer; all Indians who came within his orbit were subjected to hysterical execration.

When I was goaded to protest, he explained: 'My dear chap, you simply don't know wogs. The native employees of this hospital are the lowest specimens I've come across in the experience of a lifetime. And they're all tarred with the same brush. No respect for the white man. In the old days they would have come in crawling on their hands and knees. Now they swagger about like the lords of creation. No respect whatever. Do you expect me to tolerate that? To do so is to encourage them. If I could only get out of this bed, I'd teach 'em!' And he shook his shrivelled fist.

Once he tried to prevent me from paying for my newspaper: 'You're making a big mistake. If you pay such scum you'll never get service out of 'em.'

'I may not have change tomorrow,' I retorted.

'Let him wait for his money: it's good policy to keep 'em waiting. Take yourself off, you stinking swine,' he shouted in the retreating man's direction; 'get the hell out of here.'

Exhausted by such outbursts, he would sink back on his pillows and remove his dentures, to chew the cud of his indignation with silent gums.

These scenes were of daily occurrence, and so out of proportion to their origins that they set me wondering. The more I considered the sweeper, the sepoys, the barber and the newspaper walla, the more inoffensive they seemed. Was their insolence a figment of Hutchins's sick brain or had they, invisible to me, a subtle mode of conveying their contempt? Was not Hutchins, so insensitive in other respects, unduly sensitive in this? As far as I could see, the Indians went quietly about their work, and all I could detect of their attitude to Hutchins was a natural wish to avoid him.

'If only I had my stout Irish blackthorn with me, I'd beat a little respect into the bastards!' He sawed the air with a skinny arm, shrilling 'Whack, whack,' in a feeble falsetto, followed by 'Mercy, Sahib, please show mercy!' His glazed eyes roved the ward in quest of a laugh, but custom had staled the joke. Cackling to himself, he lapsed into one of his peculiar comas.

Strikingly different was his manner to the English orderlies. It was as near to milk and honey as he could make it. He clamoured constantly for their attention, but by now they were hardened to his ruses. All day he was wanting to have his wound dressed: there was always something wrong, the bandage was too loose or too tight. But like the sisters, they had little time for him. They knew their Mr. Hutchins: he had been an intermittent patient during the last six months and he had only himself to blame. In fact he was paying for the consequences of his own gluttony. Having been warned to avoid fats after one operation, he had simply gone home and made a hog of himself. At last he was on the mend, but none could forget the fuss he had inflicted, the thankless tasks he had imposed, his vicious cussedness.

In self-defence each had developed a special technique, rough or smooth, for dealing with him. The orderlies tended to be rough. Now and then Hutchins would let out a howl but he dared not let out a curse. He almost fawned on them.

'Now be a good fellow and fetch me some Ovaltine. My stomach won't digest this gritty cocoa.' 'Do me a favour and try to produce some toast. This bread makes me so windy I can't get rid of it for hours on end. There's a good chappie. I'll see that you get rewarded.'

Day in the hospital began long before dawn. While the jackals were still in strident session a so-called bihishty (pronounced beasty) clattered into our ward with cups and a can to distribute an infusion of tannin. Unable to sleep, Hutchins had done his best to keep others awake by yelling for the sweeper or practising a weird gamut of groans which alone would have enhanced the success of a theatrical thriller. His spirits were at their liveliest first thing in the morning.

'Wake up, wake up,' he would shout across to me. 'Aren't you tempted by a nice cup of tea? If not, let me drink it for you before it gets cold. I could do well with another cup, my tongue's like a blotter. You slackers don't deserve these luxuries.'

Having tugged his mosquito net aside he squatted in a Buddhist attitude, waiting to be washed. Though capable of washing himself, he sought every pretext of having it done for him. With a look of ecstasy he yielded his bony torso to the sponge.

One morning he waited in vain. The basin of water was dumped on a chair beside him.

'Hey, orderly, what's the meaning of this? Have you gone on strike? Aren't you going to scrub me?'

'Sister McNab says you can manage for yourself, sir.'

'But I haven't the strength,' he whined.

'Your temperature has been normal since Sunday.'

'If I tire myself it'll start jumping. Besides I'm not standing any impertinence from you, young man. Be careful or I'll put you on a charge.'

Hutchins was furious. The fumes of his ill temper covered him as in a pall of smoke, and his basin of water retained its purity.

The same morning he was told he could get up and dress and sit in a wheeled chair. He did not know how to accept this news. 'My ankles will never support me,' he demurred.

'Come, come, after all the massage we've been giving you!' Sister McNab coaxed him to make the effort.

He took a long time to dress. Then he advanced with a walking stick towards me and seated himself within asphyxiating distance. 'You thought you'd be up and out of this long before me, confess now, didn't you, my friend? You thought you would leave old Hutchins in the lurch. Well, well, we can't have it all our own way. Just look at me now. It's nothing more or less than a miracle. I've always been an agnostic. Today I'm inclined to believe that there must be a God. Before my last operation they told me I might as well give up hope, I had only one chance in a million. The blasted padre came round to offer me a hint or two —on how to behave, I daresay, when I met the Almighty. I ordered him out in no uncertain terms. It got me down at the time, I don't mind telling you. I was feeling pretty wonky after three blood transfusions, and the pack of vultures kept rubbing in how weak I was, as if I didn't know. But I swore I'd pull through in spite of the ruddy lot. I was determined to set eyes on the Norfolk Broads again.'

The monologue would have been protracted but for the arrival of his wife. She could have been his daughter, a plump young partridge of a woman with tropical features, eyes like inkpots and a tiny nose, convenient for kissing. Her accent was impeccably B.B.C. A generous soul, I thought, somewhat over-coloured, like the vegetation of the tropics. Appropriately her name was Rhoda, for she would have harmonized with rhododendrons. She had brought a hamper full of sandwiches and cakes. Hutchins looked none too pleased when she offered me some, and his expression of relief when I refused was so comical that I was tempted to change my mind. He fell upon the dainties ravenously, swallowing sandwich after sandwich with lupine eagerness.

'By Jove, my missus is tops in the kitchen,' he gasped between mouthfuls, his eyes moist with greed and gratitude combined. 'As soon as you're fit you must come and have tiffin with us.'

'What fun,' exclaimed his wife. 'I shall try out my latest recipes on you. You look fearfully fastidious. That's just what I like. It really makes cooking worth while.'

'She'll help you to eat your way back to health and Blighty,' said Hutchins. 'Another beef sandwich, dear. Congratulations on the mayonnaise. I've never tasted better in my dreams.'

As if to prove it, he was dribbling. She wiped his chin with a roguish air.

The sister on duty came in and said, 'I hope you're not leading him astray, Mrs. Hutchins. He's still on a diet, you know.'

'Don't worry, Sister, I've only allowed him the barest minimum—a few titbits to remind him of home. Dear Sister, do sample one of my chocolate éclairs and tell me how you like it.'

As the nurse's hands were wet with disinfectant Mrs. Hutchins popped one deftly into her mouth. Won over by her caressing manners, the stern sister did not enquire into the ingredients of the sandwiches, which had in any case been devoured at this juncture.

Conversation between the couple flagged after the beanfeast. Rather than sit and gaze at her too replete husband, Mrs. Hutchins tried to enliven the ward with small talk. 'You're looking ever so much better, Captain Singleton, and I see the swelling's gone.' But the Captain was too absorbed in the game of bridge to pick up her cue.

'When are you coming to visit us, Mr. Hawkins? And you must come along too, Mr. Davison, as soon as your crutches are ready.'

Mrs. Hutchins met with little response that afternoon. The ward, except for Hutchins and the bridge-party, was in one of its detached, indifferent moods, accentuated by the monsoon rain cavalcading monotonously outside. There was no alternative for Mrs. Hutchins but to face her husband until the downpour ceased. I felt quite sorry for her.

When the rain stopped she perked up a little, twittered a few sprightly nothings and kissed her old man on the lips. How she could steel herself for so repulsive a procedure, in public or in private, astounded me more than once. She must have been tough under those gentle curves. After all she had borne him a couple of sturdy brats. Probably she had come to regard him as so much leather.

Hutchins was left in uncommonly high spirits. He embarked on a fresh account of the various accidents which had befallen him since childhood, including a plane and car crash. 'But all these', he summed up, 'were bagatelles compared to the last big do. I was never more near to the cemetery. I only hope you will be spared such an ordeal, my friend. But we can't tell what's ahead of us, can we?'

We supped at six, and in spite of his recent blow-up, Hutchins clamoured for second helpings and cursed the sepoy when they were not forthcoming. The supper was more solid than usual and I congratulated him on his appetite. 'It's not appetite,' he replied. 'It's sheer necessity: I'm a married man. One must recruit one's vigour by hook or by crook.'

Next morning we were wakened abnormally early—by groans interspersed with hiccups. The groans had reached a blood-curdling pitch by the time Sister Andrews came in with the thermometer. 'Whatever's the matter now?' she exclaimed.

'I'm suffocating,' he gasped. 'It's been going on for hours. My whole inside's choked up with burning wind. A terrible cramp in the abdomen. It's absolute torture.'

As most of his fellow patients were inured to Hutchins's tantrums, they tried not to notice, but the cumulative effect was depressing. In defiance of bismuth and other potions the hiccups continued all day. Ruefully and reproachfully his eyes rested on the afternoon bridge players. It was downright callous of them to show so little sympathy. To force himself upon their attention he belched and hiccuped infinitely louder and more often than his plight could have demanded. Slowly he worked himself up into a state of frenzy: the hiccups grew desperate. He was determined to win the commiseration that he felt was his due.

Eventually a couple of sisters, a medical officer and an orderly were in puzzled attendance on him. His blood pressure was taken; a stethoscope was put through its paces; he was given an injection; and though his temperature remained normal he smiled a wry smile of triumph. He had dispersed the bridge party and again monopolized the ward. Having achieved these objectives, the sound and the fury died down. That night we all enjoyed comparative peace.

Nemesis was to come for Hutchins in the shape of a stricter diet. Henceforth sisters and orderlies supervised his scant meals with gorgon eyes, resolved that there should be no repetition of yesterday's incident. Though he fretted and fumed, he was allowed no meat except the boiled chicken he detested. The spectacle of others being served mutton and jam tart was unbearably tantalizing.

'Look here, my good fellow,' he appealed to an orderly, 'couldn't you slip a slice of mutton under all this mashed potato? Do, there's a sport. I'm famished.'

'I'm afraid orders is orders, sir,' was the laconic reply.

'But I'm starving, you fool. How can I be expected to recuperate on mashed potato? I'm not Mr. Gandhi. Call the matron. I wish to register a complaint. This is a conspiracy to keep me undernourished.'

The matron never appeared. Instead he received a scolding from Sister McNab. 'Now I've stood quite enough nonsense from you, Mr. Hutchins. You should be ashamed of yourself. There's nothing the matter with you except greed. Forget food awhile and you'll be as right as rain.'

But Hutchins was constitutionally incapable of forgetting food. After his operations it was his dominant theme. He had been admitted to this military hospital owing to some connection with Army Ordnance, but the War did not concern him. 'We're fighting those we have most in common with,' was his opinion. The rest of us left it at that.

The same afternoon a quantity of veal and ham pies were confiscated from his bearer, who got the sack for his failure to smuggle them through. 'This is just asking for trouble,' was the sister's comment. 'Mrs. Hutchins is quite aware of the regulations.'

'My wife understands me better than any of you. You're trying to get your own back on me because you know you're duds. Every fibre of me craves for meat. I'm getting more rickety and anaemic every day.'

The sister turned on her heel with an expression in which weariness had overcome disgust.

Yes, Mrs. Hutchins understood her husband. Knowing his special weakness, it looked as if she were trying to prolong his absence from home. Perhaps she was trying to get rid of him for good. Certainly she had all but succeeded on previous occasions. I observed her with increasing fascination.

Next time she called she had obtained permission to bring

some egg and lettuce sandwiches, and so absorbed was Hutchins in wolfing them that he was oblivious of his wife, who stood beside him humming a little tune. He had boasted to me that he was proof against sensual or suchlike attractions and referred to her as his 'legitimate'.

'My legitimate's a Papist—or was before our marriage. But live and let live has always been my motto, with the result that she has become just as honest-to-God pagan as yours truly. I'm pretty sure that I'm her religion now. Which is all as it should be. A woman has to worship somebody, bless 'er. Why not her better half? It suits me O.K.—and it seems to suit the legitimate.'

Fatuously basking in this illusion, Hutchins was awaiting the day of his discharge from hospital when he could gorge himself to perdition. At the same time he appeared to resent his recovery, which deprived him of his invalid's sense of power, his sway over the surgical ward. 'I should have kicked the bucket,' he muttered. 'All the doctors said so.' And his reminiscences grew sentimental. Everyone had been so kind to him, even stern Sister McNab. His eyes began to water. But his rage flared up again at the sight of what he called a wog.

Even when he was able to walk about, Hutchins seemed unwilling to leave the ward for long. Death had come to test him there: it was the scene of a personal victory he could not understand. He looked on his bed as a trophy, and our continued presence afforded him a certain gratification.

The day of his discharge arrived, not a moment too soon for his fellow patients. On his feet he appeared much taller than one would have guessed and his clothes hung scarecrow-loose about his frame. With a certain flourish he shouted across to say: 'Cheery-bye and so forth and so on. Send us a chit as soon as you're fit. I hope you don't mind my saying so but you're looking definitely greener about the gills than usual. Yes, definitely. If you don't put on a spot of colour you'll still be here by Christmas. Well, the missus'll send you a slice of our plum pudding. Between us we'll see to it that you're not forgotten! I'll be thinkof you tonight. My wife has promised me my favourite menu, "whore's dovers", game pie and chips, followed by apple roly-poly; and she usually has a surprise in store as well. And we'll open a bottle of fizz for the occasion—we've got a case of Heidsieck '38 laid by. Nothing like it for convalescence, with a cheese savoury and plenty of red pepper to bring out the full bouquet. We'll drink to your recovery. Definitely, old boy. That's a promise.'

His handshake made me feel as if I had carried off a couple of his fingers.

The sweeper who had so often performed the most menial of duties for Hutchins, such as hoisting him on to the bedpan and wiping him with cotton-wool, was drooping by the door with his mop of dampened rags. He looked only slightly more animated than his mop.

Hutchins drew himself up and struck the floor with his stick. 'If you think you're going to get any baksheesh out of me,' he bellowed, 'you're nicely mistaken, you worm.'

The worm turned. He cleared his throat as only an Indian sweeper can, reaching down his gullet deliberately and with resounding relish. The sound was so eloquent that I nearly cried Bravo. Hutchins glared and grasped his stick as if to strike him, then looked away with a defeated hangdog air. The stick fell down and he had to pick it up.

RESTING ON HIS LAURELS

'HAVE you heard the latest about Cedric?' Lilian panted over the telephone in her eagerness to be first with the news. 'He has almost killed himself.'

'Again?' No doubt I sounded callous. He had tried so often before. This time, having cut his wrists in a bath after swallowing a whole bottle of sleeping pills, he had nearly succeeded. Breathlessly Lilian continued: 'I sent my Dr. Burgin to see him. His diagnosis couldn't be more depressing. Cedric may be permanently paralysed through loss of blood. And apart from his writings he has nothing to live on.'

'Luckily, he still has Mollie,' I said.

'Who's that?'

'The girl he lives with—the one with the boutique.'

'I know nothing about that side of his life. He has always kept it dark from me. But I don't suppose she will be able to support him. I thought of raising a subscription and I need your help. You might add a few names to my list.'

Thanks to Lilian's pertinacity a substantial fund was collected by what she dubbed the Cedric Aid Committee. As time wore on, however, the subscribers began to renege. Those who went to visit him were so appalled that few of them ventured to return. He could not speak yet he made gurgling sounds which only Mollie could interpret, and he exuded an obnoxious odour. The visitor made efforts to behave naturally and carry on a one-sided conversation, while Cedric's eyes stared blankly as if he were blind. Saliva dribbled from his loose lips and Mollie wiped them tenderly. 'Don't you admire his pyjamas? I made them myself,' she said. 'Lilian gave him the dressing-gown. Isn't it gorgeous?'

'Balzac would have been envious.'

Not having heard of Balzac, Mollie looked baffled. Propped up in his armchair, Cedric continued to stare into a separate world of his own. One hoped it was not as unpleasant as one suspected. Meantime the visitor racked his brains for a subject that might kindle a spark of interest in the patient. Eventually the gurgling was succeeded by a sort of whinny combined with bleating and the glazed eyes began to goggle. The visitor drew back in alarm.

'He wants the po,' said Mollie.

'Perhaps I'd better be going.'

'Please stay. He loves seeing old friends. It's the best tonic for his morale.'

She opened his trousers and held the po in position. With an abdominal chuckle Cedric relieved himself. Further conversation was effectively nipped in the bud.

A few visits of this kind damped the most charitable intentions. Cedric vouchsafed no sign that he recognized his friends or understood their speech, and we were ashamed of uttering the usual platitudes. But Mollie insisted that our visits were therapeutic. She was a plucky young woman with an old-fashioned 'schoolgirl complexion', vivid pink cheeks all the pinker against her flaxen hair, efficient, neat and good-natured. Her health seemed all the more florid in contrast with Cedric's decrepitude. Since his last crisis her devotion to him was saintly. Her earnings supplemented the allowance provided by his friends, which barely covered expenses. At first Lilian supplied him with extra delicacies and filled his flat with flowers. Others brought books and magazines and read aloud to him though his noises were somewhat distracting. Mollie thanked them effusively on his behalf, but her gratitude could not compensate for his apathy.

For months Lilian kept up the pretence that Cedric recognized her. She was too vain to admit that anyone could fail to do so. 'His pale eyes brighten and his lips tremble with longing to communicate,' she said. 'He gazes at me so lovingly; he clasps my hand and will not let go. And his smile is so tragic that I could weep. Ours was a very special relationship.'

It was difficult to believe her. True, he gobbled the foie-gras I brought him with a gusto reminiscent of the zoo, but he never clasped my hand for his own hung limply beside him like a wet dish-cloth and he only grinned when Mollie produced the po— an invariable ritual at every meeting and, for me, a signal to depart. His chuckle as Mollie unbuttoned him became hysterical when he released his torrent. He was growing fatter and a sallow puffiness enveloped his features. Hardly any trace of his former charm remained.

The Cedric Aid Committee began to disintegrate when Lilian organized a little party for his thirty-fifth birthday—a euphemism for his thirty-eighth. She mustered a group of stalwarts who brought champagne, while she supplied a rococo cake bristling with coloured candles. 'I've a premonition that this will encourage him to speak,' she said. 'He's bound to be stimulated by the cake and the bubbly. We must all talk books to him, especially his own. It might be a good idea to read certain passages aloud. I've marked those that seemed appropriate, such as his beautiful account of the Carnival at Rio. His brain's intact: it only wants jogging. Mollie has the wrong approach. He needs a more intellectual companion.' I could think of none who would step into Mollie's shoes.

Cedric greeted us Tibetan fashion, by sticking out his tongue like an enormous sea-slug. We pretended not to notice.

'Greedy boy,' said Mollie. 'He has guessed what's inside the parcel.'

'Hush!' whispered Lilian. 'The cake is to be a surprise.' Cedric's tongue flickered at her in a provocative manner. She gave him a playful tap but was visibly put out. 'Now now, you behave yourself!' she adjured him. 'This is your birthday party and we have come to congratulate you. For all our sakes you must promise to get well. Mind over matter and no more hanky-panky!'

Cedric's upper teeth closed over his lower lip as if to pronounce a word beginning with F. His eyes glared balefully and his fists were clenched. The blinds were drawn as the candles on the cake were lighted: it should have been a cheerful scene. Lilian's husband Humphrey, who was also Cedric's literary agent, took pride in making every party go and he considered himself an expert at opening champagne. Rolling up his sleeves he seized each bottle, removed the gilded foil and cut the wire with mock solemnity, gradually coaxing the cork out with his thumb. The cork resisted his pressure and he flourished the big-bellied bottle in Cedric's direction—for luck, he said. Mollie asked him nervously: 'Wouldn't you like a corkscrew?' 'A corkscrew for fizz? What next?' As we gathered round he said: 'Keep calm, everybody. This is a serious matter: Cedric's health is involved. But we must let nature take its course, eh Cedric? Now the cork's beginning to wriggle, slowly, slowly . . .'

'For goodness' sake give me the bottle,' said Lilian, and there was a tussle between them.

'Let go or you'll bust its neck. Whew, what a stubborn little beggar! Out with you, out with you!' With an explosion the cork sprang across the room. Lilian dabbled a finger in the foam and moistened Cedric's ears. Hunched sullenly in his armchair Cedric tried in vain, like the cork, to resist, but saliva foamed from his mouth.

Though the champagne was not cold it helped to break the ice. We drank out of paper cups as there were not enough glasses. Humphrey refused the wine in spite of his comic performance.

'I've brought my own poison with me,' he remarked, pouring whisky into a mug. 'Fizz aggravates my acidity.' He added in an undertone: 'Lilian dragged me here, dammit, but what's the good? Any fool can see that he's done for. It's not as if I was keen on his writings: they've always been tricky to place. But Lilian believed in him and I relied on her intuition. She has often backed a winner.' He took a long swig of his poison. 'Was that his fifth or sixth attempt at suicide? Had he pulled it off we might have sold more of his books; he'd have been rediscovered and written up. A dramatic symbol of the Beat Generation. The snag is that he was always immature. Sexually too, I imagine.'

'My theory', interposed a young film critic, 'is that Cedric was naturally queer and refused to face it.'

'Nonsense, he was surrounded by girls of every nationality. And he talked like a Casanova: seduction after seduction.'

'I'll bet you he never got down to brass tacks. He was kidding himself. The girls were mere figures on a façade, but they became an obsession. After each failure he tried the suicide stunt, but the instinct of self-preservation won out.'

'Stop nattering over there,' shrilled Lilian. 'Cedric must cut his cake and Humphrey must give us a speech.'

A knife was thrust into Cedric's hand but he let it drop.

'Clumsy,' said Lilian. 'I'll cut it for you, and you blow out the candles.' Cedric slobbered over the cake while cups and glasses were raised to the tune of 'Happy Birthday to Cedric, happy birthday to you!'

'Silence, everybody!' Lilian commanded. 'We're all assembled to wish darling Cedric long life and health and happiness. And creation, more creation. Speak up, Humphrey!'

Her husband took another, longer swig. 'I'm a lousy speaker so I'll make it short. Lilian has taken the words out of my mouth as usual. So here's to Cedric's next opus! I'm happy to announce that *Speculations* has gone into paperbacks. We must follow it up. As soon as you're over this *contretemps*—and you're looking fine, I believe you have put on weight—you must deliver the prize baby we're all expecting. Remember you're considered the great hope of the younger generation. Fill up the bumpers, chaps, and quaff to Cedric's resurrection!'

Mollie replenished the paper cups and Lilian held one for Cedric to sip from in shuddering jerks. 'Doesn't it taste good? I hope you enjoyed the cake. I made it with my own fair hands. Give him another slice.' Mollie crammed a small segment into Cedric's open mouth where it melted into a spongy mess. Crumbs must have stuck in his gullet for he started coughing and spat it out. Lilian patted his back and the cough became frantic. He gasped, he retched, he choked: tears welled from his bloodshot eyes and his jowl turned purple as he writhed for breath. The champagne he was offered as an anodyne streamed from his nostrils. 'I'm afraid it has been too much of a thrill for him,' said Lilian, 'but at least we have testified how much we love him. I hope he realizes it.' Having recovered his breath, Cedric was clicking his tongue like a castanet against the roof of his mouth. 'You've been wonderful, Cedric, quite heroic under the circumstances! I hope we haven't tired you with our chatter. Bye-bye for the present. Look after him, Mollie dear. He is exceedingly precious. Yours is a sacred trust.'

Already there was a frenzied whinny, and those who could interpret the sound rushed hastily for the exit. It was followed by a cascade of water.

In spite of our ministrations, the party had been a flop. None of us had enjoyed it and we wondered about Cedric. He had left a dismal impression. 'Better dead,' said Humphrey Holman. 'Speechless, half-paralysed, a burden to himself and to others, I wouldn't want to survive in that condition.' Lilian was less gloomy, for she was in touch with a retired butcher in Balham who was a medium for a long-dead Arab healer, and he had promised to send forth his spiritual rays.

Gradually even Lilian began to waver in her allegiance to Cedric. The cost of his maintenance did not diminish while his health remained stationary. According to Dr. Burgin, unless his heart conked out he might live for donkey's years. Mercifully his heart was that of an ox. When Lilian spread the news, more than one member of the Cedric Aid Committee was disconcerted. Nobody had been prepared for this contingency.

Since his last attempt, Cedric manifested no further desire to die. Mollie was delighted to have him entirely to herself. She fed, clothed and nursed him and she hired a substitute during her working hours at the boutique. Nearly every penny she earned was spent on his welfare. When his friends failed to visit him she would ring them up and cajole them into coming. The majority invented specious excuses or failed to turn up. Lilian, who had founded the Cedric Aid Committee, was among the first to resign. Offended by Cedric's lack of response to her numerous acts of kindness and generosity, she complained: 'I have lots of commitments which are really more rewarding. There are my poor spastics and dear little polio children, so sweet and appreciative. The blind too, bless 'em. Such heart-rending cases, and how many of them were born that way! Whereas Cedric brought it all on himself: it was so unnecessary. At any rate, he has Mollie. That woman is an absolute martyr. I can't imagine why she puts up with him unless he is different when we're not there. Cedric has converted me to euthanasia.'

There was something to be said for putting people out of pain when it was incurable, but Mollie had told me: 'I believe he enjoys life more now than when he could walk and talk. He's remarkably cheerful and his appetite is enormous. In the old days he suffered from insomnia but now he sleeps like a log. I suppose it is because he doesn't have to worry . . .'

'He has handed over his worries to you. That's all very well so long as you stick to him, but is it fair? Supposing you want to marry and have children, what then?'

'Cedric needs me desperately and I need him. I could never give him up. And we do manage to make love now and then. I might even have a child by him. You never know. . . .'

Her cheeks reddened with her indiscretion. I remembered a rumour that she had been a gym instructress at a girls' school: perhaps it was true. Her evocation of amorous acrobatics struck me as grotesque, yet I was glad for her sake that she found some sexual satisfaction. She seemed so unsophisticated that I couldn't help smiling. As if to convince me she added with embarrassing candour: 'He's apt to get over-excited, especially when I bathe him. It's the best way to quieten his nerves. He falls asleep like a baby with a bottle.'

'Don't you get bored with the lack of conversation?'

'Not at all. He can express so much without words.' As I could detect hardly any expression on his features when I spoke to him I was astonished. And I had known him since we were at school together. I recalled that early experiment after one of his emotional upheavals. The sea was rough and he had swum far out until he was exhausted. A lifeboat had gone to his rescue and he was revived with artificial respiration. He told me that he had sunk with open eyes expecting to see the whole of his past like a film, but he only saw a mass of seaweed in which he became entangled. The experiment had disappointed him. What he called his love affairs continued to go wrong—I fancied because he was a Narcissus seeking his own reflection. None of his subsequent accidents had been accidental. On another occasion he drove his car into a tree. That had been a narrow squeak too. The car was wrecked, but he had only suffered from mild concussion. As if he attributed his failures to lack of manliness, he was still resolved to risk death to prove himself a hero. Why cling to a life in which he could neither express his genius nor satisfy his sexual desires? Was there not a superior distinction in 'flinging it away like a flower'—a flower which had lost its grace and perfume? A debonair indifference to life would expiate his human weaknesses. . . . He was undoubtedly self-dramatizing, yet that anguish of living which has been the mainspring of modern inspiration since the first world war was never apparent in his manner or his writings. His sense of tragedy was entirely personal and ingrown.

'You have a better effect on him than his other friends. Look, he wants to write a message.' Mollie gave him a pad and pencil which he grabbed with a fiendish grimace. Very slowly he proceeded to scrawl in a childish hand: 'Resting on my laurels.' He dropped the pencil and winked at me with a malicious eye.

'Well, you have plenty of laurels to rest on,' I replied with more tact than sincerity. Again his face became an impassive mask.

'I encourage him to write,' said Mollie, taking me aside, 'for I'm sure there's a masterpiece bottled up inside him. As you see it costs him an effort. Lilian said he resembled Beethoven composing a symphony. Do you agree? I can't say I notice the likeness. And speaking of Lilian, she has let us down rather badly. In fact she hasn't been near us since the birthday party. I know Cedric is cut up about it. Of course he never complains.'

'How can you tell? Perhaps he's relieved.'

'Oh, I can read his thoughts. He has no secrets from me.'

Poor Mollie was deceiving herself. Some weeks later my attention was drawn to an article signed by Cedric in *The Clarion*, a critical review of television dramatics. Albeit the Cedric Aid Committee had supplied him with a set, Mollie had told me that he seldom used it, and the style of the article had nothing in common with any of his previous writings. I presumed he had a namesake and forgot about it. More articles and sprightly replies to controversial letters appeared under his signature, altogether so unlike him that I was mystified. 'Search me,' said Lilian when I asked her if she had read them. 'I've done my bit for Cedric and a fat lot of thanks I've got. So far as I'm concerned he's out. So is Mollie. They're welcome to each other. Let them stew!'

'Surely it's satisfactory that he has taken up writing again, unless it is a ghost. To me it seems prodigious.'

'I couldn't care less. If Cedric thinks I'll drop in on him again he's mistaken. I've dropped out for good and all.'

Her reason for this volte-face was that she had telephoned for news of Cedric and an unknown contralto had answered: 'He can't see anyone. Doctor's orders.'

'But we have the same doctor. In fact I sent him to Cedric in the first place. He assured me that I could see him. Please put me on to Mollie.'

'Well, you'll have to apply somewhere else. She has left and a jolly good riddance. And who the hell are you?'

The voice had been so crudely offensive that Lilian had rung off. My own experience was similar but I refused to be thwarted. Those articles in *The Clarion* had whetted my curiosity.

Rebuffed by telephone, I resolved to call on Cedric in spite of abominable weather. A slovenly virago in slacks answered the bell, a fag-end drooping from her lower lip. Her hard eyes narrowed with hostility when I explained my harmless mission. 'You should have telephoned.'

'The line was busy. I rang at intervals but there was no reply.'

'I've heard that one before. No use: he's seeing nobody.'

'Please tell him I'm here, and I'm sure he'll change his mind.'

'Sorry, it's out of the question.'

'I've come a long way,' I pleaded, 'and look at the downpour! I'll never find a taxi . . .'

'Can't be helped. Doctor's orders. Nothing doing.'

She slammed the door in my face. Astounded at the rudeness of this reception, I steered my umbrella through sheets of rain towards Mollie's boutique in the vicinity. The teeming steaming interior was vibrant with pop music as if Carnaby Street had moved to Kensington. Mollie was dealing with a tiresome customer who could not make up her mind. She looked ill, her pallor accentuated by the blacking round her eyes which had lost their sparkle. The months since I had seen her might have been years. 'We can't talk in this place,' she murmured. 'Let's meet outside.'

'At Cedric's? What is going on there? When I called a strange woman wouldn't let me see him. She was positively insulting.'

'I've been chucked out,' said Mollie.

As she could not neglect her customers I asked her to dinner. She accepted with hesitation. 'I don't want to be pitied,' she said, 'but I can't help pitying myself.'

It was a lugubrious evening. Mollie's eyes continued to fill with tears so that the blacking stained her cheeks. Her voice was hoarse and her mouth had a nervous twitch.

'I never used to touch the stuff but now I need it,' she confessed as she swallowed her third pink gin. 'Chucked out!' she repeated.

'Not having seen Cedric lately I knew nothing about it,' I said lamely.

'Neither did I. And all the time I was making a home for him he was carrying on with that vixen on the sly.'

'Who was she—a nurse?'

'He had several detached females in tow before his last accident. She might have been one of those. Anyhow, what does it matter? She has got him.'

'Surely it cannot last?'

'That's what I'm afraid of. . . . She'll be the death of him. But there's nothing I can do about it.' Mollie broke into a sob. 'She must have hypnotic powers. She has managed to make him speak.'

'To give the devil his due that's some achievement.'

'His first words to me were "Get out!" I couldn't believe my ears but he repeated them. He shouted—it was blood-curdling: "Get out, you bitch!" And now they're engaged to be married.'

'What? In his condition?'

Mollie sighed. 'There has been a slight improvement. He can't walk yet and his joints are very stiff, especially . . . but I'll spare you the details. He was always obsessed in a way that women could sense.'

Who writes his articles in *The Clarion*?'

'I shouldn't be surprised if Lilian was at the bottom of it all. Her husband had a secretary she wanted to liquidate. Do you mind if I have some brandy?'

'You've eaten next to nothing.'

'I've no appetite. I'm done for. Cedric was everything to me: I asked for nothing better than to look after him. And now what have I to live for—a Kensington boutique?'

This young woman who had always struck me as placid and practical began to rant like a tragedy queen. Gently I suggested that there were plenty of alternatives for self-sacrifice, if that was her vocation. She had done more than her share for Cedric, who had treated her shamefully. But she refused to listen. 'I'd go back to him this moment if he'd take me,' she said hopelessly. 'I have spoken to nobody else about this. The fact is I have no friends: while I was with Cedric I never needed them.'

She had had too much to drink and when she rose she swayed crookedly. I offered her my arm, but she protested: 'Oh I'm all right. Don't worry!' In the street, however, she was violently sick while I held an umbrella over her. I accompanied her in a taxi to her hotel and helped her up the steps into the lobby. 'I apologize for being such a bore,' she whimpered, 'Remember me to Cedric when you see him.'

That was the last I saw of Mollie. Within the next few days I read in a newspaper that she had fallen out of an eighth-storey window—'a suspected suicide while of unsound mind'. I could not resist sending a telegram to Cedric expressing sympathy for his irreparable loss. In reply I received a typewritten letter signed by Cedric but surely not written by him, for it was a diatribe against the wickedness of self-slaughter. In the case of Mollie it was particularly reprehensible for she was not only young and healthy, but she was also pregnant. She had murdered her unborn child. The letter ended with a sanctimonious paean to life. We should all cultivate joy—that was the true wisdom. Cedric was happy to announce that he had discovered joy in matrimony. This had inspired his new book *Survival*.

Evidently Dr. Burgin's prognosis had been too pessimistic for Cedric recovered many of his faculties under some new treatment. In spite of its popular success I had no desire to read *Survival* or to attend Lilian's party in honour of its publication. Cedric sent me a copy which remains unopened. Memorable, absorbing, triumphant, were some of the adjectives applied to it by rhapsodical reviewers, and it galloped through several editions embellished by unrecognizable portraits of the author and his wife cheek to cheek and arm in arm. Soon a sequel was announced, but a series of obituaries were printed in its stead. Cedric had succumbed to an epidemic of Asian flu. His widow produced a sensational biography, the style of which was closely based on that of D. H. Lawrence. However, it contained no reference to Mollie. An edition of his selected letters followed, the majority addressed to Lilian, but by then the fickle reading public had lost interest and the massive volume was remaindered at a fraction of its published price.

AN OLD SCHOOL PAL

THE handwriting was almost illegible. With the aid of a magnifying glass Terence contrived to decipher the spidery sentences: 'As I shall be in your neighbourhood staying with Timothy Porter-Preston—remember him at Winchester and Lord's?—I was wondering if there were the slightest chance of my coming to see you for a night or two. It is such an age since I really had a talk with you and having just met our mutual friend Dolly Triplet it made me realize how absurd it was to reach my age and not to see an old school pal except for a drink in London on your way through to somewhere else. If you would care to put me up for a night or two, perhaps you would let me know at your earliest convenience because I shall be leaving for Timothy's at the end of this month . . .' The letter was signed Sam Weevil-Finch.

Over forty years had elapsed since Terence left school and most of his surviving friends of that period continued to see and correspond with him. Some of them were the salt and pepper of his existence. These, according to his Oxford Dictionary definition, were 'joined in intimacy and mutual benevolence independently of sexual or family love', though Freudians might attribute some sexual origin to such a relationship. Terence had shared their pleasures and pains throughout the years, and he seldom met them merely for a drink. 'Come and have a drink'— where had he last heard that casual invitation? Gradually the mists of memory dissolved and he began to identify the writer with a bespectacled bore from whom he had always fled, even at Winchester.

Weevil-Finch had seemed elderly at fifteen, a stooping figure with patchy hair, round myopic eyes, a chronic snuffle and a shuffling gait. He had been notorious for picking his nose and popping the pickings into his mouth. Scatological jokes were peculiarly distasteful in such a person but Finch had imagined they would promote his popularity. For obvious reasons he had been nicknamed Stinkbomb. Chilblains in icy classrooms with hard benches and chalky blackboards; airless evenings wrestling with algebra and Latin hexameters; indigestible and insufficient meals; O.T.C. drill and bayonet practice: the discomforts of his boyhood came flooding back to Terence, and Weevil-Finch smirking through steel-rimmed spectacles at his own smut, loomed in the background with the dreariest of them. Some years ago he had buttonholed Terence in a London club with a point-less anecdote of his puberty, but Terence had the gift of dis-missing nuisances and he remained ignorant of his adult career.

Finch's proposal to spend a night or two under Terence's roof was all the more disconcerting as he was expecting visitors with whom he had a multitude of interests in common, but he disliked inventing white lies and a night or two soon passed. His reply to Finch was courteous but cool. He agreed to put him up in spite of a dire shortage of staff.

When he broke the news to Priscilla she accused him of coward-ice. 'Why let yourself be imposed upon? Knowing him so slightly it would have been easy to refuse. Now I'll have to buy some extra blankets . . .'

Though Priscilla was half his age their harmony was due to the fact that this discrepancy did not affect them. Terence never thought of himself as sixty. He had kept his athletic figure, and his grey hair contrasted elegantly with his aquiline features. His relaxed manner concealed a fund of youthful energy. Priscilla looked nearer twenty than thirty. She had always preferred older men and, with few exceptions, she was bored by the inexperi-enced. Terence's friends had become hers, and she had introduced a spice of novelty into his circle. When Terence warned her about Finch's lack of allure she laughed: 'He must have some saving grace. You're exaggerating.'

'I can only hope he has improved with time. Some people do . . .'

She pressed his hand and said 'Darling.'

Sooner than Terence anticipated the nasal voice of Finch was demanding to be met at the railway station. 'And by the way, Rupert Lazenby can't put me up as he has caught flu. He had invited me for a week before going on to Timothy Porter-Preston's. This mucks up my immediate plans. Might I stay with you for another few days? I promise not to be difficult: Tim calls me the perfect guest.'

This time Terence was firm. 'Sorry. You said two nights, after which Priscilla has made other arrangements.'

Finch's groan of disappointment was audible on the wire. 'I suppose that means I'll have to move to an hotel. I hate hotels. Drat Rupert's 'flu, it can't be so bad as to put me to such expense. My train's due to arrive at six eleven. I trust your house is well heated. I'm awfully susceptible to chills. And who, may I ask, is Priscilla?'

'My wife.'

'I didn't realize you were married.'

'Aren't *you*?'

'No fear. I'm a bachelor by vocation.'

Traffic on the road was dense around six o'clock. It was pouring with rain and Terence was ten minutes late at the station. There was Weevil-Finch, drooping and dripping with a desolate air between two bulging suitcases, peering in every direction.

'You're rather late, aren't you? I was afraid you had forgotten me as I forgot my brolly. Well, better late than never. I could get no tea on the train. Without my tea I feel like a broken reed.'

'Don't blame me if you have chosen the rush hour to arrive in a downpour!'

'Could we stop at a teashop on the way?'

'Priscilla will brew you some, if you don't mind waiting.'

Finch pouted so that his chin almost touched his bulbous nose, showing plainly that he did mind. 'I had no idea that you lived so far out. How long will it take us?'

'Normally forty minutes, depending on the traffic.'

'I say. Quite a distance. Couldn't we stop at a road-house? I really need my tea.'

'I'm afraid it would delay us. We have guests for dinner.'

'You kept me waiting in the rain at that ghastly station. In the shelter of a drawing-room they will hardly object if we're late. They can stoke up with cocktails.'

Terence wiped his windscreen. 'The traffic's worse than usual.'

Finch lit a pipe which he puffed into Terence's face and lapsed into a silence pregnant with reproach. 'This must be a very antiquated car,' he remarked after a while. 'How many years have you had it?'

His tone was so consistently disagreeable that Terence was inclined to laugh it off. Except that he was jowly and bald it was the same Weevil-Finch he had known as Stinkbomb. The nose was redder, the ears more protuberant, and a wisp of blood-stained cotton adhered to his chin where he had cut himself shaving. The voice was still nasal but more querulous.

Priscilla recoiled at the sight of him. Seizing both her hands, he exclaimed: 'So young and winsome, and I never guessed! But surely I'm mistaken. You must be Terence's youngest daughter. May I kiss you? As one of Terence's oldest pals I claim it as a privilege.' Before Priscilla could answer he pressed his wet lips and rubbery nose against her cheek. It was as if a snail had crawled over her. Furtively she wiped the smear. Turning to Terence, Finch wagged a tobacco-stained finger at him and said archly: 'Baby-snatcher!'

'Nonsense,' said Priscilla, 'we've been married seven years.'

'And to think that Terence and I were at school together! I believe I'm actually his junior: I wish I felt it. Doesn't she make you feel terribly old, Terence?'

'Priscilla keeps me young.'

'Enviable fellow. You were born in 1910—what month?'

'If you want your tea I'll ring for some,' said Terence. 'You've half an hour to get ready for dinner.'

'Must I change? I didn't bring my dinner jacket. Rupert assured me that I wouldn't need one at The Grange. Won't I do as I am?'

'As you please. Priscilla and I change out of habit.'

'How pre-war. I was a fool to listen to Rupert. At our advanced age we should cling to the venerable customs.'

He glanced at his watch and remarked: 'By Jove, high time for a whisky! You toddle off and swap your togs, old boy. I'll pour myself a stiff drink in the meantime. Having been done out of my tea I'm thirsty for a substitute.'

'Help yourself,' said Terence glumly.

Finch poured himself half a tumbler. 'Might I trouble you for tap water? This soda plays the devil with my innards.' He sniffed the whisky with a suspicious nose. 'I hope it isn't Irish or Canadian.'

'It's Scotch all right. I'll get you some water.'

'Funny, I'd have sworn it was Irish from the smell.'

Finch plumped himself down on a delicate Hepplewhite chair which collapsed under his bulk. Terence paled at the demolition, but he managed to ask Finch kindly: 'Are you hurt?'

'Hurt? I should jolly well say so. Feels like I slipped a disc. Excruciating. Such flimsy furniture wasn't meant to be sat on.'

'It depends on the sitter,' said Terence, helping him to a sofa with an effort to conceal his vexation.

'Chairs like that are only for show in shop windows.'

'No longer, alas,' sighed Terence, who removed the shattered legs before retiring.

Finch poured himself another half tumbler of whisky. He was nodding when the other guests were ushered into the drawing-room. Terence had to shake him before he rose creakily to be introduced: Captain and Mrs. Bainbridge, Lady Sarah Parting-ton, Mr. Peter Olney. Images from bygone *Tatlers* swam before his misty spectacles. 'It never occurred to me that the county was so dressy,' he observed. 'Takes one back to the halcyon pre-war days. As dinner jackets are vanishing from London I forgot to pack mine, a pity. Gives one an inferiority complex.' There were polite murmurs of dissent before he explained: 'Terence and I were at Winchester together and we're exactly the same age. Hadn't met for donkey's years, so he inveigled me from Belgravia to talk over the happy days of yore. Nostalgia's my secret vice. I hope we won't send you to sleep with our schoolboy reminiscences.'

Lady Sarah Partington scrutinized Finch with her quizzical smile. 'I'm sure we'll all be thrilled to the core, especially if you dare to be candid. I look forward to an entrancing evening.'

'But we won't allow you to monopolize the subject,' said Mrs. Bainbridge. 'Let's all talk over our schooldays and compare impressions, the girls as well as the boys.'

'Without omitting the Adam and Eve stuff and love's young dream,' said Peter Olney.

'My first disillusion was to be undressed by an inquisitive little boy when I was eight or nine,' said Lady Sarah. 'He took a good look and said, "I don't think much of that." It took me a long time to recover my poise.'

'I didn't enjoy my schooldays,' said Priscilla. 'I only began to enjoy life since I met Terence.'

'I hope to be included from now on. I knew Terence long before you met him, in fact before you were born or thought of,' said Finch.

'It's odd he never mentioned you to me,' Priscilla said naïvely.

But Finch had a thick hide. Disregarding the ladies entirely, he meandered through a catalogue of names that meant nothing to them and little enough to Terence: Pyecroft, who had ended an adventurous career at the North Pole; Rolf Pennington, who had had six wives and been arrested for indecent exposure on a bus; Ned Rollingford, captain of the eleven, who had become a world authority on bottled waters; Buffy Andrews, who had won celebrity as a wild game hunter, killed by a hippo in the African bush. 'Which reminds me, do you still read Ballantyne and Rider Haggard as you used to during maths? After *Coral Island, The*

Gorilla Hunters is still one of my favourite novels. And Henty, what a genius! I can read him again and again.'

'You must be very bloodthirsty,' said Peter Olney.

'At any rate it's wholesome—no sexual slime like D. H. Lawrence and his ilk. Remember Ralph Rover, Jack Martin and Peterkin Gay? Good clean chaps all of them, but Peterkin was my hero. Remember when he shoots the gorilla? His first shot broke the brute's thighs, and it charged the white gunmen on its forefeet only. What a glorious description of the brute's death—the tremendous roar that shook the forest and nearly burst the white men's eardrums!'

'Sickening,' said Lady Sarah.

'It wasn't written for women,' Finch retorted contemptuously. Helping himself to roast beef, he continued: 'The barbecue feast interrupted by the lion's another purple passage. The hunters were cooking zebra round the camp fire. When we were given shepherd's pie and chunks of gristle called Irish Stew I used to dream of grilled zebra and elephant's foot. Tried to procure some from Buffy Andrews in Africa for a Ballantyne Banquet at the club, but Buffy was already kaput . . .'

'I don't see you in the role of big game hunter,' said Olney.

'I'm only a Ballantyne fan. Anyhow this roast beef is a good substitute for zebra, though I prefer it underdone. The radish sauce improves it. Delicious Brussels sprouts. Congratulations on your cook, Terence. Tell her from me she's a credit to her profession.'

All attempts to divert him from his single track failed. He proceeded to orate on the superiority of school concerts to those he had heard since. Amateur musicians beat the professionals hollow in his opinion. 'I wish I had a record of Caldicot minor playing the violin. His *Humoresque* would have made even Kreisler pull his socks up. I used to sing alto in the choir. Didn't you take part in *Hiawatha*, Terence, or was it *Rumpelstiltskin*? Old Walrus Dickinson was a champion music master. How he used to bellow through his beard while conducting! Bang, bang with the baton. "Louder, Kirkwood, can't you hear. Try again Redmond, you're singing flat. Now all together *fortissimo*: 'None ere before here / Saw common straw here' ".' Finch guffawed, splashing the tablecloth with chewed meat and vegetables. 'What about improvising a school concert of our own after supper? I'll do the conducting.' He picked up a fork and flourished it at Priscilla.

'We're no longer at school, thank God,' she said.

'You look as if you were,' he retorted. 'Anyhow Terence and I are your seniors and you'll have to obey us. What fun this is going to be. We'll start off with "Do you ken John Peel".'

The project was prevented by lack of musical instruments. 'Shame on you, Terence, not even a cottage piano?' he grumbled. 'Ladies and gents, the school concert is postponed.' Fishing for his pocket diary, he began to collect addresses. The Bainbridges owned a Tudor manor near Wimington which he recalled from an article in *Country Life*. 'I'm awfully keen on Tudor, it's just my period. Might I drop in on you while I'm in the neighbourhood, perhaps after leaving Terence? If you have a spare room I hope you'll allow me to do some historical research.' He also proposed paying visits to Lady Sarah and Peter Olney, if they could offer him spare rooms of course, as they lived rather far from London. Though he received no encouragement he was very pertinacious.

'I've only a dower house,' said Lady Sarah, 'little bigger than my Yorkshire terriers, but my rock garden is quite Alpine in its variety of plants. And I've some exceptional rhododendrons.'

'I'm awfully keen on rhododendrons,' said Finch. 'If you have no spare room, perhaps I might doss down on a sofa. I don't mind sharing a bathroom in the least.'

'But I do,' said Lady Sarah, 'as I told you my house is tiny.'

'I gather it's not far from Timothy Porter-Preston's. Maybe we could drive over for tea before I cross the Channel.' After a dramatic pause he announced: 'Next month I'm flying to Le Touquet to stay with the Harrison-Millers. I dare say you know them, shipping tycoons. They have magnificent stables and private golf links. The weight you lose on the links you gain at dinner. Bubbly before every meal and lashings of *foie-gras*. Their chef is a four-star frog: no wonder they go to Vichy every year. In spite of my zebra complex I'm partial to *boeuf à la mode*. Not that you're stinting me, Terence. Your English fare is kinder to the liver and Epsom salts are just as good as Vichy. But your claret should be *chambré*, if you don't mind my saying so. It's on the chilly side.'

'We'll warm you up with port,' said Terence with forbearance.

The port warmed him to such an extent that he fell asleep in the drawing-room. His mouth wide open, he snored and ground his false teeth. Priscilla apologized for him to her other guests, who departed earlier than usual. From her point of view it had been a disastrous evening.

Terence tried to console her with the comment that Finch's absurdity had made everybody laugh. 'Except me,' she retorted. 'Just look at the monster!'

Finch was still snoring away in an armchair. He had dropped his briar pipe on the Savonneric carpet and Priscilla leaped forward to see if it had burnt a hole. It had. Her involuntary cry wakened the sleeper. With a loud snort, like one of the jungle beasts in his favourite novel, Finch roused himself, rubbed his eyes, and blew his nose. 'Caught napping,' he muttered. 'The brandy must have been doctored. Remember when Tug Ellison slipped a cascara into Larkin's cocoa? And Larkin's revenge with the chocolate laxative, followed by civil war in the W.C.? I'm glad you woke me up. Might have choked on my dentures. Well, it's been a topping evening and I look forward to many a repeat. Rupert's flu may prove a blessing in disguise. Priscilla permitting, we must have a long pow-wow anent the merry days of yore. Have the others hooked it already? Sorry not to have said good-bye but I hope to see them soon again, a decent lot. Luckily I collected their addresses, so we'll keep in touch. What about a night-cap before hitting the hay?'

'Help yourself,' said Priscilla. 'Terence and I are early birds. It's past our bed-time.'

'Poor old Terence! A bit rough at your age to be tied to a young woman's apron strings. I could sit up all night nattering about our schooldays. So could you, I'll be bound. We'll make up for it tomorrow, eh, what? Off you go now, I won't detain the lovebirds. Mind if I switch on the radio?' He turned the button without waiting for an answer.

'He's insufferable,' said Priscilla almost within earshot. 'I dread the prospect of facing him tomorrow. You'll have to bear the brunt of it. I'll go into purdah.'

'Try to look on it as a joke, dear.'

'It's not very funny for me.'

As soon as they slipped into bed there was a rat-tat-tat at their door. 'Don't let me disturb you, but what time do you have breakfast?'

'Nine o'clock,' Terence shouted.

'I like mine at eight sharp. Could you send me up a pot of Ceylon tea with bacon and scrambled eggs? And fresh orange juice if available, well chilled. And a morning newspaper, preferably the *Daily Mirror*. Good night, sleep tight, and don't let the fleas bite, as our nannies used to say.'

Next morning Elsie, the housemaid, reported indignantly that Mr. Weevil-Finch had sent his breakfast back to the kitchen, complaining that it had been brought to him too early. They had had to cook his bacon and eggs twice over. 'I won't appear in case I lose my temper,' said Priscilla. 'We must find a way of getting rid of him.'

The way was found by Finch. When lighting his pipe he had flung the match into a waste-paper basket which had caught fire. The fire spread to a window curtain and to a bottle of liquid paraffin on the dressing-table. In attempting to smother the flames with a priceless Persian prayer rug he had only fanned the blaze, which burned the more brightly with the aid of a box of matches. Flames licked the four-poster bed and filled the whole room with acrid smoke. Coughing and spluttering, Finch tottered into the corridor. His raucous bellowings reverberated through the house. 'Call out the fire brigade!'

Terence and Priscilla came rushing with extinguishers and buckets of sand; Elsie and the cook with pails of water. As Finch had left the tap running in the bath, which was full to over-flowing, no time was wasted in dashing pail after pail over the crackling furniture. Finch stood at a discreet distance in his bedraggled dressing-gown growling 'Why the hell don't you summon the fire brigade?' while the others were scampering to quench the flames.

The rapidity and completeness of the damage made everybody gasp except Finch, who repeated: 'You'll have to get on to the insurance people at once. I've lost all the clothes I brought with me as well as my Ballantyne first editions, five hundred quid's worth all told. Let's see if there is anything to salvage. . . .'

The leather of the suitcase he had not opened was singed but its contents were intact, so he did not need to borrow clothes from Terence as he had been prompt to suggest, and his toilet accessories were safe in the flooded bathroom. But little else had been spared. Priscilla wept over the charred eighteenth-century wall-paper and toile de Jouy curtains.

'What a shambles! How did it happen—a short circuit?'

'Don't ask me,' said Finch. 'This house is evidently a tinder-box. It is courting danger to have so many inflammable chattels in a place so far from the nearest fire-station. Honestly, you shouldn't invite an old pal to risk his life in such a fire-trap. But it might have been worse. Take this as a timely warning.'

'You invited yourself,' said Priscilla. 'I was never consulted. I promise it won't happen again.'

'As soon as I can find my wallet Terence must drive me to the railway station. I won't leave without my wallet.'

The wet pouch was discovered by Elsie together with his shaving tackle in the bathroom. Gingerly he examined the damp contents. 'I suspect your maid's been pilfering,' he remarked. 'At least ten pounds are missing I'm sorry to say. Please call her in and question her.'

'I'll do no such thing. I can vouch for her honesty.'

'Well, this is your house so you're responsible. What I have here is barely enough to take me back to town. Terence will have to make good the missing sum: eleven quid to be precise.'

'We've only your word for it,' said Priscilla.

'Be careful, young woman. Are you calling me a liar?'

Rather than endure his presence a minute longer Terence telephoned for a taxi to take him to the nearest bus stop. He did not expect his old school chum to return the eleven pounds he lent him, which were accepted without thanks as a matter of course.

'If it isn't asking too much, could you contribute some sandwiches for the journey and a thermos flask of tea? Any sandwiches will do but I like my tea hot and strong, with plenty of milk and sugar.'

Resentful of his aspersions on her honesty, Elsie soaked a few slices of bread in tomato ketchup and poured barley water into the thermos. Finch was seated in the train when he opened the parcel, so she was deprived of the farcical spectacle of his explosion.

TIT FOR TAT

No, while Austin Travers was still alive Eustace had no inclination to write his obituary.

Austin had always seemed to him more vital than most people and the mere thought of killing him prematurely in cold print appalled him. However ill he might be, modern science could work wonders and Austin could afford the best medical attention. Unlike Eustace who had only enjoyed a negative *succès d'estime*, he had made a fortune with his novels and their by-products in film and television.

A stab of envy pierced Eustace when he compared their relative production and its results: he had devoted five years to a single novel which had barely sold three thousand copies whereas in the same period Austin had been as lucratively prolific as the elder Dumas. In other respects Eustace could not complain, having inherited a substantial income from Austin's wife Vera: he had not lived with her long enough to consider her his own. Fortunately his marriage had caused no estrangement from Austin. Their ways had parted amicably until they met at Vera's funeral and talked of other matters without a grain of awkwardness.

Rumour had blamed Eustace for the fatal accident. The post-mortem inquiry had left a dribble of doubt. Vera must have fiddled with the brakes before she and the motor went hurtling down the precipice while Eustace had been photographing the view. The dubious detail was that this was the first and last occasion Eustace had used a camera.

During the next ten years Eustace and Austin had spent part of every summer together either in Corfu, where Eustace had settled, or in Touraine where Austin had bought a *château*. Vera was never mentioned, but it was as if her absence had mellowed their friendship and strengthened a secret bond between them. A luxurious peace enfolded the widowers as they sat at their typewriters or swam in the sea after a morning's work. Austin paid tribute to Eustace's talent in and out of season, and the praise of so popular an author did much to compensate for the apathy of the weekly reviewers. He was as generous as he was loyal.

The *Herald*'s request for Austin's obituary had been tactfully phrased 'in case it was unfortunately needed'. Nevertheless it came as a shock and his conscience was disturbed. He shrank instinctively from so macabre a proposal. But if he refused, who could tell what sort of substitute would receive the commission. The critics were already disparaging Austin as a light entertainer without any socio-political message. They sneered at his old-fashioned narrative skill, the slick ingenuity of his plots. That his novels remained in print for decades would stimulate their envy. Dead, he would lie entirely at their mercy. A pack of puritanical jackals. . . .

Eustace crunched his breakfast toast a little too truculently and his loose wisdom tooth began to ache, reminding him of his age. Austin belonged to a younger generation yet he was bedridden in a Swiss clinic. His disease had defied the specialists. According to the *Herald*'s information it was incurable. This might explain why Eustace had not heard from him since last summer though Austin had always been a dilatory correspondent. He ought to be rescued from the jackals, Austin decided.

It was a dismal duty. The more he tried to assemble his memories, the more difficult it became to select those which threw light on his character. He had lived more inside his novels than outside them. Gradually from a tangled heap of jottings a portrait began to emerge. Like a pointillist painter Eustace touched and retouched it, a dab here and a dab there. Still dissatisfied, he plunged into his complete collection of Austin's novels. He had almost forgotten how excellent they were in their variety, and his interest warmed as he recognized this and that model thinly disguised, alternate versions of Vera before and since marriage, and an amusing caricature of himself in 'The Austere Sybarite'. The crackling vitality of his prose filled him with a pleasant glow. What a mastery of multi-lingual dialogue! He thought of his own efforts to achieve a personal style and his productions seemed as dehydrated vegetables and frozen mutton. He had overrated the importance of artistic form. Perhaps he had not appreciated Austin's achievement sufficiently on account of its too general acceptance, for Eustace convinced himself that he had no desire to be popular. He was fond of quoting Landor on the subject: 'I shall dine late, but the dining-room will be well lighted, the guests few and select.' His quiet voice could never extend beyond a contracted circle. Austin's was as that of a Caruso by comparison. Having known him so intimately Eustace had under-estimated its magnificent range.

On an impulse he telephoned to the clinic in Lausanne. He longed to tell his afflicted friend how tremendously moved he had been by his immersion in his works: it might help to cheer him. The line was busy, and when he got through after a couple of hours a secretary replied that Mr. Travers was in no condition to speak. So he sent him an express letter of closely reasoned eulogy. When he had ceased to expect a reply he received a typewritten sheet: 'Forgive dictation but I'm physically unable to write. Delighted to hear from you though from what you say I suspect you are engaged on my obituary. I hope it isn't too much of a grind. I couldn't manage it myself with such poor material. Blessings and best of luck . . .' At this point the typist had added: 'Mr. Travers has asked me to post this though he was too exhausted to finish. His voice being just above a whisper I might have misunderstood. I'm afraid there's no chance of improvement but we must keep smiling.' It was signed 'Heather Hinkson, secretary.'

Eustace wondered what species of Heather she belonged to. Most of Austin's secretaries named after flowers had been his temporary mistresses. He was beyond that now, poor fellow, his condition sounded desperate. His message, however, acted as a spur to Eustace, who polished off his obituary with unusual facility. He had exceeded the number of words required, but every additional word contributed towards a masterpiece of lapidary succinctness. Hadn't Poe said that a poem should never exceed a hundred lines, so that it should be read in one uninterrupted mood of increasing exaltation? Well, this was an elegy in prose and Eustace was proud of its peculiar aptness. Even so he returned to it again and again, altering an image, retouching a line, and revising the punctuation. Austin appeared to him in a dream and patted his shoulder. 'Congratulations!' he said, 'I couldn't do a better job if I had to write yours.' But in the dream Austin appeared plump and rubicund.

Next morning Eustace sent off his manuscript to the *Herald*. No sooner done than he regretted it and rushed back to the carbon copy on his desk. The obituary was becoming an obsession.

In due course the *Herald*'s editor thanked him for a brilliant cameo of interpretation. He trusted that the usual fee would prove acceptable and repeated his hope that the article would not be required, though his latest report was that Austin was at death's door. Having despatched the corrected proof after further anguish of indecision, Eustace picked up the thread of his interrupted novel, a modern tapestry of old Greek myths. He identified himself with Bellerophon, Pegasus with the power of words, the Chimaera with the nuclear menace, and so forth. He had got stuck in the quicksand of a scientific digression and his mind reverted to Austin, who was being kept alive by blood transfusions. If only he could mount a real Pegasus and fly to his bedside, but he loathed the chaos and cacophony of airports and the voyage from Corfu by boat and train was daunting when he might not be allowed to see Austin at the end of it. Should he wish him to eke out the rest of his days in a wheel chair when all his works proclaimed the desirability of an active life as a means to knowledge? Unless he had already reached a higher level of consciousness, what knowledge could he acquire as a passive guinea-pig? His obstinate struggle against death seemed to argue a will to survive for some predestined purpose.

While Eustace pondered the mystery it struck him that Austin had always avoided the supernatural: he had turned away from the unseeable and the unseen. He regarded life as a miraculous gift which it was one's business to enjoy, but supposing one were paralysed what could one enjoy even in beautiful surroundings? Wouldn't the beauty increase one's helpless torment? Eustace who had seldom given thought to the manner of his own death, shuddered at the picture of himself in a similar plight. Something sudden or a gentle coma, he hoped; but how selfish to be thinking of his fate instead of Austin's!

On re-reading his obituary again in a detached frame of mind he was overwhelmed with a desire to see it published. It seemed as fine as anything in the Greek Anthology. Later he was aghast at the extent of his egotism. Was it not monstrous to sacrifice his best friend to a few hundred words? To such a degree was he captivated by his pen-portrait that he was tempted to send it to Austin, who could not fail to admire its artistry.

A telegram from Heather Hinkson roused him from his morbid cogitations. 'Austin desperately anxious to see you. Urgency essential.' He made up his mind to go. It would be despicable to deny such a summons.

Miss Hinkson met him at the clinic, a jaunty little woman with a distraught expression. 'I can't thank you enough for coming. It's a great relief. Mr. Travers keeps on asking for you whenever he recovers consciousness. He wants you to be his literary executor.'

'Your wire alarmed me. This sounds more encouraging, as if he were fairly lucid.'

'He has his ups and downs. He's been up since I told him you were arriving. He's even sitting up. But make no mistake, the doctors have condemned him. He's capable of superhuman efforts, but his collapse is certain, a question of days.'

'*Vous êtes le très-bienvenu*,' said the matron. '*Le pauvre monsieur vous attend depuis toujours. Suivez-moi.*'

Tired from his journey and dreading what he might see,

Eustace was agreeably surprised to find him awake and smiling among masses of heavily scented tuberoses. He was extremely emaciated but still recognizable as he clutched Eustace's hand, tightening his bony fingers as if it were a lifeboat. It was the clutch of a skeleton. His mouth opened slowly and the voice was very faint. 'Terribly sorry to have dragged you such a distance. You look worn out.' He started coughing, a rasping rumbling sound. The nurse handed him a glass containing some milky fluid, supporting his scraggy neck while he sucked it from a tube. His head fell back on the pillow with a sigh like a weird unearthly whistle. Beads of sweat broke out on his alabaster forehead which the nurse wiped gently with a handkerchief.

'Perhaps I ought to leave him in peace,' Eustace remarked to the nurse.

'No, no,' Austin protested. Clutching his hand again, he gasped for breath. 'I'm all right . . . it's the joy of seeing you. I know what the leeches are saying. Don't believe them. I'm sure I've turned the corner, a villainous corner.' At first he ejaculated his words in spasms, but his voice became steadier as he explained that he was adding a codicil to his will. Would Eustace agree to act as his literary executor? He trusted his judgement to keep the best part of him in print. 'My stuff is unequal, the penalty of being prolific. You'll know just what to discard.' He paused to chuckle. 'As in the case of Vera. By the way I never thanked you for doing me such a good turn. Didn't want to embarrass you . . .'

Eustace stammered: 'I don't quite follow.'

The grip of Austin's rigid fingers hurt; he was grinning a death's-head grin. 'Poor Vera,' he repeated. 'What a devastating bore. Many's the time I longed to wring her neck. You had more guts than I.' He winked at Eustace with an odd grimace of complicity. 'Bravo! You did a magnificent job.'

'Honestly, Austin, you've let your imagination run riot.'

'Nonsense. Stop bluffing. What about the camera? I never swallowed that particular red herring.' His eyes twinkled and he wheezed with laughter. 'Had I been there I'd have given the car an extra push.'

'I swear you've got it wrong. I had asked Vera to wait in the two-seater. You know how impatient she was: she got tired of waiting. It's as simple as that.'

'Too simple for me, old boy. Never mind, all's well that ends well. That car rolling down the cliff . . .'

The nurse remonstrated with Eustace for making him laugh too much, but he brushed her aside in his indignation. 'I was genuinely fond of Vera. I owe her a lot.'

'She had her generous moments. I'm glad you cashed in on one of them.'

'This is grossly unfair. The whole subject is unbearably painful. . . .'

'Not to me. I put up with her longer than you did. It seemed an eternity. I was always afraid she'd come back to roost. Don't begrudge my gratitude: it's sincere. I'm allowed champagne. May I offer you a glass?'

The nurse was astonished by her patient's gaiety. 'We mustn't exaggerate. A drop of champagne and then you must rest.' Miss Hinkson poured, and all clinked glasses to Austin's recovery. 'To my literary executor!' said Austin.

Curiously elated in spite of his fatigue, Eustace invited Miss Hinkson to dine with him in a restaurant chosen by herself. 'Are you sure you want me? Oughtn't you to go straight off to bed?' she demurred. 'You've done more than your share of the good Samaritan and I'm used to supping alone. I get fagged out at the clinic, but it must have been worse for you as his oldest friend.' But Eustace insisted: he could see that she only needed coaxing, for she was bubbling with pent-up confidences about Austin's illness, the doctors and nurses, the drugs and dosage prescribed and their effects, eight pints of herbal tea daily and hot baths impregnated with imported seaweed, antibiotics and injections of camphor. 'They've given him the works. If he does survive, it'll be the survival of the fittest.'

'I hope he has plenty of pain-killers.'

'I sometimes wonder. He bears it heroically. He must have an iron constitution.'

Eustace suggested staying on until Austin was out of the wood. As if she read his thoughts Miss Hinkson declared that she considered this unnecessary. 'Mr. Travers realizes that you have many claims in Corfu. There was something he had to get off his chest and I gather that's been done. I'm glad you've agreed to be his executor. You can count on my collaboration. But you needn't feel obliged to sit here holding his hand: he has plenty of others to look after him. Even if he does recover, it will be a very slow business . . .'

Eustace decided that there was nothing equivocal in Austin's relations with her. When the topic of Austin was exhausted she had no more to say except about the weather, and since it was rainy he could only regret the unclouded sky of Corfu. Everybody in the restaurant looked damp, the food was soggy, and the rain beating against the windows washed away further attempts at conversation. Dimness was in the air, and neither knew what to talk of next. 'We must keep in touch,' said Eustace. 'I'll linger another few days just in case . . .'

'I shouldn't if I were you. It might be bad for Mr. Travers's morale. He'd guess he was on the way out. Corfu must be heavenly as I've always heard, but I'm only happy in London. I feel out of the swim elsewhere.'

Next day it was still raining. Miss Hinkson informed Eustace by telephone that Austin had had a setback. Evidently he had been over-excited, the interview had prostrated him—'though I must say he picked up miraculously while you were with him,' Miss Hinkson added. Eustace sent him some rare orchids with the aphorism: '*Les hommes ne sont justes qu'envers ceux qu'ils aiment.*' Since Austin was allowed no visitors he returned to Corfu. Perhaps, as his literary executor, he ought to revise his obituary: there was still time. But it was always a risk to repaint a finished portrait.

After a prolonged silence, a month later Eustace heard that Austin had left the clinic. An ecstatic letter from Heather Hinkson described his rapid progress since Eustace's visit. He had gone to convalesce in Barbados, the best of blood transfusions.

Austin should have been infected by Miss Hinkson's enthusiasm: instead he was unreasonably depressed. He was reminded of his obituary, though condensed into a small compass, the best prose he had ever written—scrapped. A letter from Austin followed: 'Happy to inform you that my obituary won't be needed yet awhile. I'm revelling in a new lease of life. . . . Why not join me here? I have rented a musical comedy villa which is cooled by ocean breezes. I'm sure it would rejuvenate you too. Oliver Messel is redecorating the whole island in his own inimitable style. Millionaires abound like sugar cane but they are quite civilized. Claudette Colbert is our model of perennial youth. I'm concocting a picaresque fantasy about it all. Seriously, do consider this a standing invitation. It's high time you left your hideous Achilleion.'

Eustace had retired to bed with a feverish cold and his streaming eyes were so swollen that he could hardly decipher the pallid typescript on the transparent sheets of airmail which he, lover of thick vellum, held in abomination. What the hell should he do in Barbados with an interrupted masterpiece? His Bellerophon had yet to face the Chimaera. Beside his bed was a pile of books on nuclear physics which he was attempting to digest: his imagination refused to focus on the subject and it was no use trying to force it with a temperature and a headache. His London publisher had aggravated his mood of dejection. Novels were a drug on the market, he complained. Couldn't Eustace embark on a candid autobiography? That was bound to sell, especially if he was indiscreet about his love life. Readers wanted raw facts these days, something solid to get their teeth into, and plenty of spice. Hadn't he been mixed up in a divorce, followed by a fatal accident? That was promising material. And wasn't there a lot of coprophily in Corfu—or was he thinking of one of Norman Douglas's limericks? Percy Stitchwort, of Culbertson and Becker, urged Eustace to give earnest thought to this proposal, and he guaranteed a liberal advance on royalties. On the other hand he could not agree to publish any novel unless it was frankly pornographic.

After his years of toil on 'The New Bellerophon' Eustace was overcome by a sense of futility. On the verge of seventy he could not be seduced by the electronic technique described with such gusto by novelists of the avant-garde, and he was sceptical about the vast public of which they boasted. How many dawns had been prophesied since Dada, and how many of the latest slogans were vapid variations of the old. If fiction had become a drug on the market the reason was obvious: most of it was unreadable. Cut-ups on tapes, words like syndrome, osmosis and escalation were tossed about in a bewildering ragbag of episodes vaguely influenced by films and advertisements. The purveyors of this pretentious trash blamed an antiquated social structure for their monotonous emphasis on dislocation and collapse, instead of blaming their own inadequacy.

I pity the young, he reflected, all the same what wouldn't I give to have my youth back? As long ago as the 1880s Nietzsche had written: 'Poor artist of today! With an audience of greedy, insatiable, uncurbed, loathsome, harassed spirits, and compelled to be half-priest, half-alienist!' It seemed to Eustace that the audience had changed little since then, with their hankering after strange gods and a state of timeless bliss induced by drugs. Was all his straining after perfection to end with an unpublished obituary?

The recollection of Austin, whose novels were available even in Corfu, restored his battered self-confidence. Austin was writing away with renewed vigour, oblivious of the Pop public and the avant-garde. As soon as he felt better Eustace would join him in Barbados.

As soon as he felt better . . . but he felt worse. The shooting pain in his chest was diagnosed, too late, as pleurisy. It was a stunning blow to Austin when his death was announced in the *Herald* with the comment that he was 'caviar to the general . . . a writer's writer who had faded from the literary scene. After the tragic death of his wife, the former Mrs. Austin Travers, in mysterious circumstances, he had retired to Corfu.'

'There must be a mistake,' said Austin. 'It is unlike Eustace to fail us when we were expecting him to stay.'

'I could have loved that man,' exclaimed Heather. 'Yes, he was just the sort I should have liked to marry. A man one could count on in emergencies.'

'Heather, you amaze me. Have you forgotten that he ran off with my wife? And you know what happened to her on their honeymoon. I wouldn't want the same to happen to you.'

'You've never had a truer friend. When we dined together in Lausanne he could talk of nothing but your condition. He was so upset that I feared he would break down. Poor Mr. Deacon, we shall both miss him. Now we'll have to look for another literary executor.'

'I suppose I ought to write his obituary. Tit for tat. Eustace was certainly a master-craftsman. He has left me the plot of a first-rate thriller. I'll write that next. Having known the leading characters, it won't require much labour.'

PALLADIAN PIZZICATO

A VOICE I had not heard for more years than I cared to remember was clearly audible above the muted clatter and hum of the three-star restaurant whose speciality was fish.

'What? No *alose à l'oseille*! It was a treat to which I was looking forward before I came here. *C'est navrant.*'

The head waiter's apology was visible but inaudible, and the voice I had not heard for so long rose in strident indignation: 'Lobster Thermidor! I can have that in my hotel. I'll console myself with a dozen of your small green oysters.'

His French was almost too perfect for a foreigner. It wafted me back to the evenings when he recited *La Jeune Parque* to his coterie of admirers at Cambridge, and to his melodious question: '*Mais qui pleure / Si proche de moi-même au moment de pleurer?*'

José Altamira was then regarded by those who knew him as a full-fledged genius. He sparkled with so many talents that it was hard to foretell which would predominate if he were spared by the gods. For he looked fragile, slim and hollow-chested, with an ivory complexion and very lustrous eyes. His hectic flush when he recited poetry suggested galloping consumption. Unlike most poets, however, he was supposed to be rich, and everything about him, from his Charvet neckties to his gold-tipped cigarettes, was redolent of sophisticated opulence. He came from Peru but he had many relations scattered over Europe and Paris was his second home. He spoke English fluently with an exotic accent.

Such a figure was bound to attract attention at Cambridge in the carefree nineteen-twenties. In contrast with the loose tweeds and baggy flannels of most undergraduates he favoured dark suits like Beardsley silhouettes. Already his writings were appearing in advanced periodicals, enigmatic odes and aphoristic essays that glittered with parakeet imagery. He wrote in French and Spanish as well, but we only saw his English compositions until a sumptuous selection of his poems was published in Paris with a linear profile of the author by Jean Cocteau. Trilingual poets are uncommon even now, and these seemed precociously mature under their veneer of modernity, the words pirouetting over the pages and turning cartwheels in print. We marvelled at the resources of his vocabulary. At the Semiramis Society which he founded he became our arbiter. From the blurred twilight of Cambridge in the twenties José's figure emerged more vividly than his contemporaries.

The voice protesting against Lobster Thermidor revived so many nostalgic memories that I stared in its direction, but I could detect no resemblance to José Altamira. A stout bald man was sitting with a juvenile couple of Anglo-Saxons and a florid French widow. He might have been a worldly abbé. He sprinkled his oysters with lemon and scooped them from their shells while the French widow appeared vivacious in spite of her black weeds. The English couple seemed silent and constrained. The voice that rose from the portly figure was unmistakably José's.

As I walked towards his table he exclaimed dramatically: 'Hail Julian the Apostate! You do not recognize your old *copain* of the Semiramis Society. No wonder: you have changed less than I in all these decades. Do join us for a liqueur. I cannot recommend the coffee but the Armagnac is ambrosial.' He seized me by the arm. 'Let me introduce you to the Comtesse d'Arpon and Lord and Lady Cranfield.' He seemed overjoyed to see me.

'Still writing?' I asked him.

'Spasmodically, but not for publication.'

'What a pity. I see your poems advertised in catalogues of rare books: they have become collector's items.'

'He is working on a history of the Cornarina,' the Countess informed me, rolling her Parisian r's like an amorous pigeon. 'This will be his *chef-d'œuvre*.'

'The Cornarina?' I queried. 'Wasn't she a famous courtesan?'

'She is my home,' said José simply. 'Denise and I bought the house together but now she has sold her share of it to me.'

'I have too many houses,' the Countess explained, 'and modern life has become too complicated. I refuse to be the slave of my possessions. José has become the slave of the Cornarina.'

'Have you deserted Peru?' I asked him.

'All my relatives have been obliged to return. But I cling to the Veneto with my little nest-egg.'

'He could live much better elsewhere but he prefers his white elephant. We should get rid of superfluous luxuries as we grow older,' said the Countess.

José smiled at this. 'Denise has six houses in France, not to mention her numerous apartments.'

'Those are profitable investments. The Cornarina is exactly the reverse: it swallows every *sou* of your income.'

'What else have I to live for?' sighed José.

'*Tu m'oublies. Comme tu es méchant!*'

Neither of the Cranfields opened their mouths except to eat and drink and I wondered why they happened to be there. It was already past three and I had an urgent appointment. José made me promise to call on him whenever I visited Venice: the Cornarina was barely an hour's drive along the Brenta canal.

'You will see that I live my poems,' he said. 'It has rejuvenated me.'

'And how!' young Cranfield piped in. 'It's out of this world.'

'Exactly,' said the Countess, 'so far out that one is forced to vegetate like a hermit. No social life whatever: it is just too far away from our Venetian friends.'

'Peace, rural peace.'

'Not at all. There are always dogs barking, cats howling, and cocks crowing in the early morning. *C'est le vacarme dans la solitude*. Give me the soothing steady flow of Parisian traffic.'

I could detect no sign of José's rejuvenation but he carried his paunch with dignity. His head had become that of a Roman emperor. Only his voice reminded me of his youth.

The Countess was scrutinizing the bill through her lorgnette. 'You have overcharged me for the wine,' she snapped at the waiter. 'The price written down for the Pouilly does not tally with that on your list: there's a difference of fifteen francs. And we had three *choux à la crème*, not four. And only two coffees.' Oblivious of the guests, she scolded the waiter with gusto.

'It seems to be an *addition* in the English sense,' said José. The English couple blushed with embarrassment while the Countess continued to argue. Her voice was becoming shriller when I retreated. I was almost sorry to miss the end of the act.

Browsing among the Seine bookstalls a few days later I came across a clean copy of *Equinox*. I had never heard of this novel by José. It had been published in 1935 when I was in the Far East but as I subscribed to *The Times Literary Supplement* it was surprising that it had slipped my notice. I picked it up for less than a song, intending to read it on the plane to New York. When I dipped into it I found that I could not stop reading. Although the story concerned a flight from Western civilization it was more engrossing than others I had read on that outworn theme. The prose was as magical as the landscape and the wild yet gentle people it described, people who spoke in a remote poetical language. Perhaps it was too well written to achieve popularity at a time when 'fine writing' is a term of disparagement. It had unity and profundity yet it appealed not only to the intellect but to all the senses combined. Of the many books that had won prizes and been recommended by literary guilds I could remember few which left so powerful an impression. I was impelled to send José a telegram: 'Belated congratulations on *Equinox*. It is a fine work of art.' He replied: 'Many thanks, but the Cornarina is finer.'

After the strenuous daily round in New York I found it hard to sleep at night. Beside my bed I kept a pile of soporific books which started me yawning sooner than sleeping pills. The hotel maid must have placed *Equinox* among them. I could not resist putting it to a more stringent test. Perhaps some extraneous factor —a matter of mood—had kindled my enthusiasm for it in Paris.

Once more I became so absorbed in its atmosphere that it was early morning before I dropped it to doze off.

Before leaving New York I was invited by Lenny Overton to one of his Lucullan banquets at the Waldorf Towers. Lenny was as cosmopolitan as his guests: even so I had not expected to sit next to the Countess d'Arpon. Having doffed her widow's weeds she looked ten years younger than when I had seen her in Paris.

'I have fallen in love with New York,' she told me. 'It was immediate, the *coup de foudre*. Everything here enchants me—a perpetual bubble bath! And not to be tempted by the *cuisine* is so good for one's figure. In Paris I was losing my outline. Here I can dance without feeling ridiculous and one encounters such fascinating types. Hormones in the air, and what fabulous views at night!'

'Have you heard from José?'

'His letters have become unbearable. He only thinks about the Cornarina. When we bought the place together I never dreamt it would monopolize him. Let's face it, the result is that poor José has become a bore, and he has long ceased to be an Adonis.'

'I have been enjoying his *Equinox*. I discovered it by chance.'

'I confess I could not get through it but I do not pretend to be literary. I loved José for his other qualities. It was great fun doing over the Cornarina together but he grew fonder of the place than of me.'

'I hope to see it one of these days.'

'*Cela vaut la peine*, but a lot remains to be done to it. José is restoring the frescoes himself. As he is not a painter he is spoiling them but I dare not tell him so. Let him enjoy himself while he can. He is not growing younger.'

'Unlike you, Comtesse.'

'That is entirely due to New York.'

I wished I could say the same of myself. By the time I returned to London I needed a good rest.

The Yorick Club was perhaps the most restful in London. Writers and actors of established reputation predominated over the other members who snoozed till tea-time in capacious arm-chairs after copious luncheons under portraits of their periwigged predecessors. Gervase Farnaby and Sylvester Meyer belonged to a slightly younger generation. Both were better known for their book reviews than for their experiments in fiction, which influenced their general outlook in different ways. Gervase pontificated with missionary zeal. 'Read this or be damned,' was the gist of his kinder notices. Sylvester dismissed most novels with biting contempt unless they were reprints of neglected minor classics. Any book served as a platform for ventilating his prejudices. While Gervase was always discovering new talent, sometimes where it did not exist, Sylvester would only praise a contemporary for some social reason, especially if the author owned a hospitable country house or a yacht.

I asked Gervase and Sylvester if they had heard of José. Gervase had a dim recollection of his fame at Cambridge. To Sylvester he was known as the proprietor of the Cornarina, one of the few Palladian mansions he yearned to visit though it was rumoured to be awfully uncomfortable. Neither of them had heard of *Equinox*. I assured them that it deserved to be exhumed, and who could do this more effectively than they?

Before long a new edition of *Equinox* was issued with glowing quotations from Gervase and Sylvester on the jacket. 'A master-singer of rare significance . . . thrilling suspense . . . anagogic poetry . . . an authentic and authoritative voice.' 'Like the Caliph of Fonthill the Signor of Cornarina has written his *Vathek* . . . a memorable tour de force.'

Edition followed edition and *Equinox* was translated into several languages. Ronny Peppercorn snapped up the film rights and it was widely discussed on television and radio programmes. An *Equinox Club* was founded in Texas, and it became a cult among college campuses.

José thanked me for this lucrative revival which he attributed to my friendly propaganda. His royalties would enable him to finish restoring the Cornarina. When would I pay him a visit long overdue? Apart from which he averred that the chorus of praise had left him indifferent, too many years having passed since the novel was written by a man who bore his name but who had ceased to exist outside the Cornarina.

I was pondering over this letter before catching a train for a week-end in the country. On the platform I ran into the Cranfields who proposed that we share a compartment. They too had been invited by Geraldine Portington. Pat Cranfield explained that he was Geraldine's architect as well as her nephew. He was to convert her stables into a Palladian garage and José had vetted his plan. I mentioned that I had seen his friend the Countess d'Arpon in New York.

'I hope she stays there,' said Cranfield. 'She has treated José abominably.'

He went on to describe how dilapidated the Cornarina had been before José had bought it with the Countess's co-operation. The columns and steps of the front portico were crumbling; the ground floor had been flooded and stagnant water was rotting the foundations; the ballroom had been turned into a barn by peasant squatters, and the frescoes attributed to Veronese were peeling off the walls. Yet this had been the precursor of stately Palladian buildings all over the world. Since it had fallen into such decay it had not been expensive. The expense came later.

In the first flush of acquisition the Countess had been lavish. She had ransacked the antique shops in Padua and Venice for elaborate period furniture while a squadron of masons was engaged to fortify the structure under José's supervision. Having steeped himself in Palladio's 'Treatise on Architecture', he saw to it that the original design was respected in every detail.

Prior to moving in with her lorry-load of Vuitton trunks the Countess recouped her share of the expenses by letting a film company use the place as a background for a historical drama. José protested in vain against such sacrilege.

'It will be good publicity in case we want to let it,' she told him. 'I don't mind spending money on furniture but I resent throwing it away on masons and carpenters.'

When the mess left by the cinema people had been cleared up

vast cupboards and marble-topped tables continued to arrive, stone statues for the garden and wooden figures of blackamoors for the drawing-room. Within a year the villa had recovered some of its pristine splendour. But when the Countess decided to sell her share to José she had all the furniture removed except a heavy Etruscan sarcophagus which was difficult to dispose of. The Cornarina was stripped to the bare bone but at least one could admire the purity of its proportions.

Cranfield's appreciation of José created a bond between us but their difference in age was so marked that I wondered how they had become friends. My hostess enlightened me. It was Cranfield's passion for Palladio in general and for the Cornarina in particular that had brought them together. 'Pat and Pam have a standing invitation to stay there whenever they like,' she told me.

'I don't often get the chance,' Pat said gloomily. 'Here I have to battle with town and county councillors who firmly believe that the functional ought to be bleak. Stainless steel and tinted glass, concrete with wooden shuttering, split levels, that's what they like.'

He was only twenty-five I gathered, and his first commission had been the Chinoiserie pagoda where we sat drinking tea. 'It's a heavenly bolt-hole,' said Geraldine. 'I hide here from unbidden guests—the Harpoon Countess for instance. She gate-crashed with two gigolo decorators who tried to nag me into selling them my malachite table. The cheek of it!'

'Well, you're safe from her now. She has settled in New York.'

'You mark my words, she'll turn up like a bad penny.'

After the prolonged fanfare of anticipation my first glimpse of the Cornarina was disappointing. It was certainly grand, but too grand for its position on the narrow canal. It required an avenue of trees to frame it to advantage. Without an adequate foreground or background its grandeur looked forlorn. Moreover an urban invasion was threatened on the other side of the canal where lorries, cranes and bulldozers were at work.

I had driven from Venice on a sultry morning. Seeing no sign of human occupation I climbed the massive steps feeling rather like a visitor to Heartbreak House, overawed by the vastness of the portico. Perhaps José had not received my express letter: he possessed no telephone.

The central hall was frescoed with deities who were feasting and frolicking on Olympus. The gaiety of the scene contrasted with the lack of sound. After the reverberations of the Grand Canal I had not been prepared for such silence. I walked through a series of empty rooms with lofty ceilings until I reached a pile of scaffolding. There, high on a ladder, José was restoring a faded fresco in grisaille. He was so immersed in his brushwork that I hesitated to interrupt him. Eventually I called out his name.

'Julian, how remiss of me! I'll join you instantly.' Descending a ladder, he explained: 'Since my recent heart attack I feel I must make full use of every second, and it isn't easy to bring these ghosts back to life. If you examine them closer you will see that they are doing strange things. Sometimes I fancy they illustrate my past. Certain details are in a better state of preservation than the rest. I'm toning those down to harmonize with them. Did you notice the frescoes in the Hall of Olympus? I doubt if Paul of Verona has surpassed them even at Maser. "Ceremony and splendour and an almost childlike naturalness of feeling"—how neatly Berenson summarized him!'

He led me from room to room, praising the subtlety of the proportions and proving by mathematical calculation that like Bach Palladio's invention seemed simple in spite of its extreme complexity and audacity. He had been so universally imitated that his originality was less apparent to the modern eye. José compared the Cornarina to a violin sonata, a vast composition subdivided into four movements, *Adagio*, *Fugue*, *Largo* and *Allegro assai*. The severe rhythm of the *Adagio*, like a solemn meditation, represented the façade; the Hall of Honour corresponded to the *Fugue* where all the elements were blended in perfect harmony. Details were subordinated to masses and masses to the whole: its beauty was organic. Palladio was a tireless student of organization. Here, more than elsewhere, he had mastered all its problems.

'I mustn't bore you,' he added. 'Denise complained that I was turning into a lecturer and I'm afraid it is true. So few people understand what they are looking at. One repeats oneself but I'm not afraid of repetition. Like *om mane padme om*, it can lead to illumination.'

He rang a bronze bell embossed with the Cornaro arms and a little girl toddled in with a tray of glasses and bottles. On closer inspection she was a middle-aged dwarf.

'Time for an apéritif. I have a Lilliputian couple to wait on me. Unfortunately I cannot persuade them to wear period costume like the dwarf in yonder fresco. Where is your luggage?'

'I haven't any. I must return to Venice tonight.'

'I was hoping you could stay. The Cornarina is supreme at night. Do change your mind. I have a spare toothbrush.'

'I'll have to think it over. It will mean breaking a dinner engagement at the Lido.'

'*Tant mieux*. The Lido's my idea of Purgatory. Denise used to drag me there till I had a brilliant inspiration. I had my chest and arms tattooed so that she didn't care to be seen with me on the beach.'

'Wasn't it rather drastic?'

'It amused me to become an artefact. The body may change but the tattoo has kept its brightness. To some people it is even a sexual attraction. And if I get murdered it will be easy to identify me. One never knows. Other murders have happened here.'

'Tell me about them.' I noticed that indelible mermaids were swimming up his bare arms.

'It is too early in the day.'

Cranfield rushed in and said: 'Pam begs you to come before the soufflé collapses.'

I apologized for causing the delay. 'The soufflé's already a casualty,' Pam grumbled. 'So much for good intentions. I had hoped José would make an effort to be punctual.'

'Sorry, I wasn't warned. I had ordered raw ham with melon.'

'I wanted to offer you a surprise. It's always ham and melon!'

'A simple Palladian dish. Why not leave the cooking to Giuseppina?'

Pam sniffed. 'She steeps everything in oil, and she can't resist garlic.'

'Neither can I. It is said to purify the blood.'

The table was laid under a chestnut tree near the guest house, a graceful pavilion behind the Cornarina.

'What has José given you to drink? Let me make you a dry Martini. I can see you really need one.'

'Too many double gins give the ladies double chins,' José murmured, handing me an olive. 'Believe me, Julian, my vermouth is much safer.'

Pam Cranfield was ruthless. 'Chuck that liquid glue into the canal,' she said, her breasts wobbling to the rhythm of the cocktail shaker.

José's eyes flashed with anger but he coolly remarked: 'Cocktails do not suit the Cornarina.'

'Perhaps I don't suit it,' Pam retorted. 'You can get drunk on Palladio. I prefer a good cocktail.'

'Anyhow Pat is a great compensation. Palladio would be delighted with him.'

Between Pam and José there was an undertone of bickering throughout the meal. 'Another sleepless night?' he asked her.

'Your tablets were no good. The howling started again as soon as I dropped off.'

'It must have been the owls. They can be horribly human.'

Giuseppina staggered round the table under platters of *tortellini*, followed by grilled chicken with stewed peppers and purple figs with cream. José's paunch was easily accounted for. By the time coffee was served I was drowsily replete but José was still eager to show me the premises and I had to play up.

After another hour I began to wilt, so that I failed to assimilate half his information. He made the Cornarina seem a lesser Versailles where the Cornaro dynasty had held extravagant court, their guests arriving from Venice on the family houseboat, each dame accompanied by her *cicisbeo*. Before those recognized gallants had come into fashion a lady of the family had been caught by her husband *in flagrante* with his favourite singer. Enraged by the seduction of his protégé, he had imprisoned her in an attic with a baboon which had bitten her to death. 'Pam fancies that she can hear her screams and I encourage the illusion when she's tiresome.'

'She seemed a bit unstrung.'

'I wish she'd migrate to the Lido. Here she's rather a fly in my ointment. Since my days are numbered I need Pat's collaboration more than ever.'

'All our days are numbered, José. Why give it a thought?'

'You needn't but I've been warned by the doctors. That's why I'm so anxious to finish my work. And that's why Denise left me.'

'No doctor is infallible.'

'I pin my faith to Palladio. He keeps me going. Perfection of proportion and purity of detail. Excuse me a moment. I must give myself an injection.'

At a trestle table in the gallery I found Pat Cranfield. He was reproducing Palladio's design for the Cornarina which had suffered from exposure to the damp. 'I'm enlarging it so that the steps on each side of the portico can be seen more clearly than in Leoni's edition,' he explained. 'His measurements differ from mine, or rather from Palladio's. One keeps on discovering variations. I don't think Scamozzi had anything to do with it as Bertotti suggested, much to José's annoyance.'

'José seems worried about his health. Is there any real cause for anxiety?'

'He has been a hypochondriac since I've known him. The Countess didn't improve things by hinting he had cancer. She sent him to a Balkan quack who gave him pills, and to a smart Parisian who prescribed injections. But he has such stamina that I can't believe there's much the matter with him.'

Giuseppina, flustered and gibbering, announced the arrival of a busload of visitors, all members of an architectural association, and José reappeared to act as their cicerone. His patience in answering their questions was inexhaustible. He pointed out that

Palladio was not a slave to his own rules regarding the proportion of classical columns and their entablatures and went on to remind them that the Master had begun his career as a sculptor.

'How useful if all architects had experience of sculpture, and saw buildings as extensions of the human form,' he remarked.

The human forms he was addressing were not classical specimens. Sloping shoulders, protuberant bellies, flopping breasts, ill concealed by clothes that were chosen for comfort rather than elegance, one could see why they were translated into cubic shapes by modern artists. They contrasted none too favourably with the frescoes on the walls. Had Veronese idealized his models? Some members of the party took notes, others took snapshots. One little man bounced forward and declared in a squeaky voice: 'I'm sure these frescoes were never painted by Veronese.'

'I beg your pardon,' said José. 'Having studied his work for years I think I ought to know. Besides, I have documentary evidence.'

'Fiddlesticks. The quality's lacking, the individual touch. These are paltry pastiches. You can't hoodwink me!'

'And who are you, sir?'

'I'm the lecturer on art history at Westmacombe University. Here's my card.'

'For documentary evidence? Had you told me you lectured on economics I should have been less amazed.'

The little man snorted: 'Even third-rate frescoes should be handled carefully and these have been botched.'

'So you don't believe in restoration?'

'Only by a skilled practitioner. I could give you the names of several but the mischief has been done. Come along, ladies and gentlemen, the highlights are still ahead of us.'

'Don't let me detain you,' said José, tearing up his printed card.

As soon as they departed another group arrived. This consisted of the technicians of a television company. José tolerated the invasion for the Cornarina's sake. He wished all the world to admire if not to share his true love, but evidently it cost him an effort. He led them from the kitchens in the basement to the granaries under the roof.

'Is this a sample of your daily life?' I asked him.

He smiled. 'I like to think it may give these people a sense of eternal values.'

'What an altruist! When do you ever find time to write?'

'I sleep very little, and my writing is merely factual.' A hooting of horns was followed by a fresh incursion. A party of Pamela's friends wished to drag her off to the Lido. Though Pat and I were urged to join them we excused ourselves for José's sake.

While Pam was present she had struck me as a discord, but when she left us I realized that she had contributed a note of reality to an atmosphere vaguely unreal. Pat and José were like temple priests performing a ritual of adoration. New worlds might be born and shattered but they would continue to worship at the shrine. Pam was too young and too modern to participate.

'Palladio is pickling my husband,' she had complained. 'It's all very well for José: he's pickled already. But Pat's still under thirty and I don't approve.'

I fancied she was exaggerating, but when Pat was alone with José I could see what she meant. He resembled a mediaeval monk bent over his drawing-board. José sat beside him scribbling in a notebook with an abstracted expression. As for me, I felt like a coarse intruder in a cloister. Suddenly José rose and exclaimed: 'Time for another injection. Just when one is about to be united with the Master a clock strikes "Not yet!" I've been trying to formulate my conclusions but the words refuse to obey me. Spanish, French, English, each language used to supplement the other. Now they confuse me. I have also been perturbed by a cable from Denise. She wants me to send her Etruscan sarcophagus to New York.'

'You'd have to obtain an export licence. That will take some time. I should procrastinate till she forgets about it.'

'When her mind is set on a thing Denise can be very persistent. I suppose she intends to sell it to a museum.'

'Tell her to apply to the Fine Arts people in Rome. They'll keep her waiting.'

'Pat advises me to disregard it. After all these years she might have let me keep it for my burial.'

Twilight was gathering and the frescoes on the walls assumed a new life. The gods and goddesses took command of the hall we sat in which seemed to expand in the glow of candles lighted by the dwarf. José became another person, as the saying goes: the outside world had ceased to concern him. His talk floated back to Palladio and Paul of Verona: almost he seemed to melt into the walls and soar towards the ceilings as if he were disembodied, a ghost of the long-dead architect, while we listened to footsteps echoing in the distance and the hooting of an owl. I decided to leave, but something detained me as if I were drugged. I had lost count of time when another visitor was announced by the gibbering dwarf: a journalist who was to interview José for a radio programme. José stirred from his meditations and said: 'Forgive me, I had forgotten this appointment. Anyhow the man is so late I can hardly be blamed. Please don't leave me to his tender mercies.'

The interviewer stalked in with a mechanician and a recording machine. 'Sam Simmons,' he introduced himself. 'And this is my colleague Bert Fuller. Better late than never. There was a bomb scare on the plane and we were held up at Malpensa. I tried to ring up but it appears you're not connected. Why's that?'

'If you look around you'll understand. There are pleasanter methods of communication.'

'I don't get you,' said Sam Simmons. 'I couldn't live without a telephone.'

'How tragic!' José sighed. 'My heart bleeds for you.'

'It needn't. I'm in clover. I've interviewed scores of celebrities dead and alive.'

'You have actually conversed with the dead?'

'Dead now—since I interviewed them.'

'That sounds ominous. As I'm no celebrity I hope to survive

the ordeal. May I ask why I have been selected for this dubious honour?'

'Who is being interviewed, you or me? Fact is the public happens to be interested in originals. Not one in a million lives like you in a famous Palladian mansion. Speaking for the general public, we want to know what it does to you, how you react, the why and the wherefore you chose to settle in such a spot. But before we get down to it, Bert and I have a thirst on after our drive from Milan. Might we trouble you for a drink?'

José sent for some *grappa* which they gulped, little suspecting how fiery it would become inside them. They gagged and gasped for water. But they replenished their glasses when José proposed that they should see the house before the interview. 'It is so much the best part of me that I often wonder if I exist outside it.'

'Okay, but make it snappy. Drink up Bert, this may give us a new angle.'

José preceded them from room to room with Giuseppina carrying a lighted candle. Their footsteps echoed through the empty rooms which appeared much larger than in the daytime. Again José expatiated on Palladio's aims and achievements, as illustrated by the example before their eyes. Simmons muttered to me: 'I wouldn't exchange my flat in Highgate for this barrack. I like my comforts and here there isn't a decent armchair. It doesn't look lived in. Granted the size is arresting, but what does it add up to? Well, our host has the gift of the gab, and that's an advantage. Having come all this way we must have something to show for it.'

'I call it spooky,' said Bert.

'It swarms with ghosts,' said José, 'historic spectres from the Venetian past.'

'Well, we must get back into the present. Let's start recording now. Are you ready for my questions?'

'Fire away,' said José wearily.

The face of Simmons was transformed as if he had put on the

mask of an inquisitor. His voice became rasping and truculent. 'Supposing this recording machine were a bomb to blow this place up, what would you do? It is bound to occur eventually, don't you agree? Sooner or later we'll all be blown to smithereens. The atomic bomb is with us to stay, and I reckon it makes us live more intensely. Do *you* live more intensely? Do you honestly consider that you are leading a full, useful and well-balanced life?'

'Since I have shown you the Cornarina I consider your question inept. As architecture nothing could be better balanced. And I feel it has been and will be useful—not only to the specialist. Restoring it has been the climax of my life.'

'In other words you're an escapist from the world other people live in.'

'Do the prisoners in modern concentration camps, the slaves who chop down trees for twelve hours a day, starving and half naked in a temperature of fifty degrees below zero—do they lead full, useful and well-balanced lives?'

'Some people think they do. Anyhow they're a minority.'

'So am I.'

'You refuse to recognize the central trauma of our time, the imminent prospect of universal rubble. But you must admit that your unconscious mind has been influenced willy-nilly. It's fairly obvious that you're trying to hide from the bomb. Take it from me it's not a bit of use. The bomb is everywhere, like God.'

'Like the devil, you mean.'

'Perhaps that's more apt. It amounts to the same thing.'

'Evidently we speak a different language. To me God is perfect beauty, the supreme architect, though I cannot pretend that my knowledge of Him is other than indirect. The bravest of us experience His presence by contemplation. St. John of the Cross did this, and his words are charged with supernatural sense.'

'Supernatural nonsense,' snapped Simmons. 'Bow wow wow. This is getting us nowhere.'

Turning to Bert Fuller, José inquired: 'Does the animal bite? I'm terrified of rabies.'

José's face was so white and drawn, his breathing so stertorous, that I urge Cranfield to fetch a doctor. In the meantime I made signs to Simmons to stop the interview, attempting to explain by dumb show that José was ailing, but Simmons callously persisted: 'Carry on, Bert. The public will enjoy the sparks. I've several more questions to wind up with. I suggest that Palladio, or your romantic idea of him, has blinded you to the creative architecture of our age, to the more significant achievements of Le Corbusier and Mies van der Rohe. I suggest that you are following a phantom that leads to nowhere and nothing. Doesn't it all boil down to the fact that you're a cowardly escapist?'

'Only in so far as I want to escape from you,' said José with a groan.

Sam Simmons laughed a stage villain's laugh. 'You might as well try to dodge your destiny. I stick to my guns and I've killed off most of the people I've interviewed. You're doomed like the rest of them. Now tell us about your hobbies while the going's good.'

Fiend or fool, the man gabbled on without noticing that José had fallen back in his chair, unconscious.

'Gosh, he has already collapsed,' he remarked complacently when Cranfield arrived with the doctor. 'Bert and I had better be off. We've an interview in Venice before that collapses too.'

According to the doctor José was merely suffering from nervous exhaustion. His pulse was *pianissimo*. Apart from his labours at the villa he had been seeing too many people—bloodsuckers. He recovered consciousness after an injection. 'Have the brutes gone?' he asked. 'It is useful to have a weak heart on these occasions, but I'm not ready for the Etruscan sarcophagus. By the way, Denise . . .'

'Forget her. The latest is that she has fallen in love with a hippie in San Francisco,' said Pat Cranfield.

'Peace, rural peace,' José murmured with a smile.

I thought of the cranes, lorries, bulldozers and petrol pumps across the canal. Fortunately José was oblivious of them. He wanted to join us for dinner but the doctor persuaded him to lie down.

THE MACHINE IS BROKEN DOWN

SIR OSBERT SITWELL was a brilliant painter in words and one of his earliest portraits is that of Hugh Dearborn in *The machine breaks down* (1924), but the portrait, fine as far as it goes, remains incomplete, for it ends with a nervous breakdown. Hugh is left jabbering to himself till three o'clock in the morning, pleading in vain with his fickle Muse to return to him. Evidently he had recovered when I met him several years later. A little more wrinkled perhaps, the Edwardian dandy was as immaculate as ever, and though he was never visible before five in the afternoon, his vitality was unimpaired. He was to be seen in the most unexpected places, and before he was seen his voice could be heard, rising rather than falling.

Already in the eighteen-nineties Hugh Dearborn had achieved fame as an artist of the spoken word. So polished were his periods, so dramatic his timing in the development of an anecdote, without any hesitation except to heighten suspense, that he could have been mistaken for an eminent novelist or actor, but he had no ambition to shine in any field outside his own.

While he was drawn to the writers who envied his verbal dexterity he confessed that he seldom dawdled over a book. This was odd considering the literary flavour of his language. He was proud of his friendship with Proust but he could not read him. 'Such interminable sentences!' he complained, forgetting his own prolixity. His first edition of *Du côté de chez Swann*, with a flamboyant inscription from the author on the title-page, was still uncut. The only novel he admired unreservedly was *Mademoiselle de Maupin*. 'I know it by heart,' he said. 'It is absolutely me.' A delicate drawing of the heroine by Beardsley hung beside his eighteenth-century bed. In accent and tone his French was as faultless as his sartorial style. This influenced his gestures and mannerisms: in spite of his name and antecedents he never seemed quite English.

The fact that he had known Proust and the original of Albertine was sufficient to interest me; he had also known Whistler and Wilde and the luminaries of *The Yellow Book*, and he would embark on vivid anecdotes about them, mimicking their idiosyncrasies, if offered the slightest encouragement. Since his last breakdown, however, he had brought his stories up to date: the *Boeuf sur le Toit* and its patron Moÿses, Cocteau, the Paris Six, the Fratellini brothers and Count Etienne de Beaumont replaced the old Café Royal and its ghostly clients. Albeit he struggled and strained to be contemporary, introducing the latest slang into his speech, which sounded curiously exotic on his lips, his whole manner was too ornate for the nineteen-twenties. I doubt if anything like his talk can be heard in England today. Its nearest equivalent would be the dialogue of Henry James in *The Finer Grain*. In the ambience of the so-called Bright Young People it sounded prehistoric, yet he was a familiar figure at their favourite haunts, where he was treated as a sort of lucky mascot.

Hugh's fame had revived with the success of *The Green Hat* in which he figured as a minor character. Michael Arlen was a far cry from Marcel Proust, and I wondered if Hugh was aware of the gulf between them since he said he considered Michael Arlen more readable. Perhaps he put all the writers and painters he knew in the same class with the boxers and tennis champions he cultivated with equal assiduity. Sometimes I fancied he was more enthusiastic about the latter. His apparently fragile physique, with the snuff-box-like finish described by Osbert Sitwell, was eminently aristocratic, but he was democratic in his sexual tastes —to such a degree that he had been dropped by the more exclusive London hostesses. Though social tolerance had increased in the Waste Land period between the wars, society was still far from 'permissive', and Hugh Dearborn had been noticed once too often in company that contrasted too stridently with his sophisticated self. Never mind how sparkling his conversation such questionable associations might lead to scandal. In fact his few intimate friends were opulent married women, preferably with a purple past. He was indifferent to men save as casual exponents of virility or as attentive members of his audience. The Bright Young People were entertained by his panache and vitality, which most of them lacked. He introduced a note of period distinction to their cocktail parties; like them he was always ready for a lark and he certainly had more to say. Agatha Runcible and her set were listless and monosyllabic.

Already the art of conversation, like that of writing letters, was obsolescent. Few had patience with the former or time for the latter, which had almost been supplanted by the telephone. The staccato darts of Noël Coward or the falsetto pipings of Bloomsbury had silenced the performances of the professional raconteur with one or two exceptions like Hugh Dearborn whose sing-song voice soared above the snatches of dialogue at crowded cocktail parties and night-clubs. It was modish for the young to seem bored even when they were enjoying themselves and Hugh stood out among the throng of bored faces on account of his patent zest. He stayed on to the end of every party, the last to leave, still talking away, uncrumpled and eager-eyed. As if he dreaded being snuffed out like a candle, he prolonged any departure with another of his sprightly anecdotes, a comment on some ludicrous episode that had passed unnoticed by less observant eyes. In common with the very young this septuagenarian seemed to live for parties, and these had become much of a muchness, whether in fancy dress or traditional costume, until Florence Mills and the Blackbirds took London by storm.

Not all the coloured boys and girls who were suddenly lionized belonged to that popular troupe: many sang and danced in vaudeville shows and night-clubs. After the diluted jazz of the Savoy Orpheans and other genteel dance bands, they imported the riotous rhythms of the American deep south with more than a hint of African jungle origins. Never had the saxophone risen to such paroxysms of passion. Frenzied couples kicked out their legs to the strains of the Charleston, hugged each other hectically to the Blues, wobbled and jerked their anatomies to the Black Bottom; the foxtrot was transformed. And always where the couples were thickest on the floor Hugh Dearborn was footing it like a mechanical marionette in frantic competition. Whenever he passed the orchestra he would wave to a different musician or lean over to ask for the Mississippi Blues and invite him home for a drink. He had a waggish word of greeting for each as he twirled or side-stepped closer to the drummer, drawn like an intoxicated moth towards so many black flames. One of them riposted: 'Hello Josephine!' For this was the heyday of 'la Bakère', flopping her bananas like cowtails in fly-time as Taylor Gordon said.

Night after night Hugh haunted the Café de Paris where the Snowballs were the principal attraction. The dynamism of these musicians, coloured rather than black since their complexions were as various as a tulip-bed, heated his cooling blood even more than the Strauss waltzes of his prime. Round and round he spun till his partner was limp and dizzy, only slowing down when he approached the band. He achieved this amazing feat of endurance entirely under his own steam. Unlike the others, all so much younger than himself, he consumed little alcohol. An occasional sip of champagne when he was thirsty sufficed to refuel his system. Between one dance and the next he never stopped chattering.

'Why do people invite that raddled piece of antiquity? He gives me the creeps,' said Percy Beamish, who looked older than his twenty-five years in spite of his make-up.

'I think he's rather divine,' said Agatha. 'I mean without him this wouldn't be nearly such fun.'

'Death and the Maiden,' said Percy. 'Too macabre.' Percy had been running after the Snowballs ever since their engagement by the Café de Paris: he knew all their names and nicknames and entertained them frequently in his Mayfair flat. Consequently he assumed proprietary airs towards them. Like most of his friends he was free from racial prejudice but he tended to exaggerate his penchant for Negroes, as they were then called. Often he was the only white person in their midst and he was as proud of this distinction as if he had been admitted to some esoteric club. His was a form of inverted snobbery though Freud might have offered a different explanation. Needless to say he collected African art: his flat was full of carved phallic gods and pregnant goddesses, totems of ancestors, initiation masks, fertility charms, spears, war-drums, and Congo ivories. The Snowballs, who considered themselves citizens of the United States, were puzzled rather than appreciative of these archetypal images and curios, which in their hearts they thought ugly and barbaric. They had never heard of Waregga warriors or the great Bushongo represented in Percy's collection, and they were incredulous when Percy mentioned the high prices he had paid for these objects which nothing would have induced them to buy. They felt as little at ease among them as if they had been in the African bush. However, they voted Percy a real nice guy, a bit screwy but generous with his liquor.

Hugh Dearborn's flat made a cosier impression on the Snowballs, with its comfortable sofas and prevailing pinkness, apart from the eighteenth-century engravings of saturnalia on the walls. Hugh's cocktail party in their honour was a greater success than Percy's. With Hugh there was no nonsense about being African. Percy constantly exhorted them to 'be African' and remember their distant ancestors. The only ancestors they could remember had been slaves or domestic servants and those they would sooner forget. Hugh's stories exerted the fascination of a well-acted monologue in some foreign language, accompanied by gestures and grimaces which made them split their sides on top of the Martinis they had swallowed. And they were vastly diverted by his engravings illustrating *The Decameron* (since Hugh Dearborn was not a collector of books), so much livelier in their elegant eroticism than Percy's crude figures with erections from the Congo.

When Dapper Dan the Drummer described what a swell party

Hugh had given, Percy was doubly annoyed since he had not been invited. Dapper Dan was Percy's favourite, a six-footer of dark mahogany with the face of a primitive cult mask and a happy rolling stride. He called him his Black Prince. Mixing his drinks as promiscuously as he mixed his friends, Percy expressed his resentment and jealousy of Hugh by butting into him on the dance floor of the Café de Paris, and as Hugh paid no attention he kicked his shins. With a groan Hugh limped towards him and said: 'Little leprechaun, go back to the woods where you belong!' Percy was spoiling for a fight, but others stepped in to restrain him while Hugh stood glaring defiantly: 'Back to the woods, little fairy!' The scene shocked those who had remnants of respect for old age. Poor Hugh looked white and haggard, but he tried to laugh it off. 'It's really complimentary to an old buffer like me, as if I could compete with such a bright young thing! Which makes me wonder how the adjective "bright" became attached to such specimens. *Au fond* they're pretty dreary: they don't know what to do with themselves. . . .'

Aware that he had been compromised by this public outburst, Percy bore Hugh a grudge, and as they were equally ubiquitous they could not help meeting. Percy kept his eye on Dapper Dan as he beat his drum like a Waregga warrior. 'How gorgeously African!' he murmured to Agatha.

'All niggers look alike to me,' she replied.

'A true case of colour blindness,' he remarked. 'I wish I could add his statue to my collection. It would be my masterpiece.'

'How you do carry on. You're getting like Hugh Dearborn.'

'Don't libel me, duckie.'

At that moment Percy noticed Hugh confabulating with Dapper Dan and his anger against him returned. He was already vexed that Dan had a date, as he told him, after the show. When he discovered that the date was with Hugh he was rabid. That anyone should prefer a creature who had reached the biblical quota to his glamorous self, still under thirty, was deeply humiliating.

'What on earth do you see in that decrepit dowager?' he asked Dan.

'I get a kick out of his conversation. He talks so refined and he makes me feel at home in little old Europe. Gave us fellers the grandest time in his old-world parlour last Sunday with champagne from glass slippers.'

'Well, if you want to give *him* a good time just beat him up. That's what he's after, the drooling old masochist.'

Dan's eyes grew larger. 'What's that?'

'A freak who loves a licking.'

'You don't mean to say!'

'Why not chuck him and come over to my place. I can promise you more amusement.'

'I'm strictly moral about keeping a date,' said Dan with a twisted smile.

'Join me for a drink beforehand. You'll need it,' said Percy.

Dan was half lit up with double gin fizzes when Hugh took him round to his flat. Hugh told him his naughtiest stories and he laughed uproariously. But Dan's mood changed abruptly after the next drink and his expression became truculent. 'Percy gave me the inside dope on you, you old faggot. So you want a licking? I'll make you holler. I'll give you the licking of your life.'

'Percy's a practical joker. He was pulling your leg, Dannie dear.'

'Bull. I ain't your dear. A peckerwood like Percy would never dare pull the leg of a sweetback like me. He sure was telling me the truth. Here, gimme another drink before I crack your skull.'

Hugh kept his composure, but he was alarmed. 'Come, come, what's the matter? You're not yourself, Dannie. Something must have upset you. You couldn't take Percy seriously, especially when he's blotto. Sit down and make yourself comfortable.'

Having poured himself another stiff gin the black man towered over him with clenched fists and bloodshot eyes. While Hugh tried to calm him down he could not help admiring the fierce animal intensity of his posture. What a model for a Michel-angelo! he thought. 'Sit down,' he entreated. 'What has got into you?'

'Be careful. I know what you're thinking,' said Dan. 'I'm just a low nigger to you. Yeah, you're feelin' so white and superior and you want me to give you a thrill.'

'Don't be absurd. I would never have invited you and your mates here if I had any racial prejudice. On the contrary, I think you're magnificent.'

'You can't kid Dapper Dan. Your folks kept mine in chains. We're just a pack of ignorant slaves to do your scrub-work. You'd like to run us back to Africa, I guess.'

'This is most unfair,' Hugh protested.

'Where's the victrola? Put on a hot ragtime number and make it snappy.' Hugh meekly obeyed. 'Now dance for me. I want to see a belly-dance like in the Oscar Wilde opera you described. Salome stuff.'

'I've danced enough tonight. Do you realize it is nearly four a.m.?'

'Well, you must start again in my honour. One, two, three, hop. No foolin', shake those shanks! Maybe it would be funnier in your birthday suit. Remove your garments.'

Fear and fatigue had numbed Hugh's spirit and dried up his power of speech. Mumbling and grumbling, he flopped down on the cushioned divan. 'I'm tired I tell you. It's too late. Time for you to be going. You've had enough to drink.'

'I'll stay right here till I've had more. I'm mighty thirsty.'

Dan unfastened his belt and began to lay about him. 'Keep dancing sister, or I'll make you bleed like a stuck hog!' Hugh's cries for mercy excited him to greater violence. The gramophone drowned Dan's whacks and Hugh's weak groans. 'I hate all white skins,' the black man growled. 'Say, who's the slave now?' With maniacal ferocity he belaboured Hugh with his thick leather belt. 'Go down on your hands and knees and crawl before me with your tongue out. I haven't done with you yet. . . .'

When Mrs. Duffy the charlady called later in the morning she found Hugh senseless on the Aubusson carpet. His clothes were torn and bespattered with blood; his face was barely recognizable, so bruised and swollen, his nose and mouth cut up and clotted. But he was still breathing. Horrified, Mrs. Duffy sent for an ambulance and Hugh was taken to hospital. As he was also badly concussed it took him a whole month to recover. He pretended he had been in a motor crash, so swift and so sudden that he was vague about the details.

Percy heard from Dapper Dan what had really happened: 'I carried out your suggestion, beat the hell out of him.'

'Jolly good show,' said Percy with a malevolent leer. But Dan was secretly ashamed of his behaviour and he blamed Percy for getting him all drunked up. Surely the devil had got into him and Percy was his agent. He avoided him in future.

Hugh's hospitality was missed by the other Snowballs. Agatha Runcible traced him to his nursing-home and sent him flowers. But he was unwilling to receive any of his bright young friends until he was more presentable. He wore dark spectacles to hide his swollen eyelids and half his face was swathed in bandages; his speech came muffled through his broken teeth. His good charlady asked if there was anything he needed in particular, any special food he fancied. (Hugh never ate much: he ate even less since his 'motor accident'. As Mrs. Duffy was wont to describe him, he was 'nothing but skin and bone'.)

'No thank you, dear, I've got to keep my figure,' he replied. 'But be an angel and bring me the book from beside my bed. There's only one.'

'The Bible?'

'My Bible. It has a French name: *Mademoiselle de Maupin*. And if you meet Father Maloney, please ask him to pay me a visit. It's high time I confessed my sins.'

'Bless you, sir, you're more sinned against than sinning I'll be bound.'

Mrs. Duffy had brought him a bunch of violets which had set him dreaming of his youth. How many voices speaking from the past! He spent hours focusing their blurred faces. A drop of

Guerlain on his handkerchief evoked the Paris he had known before 1914 when pleasure had been taken seriously and he had decided that his mission in life was to charm and amuse. With only a modest income he had enjoyed half a century of social triumphs entirely on the strength of his talk. On a limited scale he had savoured the supreme satisfaction that statesmen and kings and queens of the stage derived from a vaster audience, but while the speeches of statesmen are prepared and actors interpret the words of other men Hugh had improvised and extemporized on the spur of the moment, imposing a hush on formal receptions, causing ripples of laughter to spread like a wave and swell to a roar of applause.

International society had been more compact and selective in his youth and Hugh had gravitated towards it wherever it forgathered. From Deauville to Biarritz, from Baden-Baden to Homburg, from royal courts to the boudoirs of courtesans, he had woven his narrative spells. Sem had caricatured him in a white hat swinging his binoculars at Longchamps; Jacques-Emile Blanche had painted him in a characteristic pose, little finger raised to emphasize one of his witticisms; and the divine Sarah had christened him Ariel. Yes, he had been fêted by the famous, but everything had changed since 1914. That had been the end of the Second Empire and of the *douceur de vivre* when to give pleasure had been his superlative duty. Hugh had survived the holocaust, determined to keep abreast of rougher times, but the technique he had perfected by unremitting practice and the vibrating accents and modulations of his vocal instrument, were wasted on those he was anxious to beguile. Sarah Bernhardt, Réjane, the Guitrys, Boni de Castellane's party in the Bois de Boulogne lit up by eighty thousand Venetian lanterns, the tunes of Offenbach, the four-wheelers and whiffs of the stable on Parisian boulevards: he saw and heard these again in spasmodic flashbacks behind his dark spectacles.

Shifting between and dominating all other memories was the image of Dapper Dan, and Hugh shuddered voluptuously at the sculptural grace of that massive body running wild in his quiet flat. He could not banish that powerful image, and the ache of his bones and bruises of his flesh gave him a sensation akin to bliss when he linked them with that glittering black angel. He had been made to suffer for his love of beauty.

Though it was not an experience to repeat or a story to add to his repertoire he dwelt fondly on the physical details and sublimated them in his imagination. Surely he must have been loved to excite such violence.

Father Maloney was appalled by his confession. 'You have been cruelly punished,' he said. 'It must have been a nightmare. Take it as a terrible warning.'

'No, father, it was absolute ecstasy. I never felt nearer to Heaven. I felt disembodied, etherealized, floating on air like the saints.'

After all the confessions he had heard in his austere life Father Maloney had become very tolerant. There were many ways to Heaven, he reflected, but this was indeed the strangest.

'*Si vieillesse pouvait!*' Hugh murmured plaintively, 'I'd go through it all over again.'

In the street outside the nursing-home a tired hurdy-gurdy ground out the music of 'Bye-bye Blackbird', missing a note now and then. The tune was poignantly sad in the gathering dusk. To Hugh Dearborn it sounded prophetic.

HIS SERENE HIGHNESS

THE vicinity of Rome abounds in glorious villas designed by great architects for bygone cardinals and papal nephews, and La Trappola is not the least famous of these with its sunken flower-garden surrounded by groves of umbrella-pine. Perhaps because it had always been lived in, La Trappola retained an intimate charm which its more grandiose neighbours lacked. This was chiefly due to its last owner Prince Aleco of Transylvania, who had inherited it from a maternal aunt, the Grand Duchess of Swabia, soon after his enforced exile.

The Grand Duchess had been more interested in her para-mours than her property and had allowed it to run down in partial if picturesque decay. The statues about its ochre façade were mantled in moss and many had lost a limb. The clogged fountains were silent and the fishponds were coated in stagnant slime; the rococo aviary was empty. Indoors the tapestries were in sad need of repair; the frayed carpets seemed to have been nibbled by mice; and the elaborately framed looking-glasses were stained and mottled—some said because the Grand Duchess dreaded the sight of her own reflection since her hour-glass figure had collapsed in rolls of flesh. This lamentable neglect had not been caused by lack of funds, for she bequeathed a large fortune with the property.

A man of scholarly instincts and fastidious taste, Prince Aleco proceeded to restore La Trappola to its pristine splendour. Several years were devoted to refurnishing its interior room by room, making a clean sweep of the mechanical toys and gewgaws dear to the Grand Duchess and replacing them with the Renaissance furniture, paintings and sculpture which his aunt had banished to dusty attics and damp cellars. Every other day he retrieved a precious relic of antiquity from some unexpected corner: Etruscan vases and cinerary urns were found in the straw of long-abandoned stables. La Trappola soon became a living museum pervaded with the personality of its owner, and a charm distilled from several civilizations.

In spite of his sciatica Prince Aleco would welcome guests at the top of a wide double staircase and lead them through a pillared gallery to the frescoed drawing-room after introducing them to his favourite view of the terraces espaliered with lemons. Everything seemed to blossom in his presence. The central loggia was a-flutter with cooing doves and scented with jasmine.

An imposing butler hovered in proximity. It was obvious that he took pride in his position: he bowed like a courtier, marched with measured tread, and articulated the words 'Serene Highness' with operatic relish. To visitors his manner was suave but faintly condescending. During meals he watched the Prince's every move, ready to replenish his wine glass with a twirl of the crusted bottle, for His Highness had also inherited a venerable cellar.

An insatiable collector, Prince Aleco never relaxed from his pursuit of finer treasures for La Trappola. This brought him in contact with other collectors, above all with his old Oxford crony Vincent Webb, who had settled in Rome after retiring from the diplomatic service. Together they spent many stimulating hours in antique shops and at auctions. The hunt kept both of them young: having had a surfeit of politics and social agitation they cared less for people than for works of art. They formed an incongruous pair in the Via del Babuino, Prince Aleco lean and dark, Vincent Webb tubby and rosy trotting beside him, peering into the shop windows and discussing which to enter. 'Nannucci never had anything for me,' the Prince complained, 'his emporium is swamped in art nouveau nonsense of the type I've had to discard. But I've noticed two Empire candle-sticks that might appeal to you.'

Vincent specialized in the Napoleonic period: eagles, pyramids and sphinxes vied with each other in the neo-classical rooms of his small palace near the Pantheon. Prince Aleco used to laugh at his preference of Canova to Michelangelo, and as their tastes differed so widely one or the other seldom returned empty-handed from their expeditions. Vincent's was the more easy to satisfy. He would puzzle an antique dealer by announcing: 'I have come to you to be rejuvenated. What is your tonic for today?'

Whereas Vincent was a bachelor Prince Aleco had three lusty sons, none of whom appreciated La Trappola and its rare contents. On their brief dutiful visits they regarded it as a dismal yet extravagant backwater. Fortunately Princess Ingrid, his wife, was fond of gardening and galloping in what remained of the Roman Campagna but she was unsympathetic to her husband's acquisitive mania. When the Prince had finished restoring his domain he was shocked to discover his children's aversion and ill-concealed resentment. Everybody else raved about the wonder of his achievement, the poetical perfection of its situation within easy distance of the Eternal City, but his sons only hankered after London, Paris and New York. When he had lavished such loving care on the place they grumbled about its material cost, little realizing that he had tripled its value even from that point of view. 'Why, instead of a new Mercedes he had bought a bulky old Bernini.'

Depressed and crippled by bouts of sciatica, Prince Aleco decided to sell La Trappola and most of its contents. Too late he regretted this decision, for although the estate was sold for a staggering sum and the auction of its furniture far exceeded the sanguine expectations of all concerned he was obliged to seek another home and he would never find one so beautiful. It was a second exile, from the serene security of his wrought-iron gates to the nerve-racking din of the future, from a sense of eternity to a realization of the ephemeral. Considering his seventy years of age he felt he had lost more than he had gained. His children of course were delighted: they invested in speedier motor cars on the strength of the sale. Vincent suggested that he move to Rome, but Rome was too poignantly near his beloved Trappola, now threatened with 'development' by an international hotel company.

Eventually Prince Aleco moved to Cannes. Not the least of his vexations was having to part with his loyal retainers, beginning with Cesare his majordomo, who had served him devotedly for twenty years.

Before leaving he strongly advised Vincent to engage this paragon of butlers who in spite of all his inducements refused to leave Italy.

'I fear he's too grand for me,' said Vincent. 'Besides, he will certainly want to rejoin you as soon as you get settled.'

'No hope, he's mulishly stubborn. Let me arrange it. I'm pretty sure you would suit him.'

'But would he suit me, sir?'

'You are always complaining that your servants break things. With Cesare nothing will be broken. I recommend him as the last of a dying species.'

Though he had been pensioned off with princely munificence Cesare was reluctant to retire into private life and the prospect of employment by a quiet bachelor did not displease him. It was a pity the bachelor lacked a title but he seemed to have patrician connections. He had seen him often at La Trappola and Prince Aleco's recommendation was sufficient. Vincent could barely afford to pay so high a wage but the Prince persuaded him that this would be a solid form of insurance.

Since he had been in control of La Trappola during the hurly-burly of the sale (described in the Press as 'the sale of the century') Cesare required a month's rest from his exertions. After an inspection of Vincent's palace he was outspoken in condemnation of the servants' quarters. These might be modernized but not enlarged, so he demanded as a *sine qua non* one of the guests' bedrooms and a bathroom for himself. Among other conditions his meals were to be served separately and a maid was to clean his room and make his bed. Instead of the traditional tails he would wear a linen jacket with gold epaulettes. Not without misgiving Vincent agreed to these and other stipulations, remembering Prince Aleco's parting message: 'Don't let him slip through your fingers!'

Cesare's interrogation made Vincent feel he was in a witness-box. Evidently the hours he kept were too early for Cesare's liking. 'What, sir, breakfast at eight? His Serene Highness never had his before nine, more often at ten which he called a more civilized hour. Do you take tea or coffee, sir?' 'Coffee.' 'His Serene Highness always had China tea with lemon and two slices of thin buttered toast. I presume, sir, you are accustomed to a classical English breakfast of orange juice, cereals, ham and eggs, marmalade, and so forth?' 'Dear me, no. A fresh roll with my coffee perhaps. . . .' Cesare looked disappointed. 'How strange. The young Princes had hearty English breakfasts. It was a treat to see them tuck in, and they had plentiful snacks between meals. Her Serene Highness only took fruit with an infusion of camomile but she suffered from gastritis. . . .'

Whenever Vincent acquainted Cesare with some personal taste or habit he would allude to those of His Serene Highness and his family as if Vincent ought to emulate such distinguished examples. Hitherto his excellent cook, who called himself the chef and dressed accordingly in spotless white, had always submitted to him the daily bill of fare. Cesare insisted that this was *lèse majesté*: the cook's function was confined to the kitchen. Considering himself best qualified to act as culinary ambassador, he would fling open the door—it was *infra dig* to knock—and march into the room with the menu on a silver salver to recite the details with a copious commentary:

'Cheese soufflé as an overture: permit me to add with a flavouring of white truffle and minced ham (that is how His Serene Highness liked it), followed by a fricassee of veal—a little too heavy, if you know what I mean, on top of a proper soufflé. What about breast of tender chicken with madeira sauce, braised endives and sauté potatoes? The chef has written down a choco-late mousse but with due respect the texture of mousse is too similar to that of a soufflé. I would propose a baba au rhum or a Mont Blanc of grated chestnut and whipped cream to wind up with. The Princes used to squeeze out the rhum and leave the baba, and how they loved whipped cream! We had our own cows at La Trappola, the butter and cream were always fresh. His Serene Highness was indifferent to sweets but he was partial to a purée of apples flavoured with lemon. Often he only had that for supper followed by a slice of Brie or Camembert. The cheese had to be ripe and runny or he wouldn't touch it. . . .'

Vincent's taste was too plebeian for Cesare. He disconcerted him by ordering grilled steak with a single baked potato. Ever 'with due respect' and an air of demure deprecation Cesare attempted to impose saucier and more fanciful dishes on the indignant cook. However, his arrival enabled Vincent to dismiss the butter-fingered dolt he nicknamed The Iconoclast since he had smashed the spread wings of his noblest Napoleonic eagle. He had pardoned his other breakages once too often. At least Cesare should spare him such frequent pangs.

But the crashing of glass still haunted his ears. Cesare pointed out that most of his china was chipped and that dozens of his Venetian wine glasses were missing, not a single set was intact. 'And a word about your wine, sir. The Chianti you drink is unworthy of your palate and, with due respect, even of mine, sir. Too acid for delicate stomachs. And the Frascati—frankly, I'm ashamed of serving such stuff, only fit for lorry drivers. His Serene Highness favoured French vintages with his meals, varying them with Johannisberg or Tokay. For table water he preferred Vichy. In hot weather he would quench his thirst with German lager. With Your Excellency's permission I might telephone the Prince's wine merchants for a few cases of claret and burgundy on the same reasonable terms. But the Johannisberg and the Imperial Tokay of La Trappola were incomparable: we shall never see the like again, pure hen's milk as we Romans say' —he kissed his own fingers in a rapturous gesture. 'As His Serene Highness only drank a glass or two we others were free to enjoy the rest of the bottle. The Princess only drank fruit juice and the

young Princes preferred Coca-Cola.' Cesare burst out laughing.
'They also had a passion for ice-cream cones. They would stop at
the village café and feast on them every day. Once they urged His
Serene Highness to sample one and it made him sick. I had to
give him brandy to take away the taste. My boys have tried to
poison me, he said with a shudder. His own particular weakness
was for raw spring onions and he insisted on smearing the salad
bowl with garlic. By the way, your cook's salad is not up to
scratch. He leaves too much water on the lettuce and he's ignorant of the right proportion of oil to vinegar. I must teach him
how to prepare it *alla Trappola*. The lettuce should be a founda-
tion for radishes, black olives, celery, tomatoes, carrots and a few
beans. Chopped onions according to taste but a soupçon of garlic
essential. The Princess used to eat raw onions at bedtime as she
said they helped her to sleep. Are you troubled by insomnia, sir?
If so, let me urge you to try Her Serene Highness's remedy. I
have found it effective myself though onions do tend to repeat the
next day. Which can be embarrassing.'

Vincent listened to such dissertations with the patience of an
old diplomat for Cesare, like the onions, tended to repeat himself
and he had Prince Aleco on the brain. His cook Gino was less
patient. Having ruled Vincent's kitchen for fifteen years he had
grown accustomed to his daily chat with the master, which
afforded him an opportunity to air his views on current
affairs as well as the *plat du jour*. Deprived of this privilege
and subjected to the newcomer's interference, he exploded like
a rocket.

'Let me try to coax His Serene Highness's former chef into
your service,' Cesare whispered behind closed doors to Vincent.
'His wages may be higher but you will save on the books. He's a
cordon bleu: you will soon appreciate the difference. At present he
is employed in a restaurant where he earns double but the work
is more fatiguing. I should be glad to undertake this mission on
your behalf. With due respect I've been suffering from wind
since I came here: my intestines never did so much rumbling in
all the years I lived at La Trappola.'

'I'm sorry about your wind. Maybe you should go on a diet. Gino's cooking happens to suit me personally.'

'No doubt we were spoiled at La Trappola. The Princes were crack shots and we had enough wild game to feed a regiment. We even had our share of foie-gras and other delicacies.'

'I suspect that accounts for the state of your liver. I like my food good and plain.'

'I was forgetting your nationality,' said Cesare. 'Pending negotiations it would be wiser to say nothing of this to Gino. He is capable of poisoning my soup.'

Gino having departed in a huff, Cesare succeeded in procuring the superior substitute he had proposed. Monsù Nazareno, as he was called, was a garrulous and exuberant Neapolitan who considered himself entitled to dictate the bill of fare. From now on Vincent never had any inkling of what viands were in store for him. Monsù Nazareno was a master of gastronomical surprise. He took infinite pains over the preparation of his dishes, all of which were so elaborate as to be unrecognizable. Liver *pâtés* in the shape of stars nestling in jelly with sprigs of parsley and other herbs, Russian salads like Byzantine mosaics covered with a swirling calligraphy of yellow mayonnaise, circular fish nibbling their tails among clusters of shrimps and segments of lemon, oxtail in hillocks of rice tinted with saffron and tomato, variegated pastry with scrambled egg and anchovy, multi-coloured ice-cream in baskets of nougat and spun sugar—Monsù Nazareno arranged them as for a Dutch still life. It seemed a pity to destroy such exquisite creations, which would collapse in a heap with the first helping.

After every meal the chef would pop in to ask Vincent if he had enjoyed his latest invention, but Vincent was never given a chance to reply. Monsù Nazareno was even more garrulous than Cesare, boasting of the gala banquets he had served and the celebrities who had congratulated him on his genius. He showed him an album of photographs illustrating the highlights of his career, and when Vincent gave a dinner for a cardinal or ambassador he brought in his nephew to take coloured snapshots of the main course. Crêpes Suzette were his special pride: with the speed of a prestidigitator he performed the rite of flicking them over the flame with a broad grin on his flushed face. Whenever there were guests for luncheon or dinner he worked himself up into orgasms of excitement. He talked much to himself and his melodramatic voice reverberated through the palace.

Cesare rejoiced in his triumph. Having imposed a *cordon bleu* on Vincent he attempted to revise his visiting list. 'Who is Your Excellency expecting today? Pardon me for asking, but it warms my heart to welcome old acquaintances from La Trappola.' When he recognized a friend of Prince Aleco's he would shake hands with him like a master of ceremonies and enquire about his health and family. During the meal he listened to the conversation and cackled like a hen when it amused him. Later he would comment on the success or failure of the party with impressions of individual quests. 'Oh sir, the Marchesa gave me quite a turn, she's dreadfully changed. I remember her when she was a radiant beauty, the toast of the Caccia Club. All Rome was crazy about her. I fear she drinks too much. Before she sat down she beckoned to me to fill her wine glass. She walked so unsteadily that I was afraid she would fall down any minute. I had to help her to the door. . . . With due respect, I don't think you ought to invite the Duke of Ponza after what I've been reading about him in the newspapers. Maybe Your Excellency missed the latest scandal. This time he's involved with a notorious black masseuse. Before you know it he'll try to foist her on you. Last time it was with that night-club dancer who drowned herself in the Tiber. Blood will tell, and that person is not what he pretends to be. He was adopted by the old Duke, some said because he was his natural son, others because of a less natural connection. I felt it my duty to warn you. His Serene Highness would never receive him though he tolerated the old Duke, who was perfectly legitimate of course. We were very particular about the people admitted to La Trappola.'

Often when Vincent dined alone Cesare became so absorbed in one of his monologues that he forgot to serve him. Vincent would sit before an empty plate, afraid of interrupting the speaker, who was apt to sulk if Vincent called him to order. Every topic, even the weather, led Cesare to embark on one of his nostalgic disquisitions. Over the payment of a bill, for instance: 'You had to know His Serene Highness as intimately as I did to appreciate the virtues of princely blood. Never the slightest fuss over an account. He paid for everything on the nail without a murmur.'

'Antiques excepted,' said Vincent. 'He haggled over them with Oriental pertinacity, always getting the best of the bargain.'

'I was referring to his household. The harmony of La Trappola was based on trust. His Serene Highness trusted me in everything . . .'

If something slipped Cesare's memory he would sigh: 'Ah me, I'm not so young as I was but that is no excuse. His Serene Highness was no younger yet he had a wonderful memory. It never failed him and, by Bacchus, he had plenty to remember. Every item in his vast collection was printed on his mind. Goodness, how this made him suffer during our great sale! All those treasures he loved like a jealous mother exposed to the common herd. Hucksters and harlots prying into his bedroom and bathroom, stamping cigarettes out on the pavement, mauling his tapestries, tapping his chairs and turning them topsy-turvy—the mere thought of it all made him ill. And the horrible publicity—journalists raking up the love-affairs of the late Grand Duchess. At the very last moment he wanted to stop the sale, but he had signed a contract with the auctioneers.'

After a few weeks Cesare limped painfully into Vincent's study and begged for sick leave. He, too, was stricken with sciatica and he could not stand without wincing. 'At least you are in princely company,' Vincent observed.

Cesare remained in bed for a month with an electric pad to soothe his aching nerve. He appeared much thinner with sunken eyes when Vincent visited his stuffy sick-room. Framed photographs of Prince Aleco and his progeny stood on his night-table, and indeed only one subject could distract him from his twinges.

'When I had a similar attack at La Trappola four years ago His
Serene Highness came to see me every day and my room was a
bower of roses. It brings the tears to my eyes to think of such
gracious kindness. His Serene Highness said to me with his
beautiful smile—even his teeth were unique works of art—"I'm
afraid my own sciatica must be infectious." He put a sunnier
room at my disposal, sent me muscat grapes and peaches from the
hothouse, lent me his own machine for ultra-violet rays as well as
a radio and television set. In short I lacked nothing except health,
which soon returned thanks to the dear good Prince. He cheered
me up with his jokes but at times it was hard to tell whether he
was jesting or in earnest. "You need never fear loneliness," he
would say, "since you are not married." Mind you, sir, he was
devoted to Her Serene Highness, the sweetest of ladies, though
she cared nothing for antiques. She had an itch for novelty, the
latest thing. How she enjoyed herself when I accompanied her to
the supermarket. She swept all the tins off the shelves and wanted
to open each of them on the spot. We spent a whole morning
there and I could hardly tear her away. She had a strange enthusiasm for vacuum cleaners. Yes, Her Serene Highness also
had a whimsical sense of humour. Once she hid a couple of
rubber frogs that croaked like real ones under the Prince's pillow.
How she giggled when he leapt out of bed with a yell—she was
standing outside in the passage with the young Princes. Another
time she mixed some marble fruit with the real ones for dessert.
The Prince took one absent-mindedly and cut his hand trying to
peel it. He might have broken a tooth . . .'

Luckily for Vincent, Cesare's distemper happened to coincide
with his annual visit to the Bahamas. For once he left his palace
without the worry and tension of previous years. Between Cesare
and Monsù Nazareno he had ceased to feel quite at home there
and it was a relief to escape from the Eden of Cesare's memories.
If Prince Aleco had been a hero to his butler, the minutiae of his
existence at La Trappola had become an obsessive bore to his
Oxford friend. A change of diet, moreover, was imperative, and
the climate of Nassau was predictably anodyne. The contrast with

Rome was complete. Inhibitions and rheumatism soon vanished in that balmy air: it was a return to nature and the people who had never left it.

Deeply suntanned and brainwashed, as it were, by the brainless tropical life, Vincent returned to Rome in glowing spirits. Cesare and Monsù Nazareno greeted him as if he were their honoured guest. Everything seemed to be in its former place yet everything looked different. While Cesare led him through the rooms of his *piano nobile* which he had subjected to a thorough spring cleaning Vincent blinked in dismay. The mellow gold of his frames, tables, chairs, eagles, sphinxes and candelabra glittered as if they were new; the soft ivory tones of his statuettes appeared to have been skinned or whitewashed: all the patina of the Napoleonic period had vanished, and it would take an age to recover from the drastic scraping and scrubbing it had received. Only the paintings retained their original glazes, and Cesare expressed regret that he lacked the proper varnish to deal with these in similar fashion. The neo-classical *jardinières* had been filled with frilly ferns and aspidistras.

Vincent paled with the shock, but there was nothing to be done and nothing he could find to say: he could only repress his tears. Finally he blurted out between gasps: 'But everything looks brand new.'

'As it *should* look,' said Cesare, rubbing his hands in self-congratulation. 'You have no idea of the dust and dirt Monsù Nazareno and I removed between us. We were at it all day long during your absence though I still have a twinge now and then.'

Vincent remembered Prince Aleco's assurance that nothing would be broken under Cesare's care. He would have preferred a few breakages to this wholesale renovation which made his rooms resemble some gaudy luxury hotel. He sighed heavily.

'What's the matter, sir?'

'I'm feeling very tired after my journey.'

'You must be hungry too. The chef has prepared a capital dinner but I promised not to tell you what. It is to be a nice surprise.'

Vincent had no appetite. He had had a surfeit of surprises. Presuming that he had languished for pasta in the barbarous Bahamas the chef had prepared a steaming bowl of green *tagliatelle*, followed by fatty chunks of Roman lamb and an apple meringue pie. But the dining-room still reeked of furniture polish.

'I don't want to hurt the chef's feelings,' he remarked to Cesare. 'Please eat this up in my stead.'

Nothing loth, Cesare made short work of the copious meal. For once he had neglected a reference to His Serene Highness.

Vincent had a sleepless night, haunted with forebodings about his domestic predicament. In vain he strove to change the train of his thoughts, which revolved in dizzy circles until he dozed off. He awoke sweating from nightmares of Cesare and the cook playing havoc with his curule chair, a priceless piece in massive mahogany with the heads and feet of lions in gilt bronze designed by David for Napoleon. 'Prince Aleco help me,' he prayed, as to a patron saint.

Prince Aleco did help him in an unexpected manner. When it was published that he had been injured in a car crash Cesare announced that he would have to join him immediately. 'After all he has done for me in the past,' he explained, 'I'd never forgive myself if I failed him in time of calamity.' Though it was reported that the Prince was out of danger Cesare was determined to fly to his bedside. He looked very dapper in well-cut tweeds with a gardenia in his buttonhole when he came to bid Vincent adieu. His departure was too sudden to be convenient but it was a relief to be spared further disquisitions about His Highness. These, and the damage done to his Empire furniture, seemed too heavy a price to pay for such ministrations as Cesare deigned to bestow. In the meantime he sought an adept in faking who might restore the old gilt to his brass ornaments and tone down the chalky white of others. His thoughts often reverted to Prince Aleco on his habitual rounds of the antique shops. He had not followed his note of sympathy and good wishes with further enquiries, unwilling to appear obtrusive. Eventually he received a glossy postcard of the Boulevard de la Croisette with respectful *Saluti* from Cesare and a bantering letter from the Prince. 'What have you done to Cesare?' he queried. 'He has become impossible. He never stops talking about you and your palazzo. While I'm in plaster he refuses to leave me but the boredom of his company is crushing. At least he has made me realize that I'm better off in the relative tranquillity of Cannes. Please send for him at once. Relieve me of this incubus before he drives me mad.'

Very tactfully Vincent replied that Cesare was of an age to retire as he himself had from another branch of the diplomatic service.